My Uncle's New Eyes

Joseph Hirsch

Black Rose Writing | Texas

ISBN: 978-1-68433-513-8
PUBLISHED BY BLACK ROSE WRITING
www.blackrosewriting.com

Printed in the United States of America
Suggested Retail Price (SRP) $17.95

My Uncle's New Eyes is printed in Baskerville

*As a planet-friendly publisher, Black Rose Writing does its best to eliminate unnecessary waste to reduce paper usage and energy costs, while never compromising the reading experience. As a result, the final word count vs. page count may not meet common expectations.

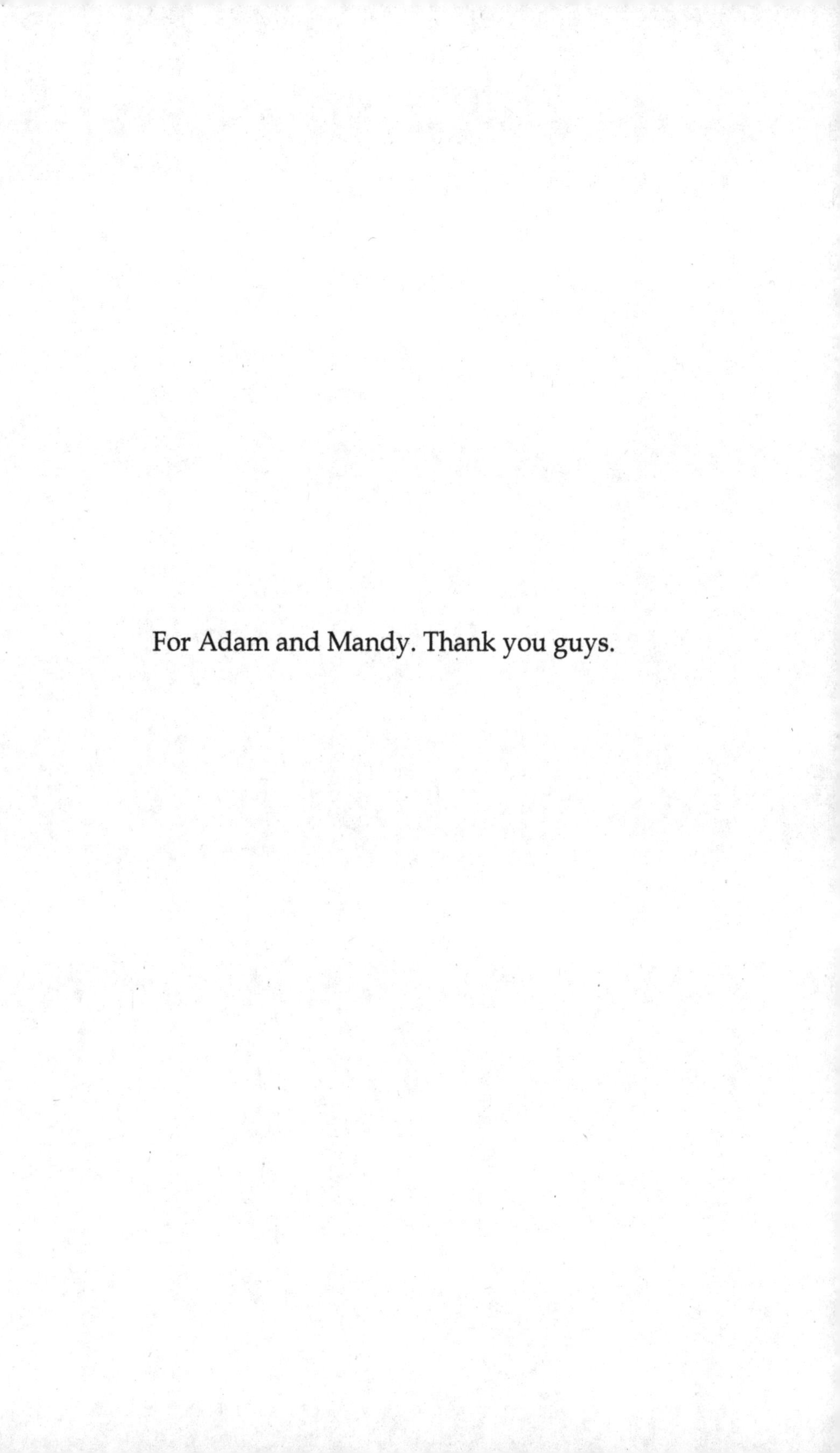

For Adam and Mandy. Thank you guys.

MY UNCLE'S NEW EYES

"The graveyards are full of indispensable men."
-Saying of unknown provenance, attributed to personages as varied as
Charles De Gaulle and Winston Churchill

"If they cut my bald head open, they will find one big boxing glove."
-Marvelous Marvin Hagler

"Why am I not young?"
-Gustave Flaubert

CHAPTER ONE
WELCOME TO REDROCK

My mom was not happy that she had to pick me up when I got suspended from Redrock Retreat, after my friend and I got caught during a random pat-down on the return to the tour bus during a field trip and one counselor found our shrooms on me.

The school called her where she lived with my stepfather on his cattle ranch in Flagstaff. She wasn't home, and so the maid forwarded the message to where she had been vacationing on the Seine, eating chocolate and sampling the local shopping and theater until her screwup son put the kibosh on that and she had to fly home.

I spotted her ivory-white Range Rover churning up graded sand in its tires on the horizon, as she passed by the rusted windmill that separated the rehab clinic/boarding school from the surrounding barb-wired homesteads. Administrator Stevens stood with me in the shadow of the hacienda's colonnaded walkway, a clipboard in his left hand and his right hand balled into a fist.

I watched that right hand reflexively close and open, covered with black hair up to the knuckles, the gemstone on his class ring catching light from the hot sun.

"You use this month," he said to me, "to improve yourself." He gritted his teeth until I worried he might lose a bit of the ionized white on them. He couldn't afford to do that, since his eyes were already flinty and his skin sapped of life by the sun, and if he broke the teeth grinding them down he'd look more like a warden than a game-show host.

"Yes sir," I said, and stood there with my black duffel bag.

A thin reddish dust the Range Rover's tires had kicked up covered the car, the clouds the same color as the adobe bricks on the buildings of the campus. The car stopped next to the flagstone fountain in the courtyard, and the principal and I went out to meet my mom.

The fob on the Rover chirped, and the trunk opened. I tossed my crap inside, next to some plastic-wrapped antiquing acquisitions Deborah had picked up on her trip down here.

"Careful," she said, turning to me from the front seat. Oversized Dolce & Gabbana glasses with smoked rose frames covered her eyes. "That's real French Provincial."

I settled my bag next to the nearest wooden chair. "I guess you picked this up over in France then, and not down here?"

"They forgot to mail it the last time I was at the Pied-à-terre, even though I left specific instructions to have it forwarded."

"Well, you've got it now," I said, "and all's right with the world."

She pouted as much as the collagen allowed and frowned to the extent the Botox permitted. Debby pulled a smile for Stevens and signed the release form with a quick flourish. "We're terribly sorry about this."

He smiled back at her. "He's a bright kid, with great ability. He's the star pupil in his English and history classes." Stevens' eyes closed, in a gesture that was half-wink, half-wince, meant to show his forbearance developed over the course of a long career dealing with kids as difficult as me, and sometimes worse. "We'll try again in a month."

The smiles dropped from both their faces as they parted and let me make my way through their ranks to the car. I settled into the ribbed leather of the backseat and prepared myself for the long drive.

I figured one of two things would happen when Debbie shut her own door and we drove off. Either she would hit me with both barrels, or we'd do the stony silence routine.

The sigh would be the opening salvo, and ready me for whatever came next. The door slammed shut, and she put the car in gear.

The Streisand on the ten-disc changer was loud enough that I couldn't tell if Debby was fuming. The sizzle of a match coming to life didn't make it any easier to tell how pissed she was.

She drank smoke from a Gauloises Blond and puckered her lips to blow it out. Then she cracked her window and waved the stream of blue smoke out into the desert. She opened the sunroof just to make sure the crosscurrent was strong enough to hide the smoke from Jim, should he drive her car instead of his silver Porsche Boxster.

"Jim was thinking about letting you manage one of his Subways part-time when you turned eighteen."

"Can't work around food, mom." I slapped my gut beneath the raglan of my Polo shirt. It jiggled a lot less than last time she'd seen me.

"You look fitter." She flicked her cigarette out of the window into some sagebrush that resembled snow whenever the sun was this bright and there was nothing to keep it from bleaching the scrubland.

The Paiute name for this place actually translated into something like "The Land the Lord Forgot." The Mormons who'd passed through here maybe a couple hundred years ago seemed to concur, for after a short stay they'd pulled up stakes and hitched wagons, leaving behind the blockhouses to stand empty for ages. Some decades later the widow of some captain of industry opened up a school dedicated to Christianizing any local redskin heathens not already killed or herded onto reservations.

How that eventually morphed into a boarding school / rehab facility for the screwed up kids of the wealthy is something you will have to ask someone better educated in Redrock lore.

"You want to tell me why you did this to me?" she asked.

The tires went from rock to asphalt, and now aside from Streisand's pleading to her wayward father there was only the growing silence between me and my mother.

"Debbie, I think I'm the one who ingested those mushrooms. I didn't do it to *you*. I did it to me. Or for me."

"Okay, *Michael*." She put some sneer on that. She didn't like it when I called her by her name instead of "Mom," and especially not when I shortened "Deborah" to "Debbie." That reminded her too much of our white trash roots, how she'd been a keno runner who had lassoed herself a high-roller by playing her cards right, saddling up to the well-heeled rancher when he was on a winning streak and tipsy from the comped whiskey sours.

Hell, she'd played her hand better than right. Perfect, in fact. They didn't even have a prenup.

"Why did you do something this stupid?" She asked. "You had a problem with hard drugs. I could understand a relapse, but this…" She shook her head. I hung mine. She had a point. The anger was subsiding, and the pain was coming, the realization that she was human and I was hurting her, that even if she was a gold digger, I didn't blame her for that. It was a cold world, and she was just trying to survive, and a lot of the pain she'd absorbed had been to shield me.

"Adam," I said, and didn't get to say anymore.

"That little kid who you brought back to the ranch last time you were home?" She winced.

Adam had a glandular problem that made him look much younger than he was. They'd held him back twice as a sophomore, and he was actually now nineteen as a senior, but he still looked like a towheaded prepubescent.

"Yes, Adam."

I looked up at the square of blue cloudless sky visible through the sunroof. "He said that if we watched the sky at night on mushrooms, it would let us see the UFOs that are supposedly invisible, going back and forth to Nellis Air Base on maneuvers. They cloak while doing recon," I said, "but the shrooms give you the vision to make them visible via the magic of the opened third eye."

I was ready to elaborate, tell her about our talk of Castaneda beneath the stars, but she jammed the brakes hard enough that I lurched in my seat, given a touch of whiplash as my forehead almost pressed the leather cushion of her headrest.

Cars passed the stationary Range Rover, honking boxes of steel rage, blurring metal monsters rushing left and right, causing the thing to feel as if it could tip over on its tenuous bearings and fall into the culvert at the side of the road; I'd heard these cars weren't good in rollovers. I'd come close enough while driving drunk to test those physics firsthand.

She lay her head on the steering wheel, and her platinum'd hair uncoiled like a synthetic version of Medusa's gorgon coif. When she next lifted her head to take another hit of the smoke, her mascara spilled from her eyes, running streams of black blood, the stigmata of a middle-aged Milf at wit's end with her wayward wretch of a son.

"Michael, I don't know what to do."

I didn't say "Send me to live with my father," even though La Tuna FCI was only a state away and I might head to prison at some point anyway (though probably for something less white collar than my father's embezzlement scheme, if I kept up the way I had been before going to Redrock).

I honestly didn't know what I should do, except maybe get high.

I still had a half ounce of British Columbian purple weed wrapped in a Ziploc bag tucked in my black duffel, which meant I could get stoned enough for the short term to delay thinking about the question at hand, the one weighing on both of us.

I didn't have a pipe on me, but back at Jim's "Rustler's Retreat" I had a couple ceramic pieces along with my bong molded to look like a wizard's staff. I hid my pipes in strategic places throughout the ranch, a one-hitter in the tack shack near the agave patch, some rolling papers stashed on a shelf next to a can of WD-40 in the pool house, around which the pear cacti prickles made it unsafe to walk without flip-flops.

Suicide was also an option. As was running away.

But I wasn't Huck Finn, and the river wasn't what it once had been. Besides that Big Jim had connections on account of his stake in several grind joint casinos in Glitter Gulch and a piece of a slot vending concern with contracts stretching from Macau to Hamburg. That meant he had eyes and ears all over the planet and the best network of house and roving detectives in the world on his payroll. Wherever I went, I wouldn't get far.

I'd be an adult in the legal sense in little more than couple years, anyway. All I had to do was wait it out, and I'd be free.

"Mom, I'm sorry," I said.

I was.

She held up a hand, and I couldn't tell if the gesture conveyed an apology accepted, caught like a dream in one those looms they sold in those roadside junk shops, or if she was telling me with her flick of the wrist to be quiet.

I shut up just in case, stared out the window, but since it was tinted and the sun was so bright, I saw more of my reflection than the landscape.

Debbie hadn't just been messing with me. I had lost a ton of weight.

My face had always been round, moony, but all the hiking and the low-cal diet along with puberty had stripped me of the cherubic fat and made me look closer now to a man than a child.

I could see high cheekbones that seemed to grow overnight from nowhere. I had only a light smattering of pimples on my face, for which I was grateful, since I knew some guys afflicted with the things like they were like buboes on the face of a Medieval peasant.

Not being fat also let me see what features I'd gotten from my parents. I could see the ones I'd gotten from my mom. I had her sandy-brown hair, which she'd irreparably poisoned with dyes and treatments, and I'd also gotten her coppery tone that meant I didn't burn but darkened to a deep olive more like an Italian or a Greek when the sun was really out and pounding the desert.

As for what I'd inherited from my father (aside from a taste for the needle), it would have been hard to say, since it had been a long time since I'd last seen him, and even then he had changed to be almost unrecognizable from the previous time we'd met.

Que sera, sera, as they said in Debbie's adopted home of Paree.

Her crying had tapered off to sniffling, and she had finished her cigarette. She watched her side-view mirrors, saw nothing but desert and an unfurled ribbon of grey road behind her. She put the luxury auto into gear again and drove, this time in the other direction.

I sat up, on edge. "Where are we going, Mom?"

I hadn't planned on calling her "Mom" again. It had just come out.

"Your uncle's." She reached into her alligator Coach bag on the passenger seat, snapped open the golden hasps and grabbed a Kleenex from the box. It wasn't a surprise to see that she kept tissues there, and I imagined she did quite a lot of crying that had nothing to do with me.

As much of a little shit as I could be, I think I was also ultimately aware that I was the unhappy result of something rather than the source of that unhappiness itself. "Mom, I thought he was in a rest home."

"He was." She nodded, blew her nose into the Kleenex with her right hand while she worked the woodgrain steering wheel with the left. "He had some friends from the old days pitch in to get him out and set him up. He's got a live-in nurse."

I opened my mouth, tried to stifle the words. "I knew Jim had bought you but I didn't know he was buying up the whole family."

I'd always been too smart by half, and I'd sat more than my fair share of days in detention back at Redrock for speaking when I shouldn't have.

"Money matters, Michael," she said, not even angry with me for my jab, pitying me for viewing myself as above whoring, as if, in its own way, that wasn't what everyone was doing. And maybe they were.

I'd seen Jim glad-handing and flesh-pressing when he didn't want to, smiling his face sore and working oily guys in snakeskin boots and turquoise bolo ties. Old Administrator Stevens was good at bootlicking the parents who had the money to invest in Redrock's expansion, maybe a new wing here, or a satellite campus there, with even some talk of a planetarium when he was at his oleaginous best. He'd trail them as they made their tours of the rocky grounds like a stag following the scent of female estrous in rutting season.

Gotta serve someone, as the curly-headed bard and Nobel-laureate Robert Zimmerman once put it.

"Besides," she added, open-toed pump pressed down on the gas pedal. "Your uncle has friends in high places. He doesn't even need Jim or his money." She stared through the tint of her glasses and that of the windshield, toward the sun turning the air to rippling warm waves on the horizon. "People loved him in Vegas when I worked there, almost as much as Benny Binion."

All I knew about the guy was that he had been a boxer, a great one even, but then he'd gotten his brains beaten to mush, lost his title, lost his faculties and his wife, lost everything.

Now at least he had a house, and I was going there to live with him for the next month. I could have argued with Deborah more, but I knew her life was hard enough without me and my big mouth.

And I still loved her a bit more than I hated her.

CHAPTER TWO
CASA DE LUNA

The man was technically my great uncle, since he was my grandfather's brother, but it was easier to just go with the flow and call him my uncle when talking with Deborah. I couldn't exactly say why she kept in contact with him, except that perhaps unlike the rest of the male relatives in her family he had never tried to hit on her or borrow her money or car. Whether that was down to him being punch-drunk or if he had been a nice guy before that was also something I didn't know.

"I'll come get you at the end of the month, drive you back to Redrock."

"Sounds good," I said.

The weather was strange. Ripples of lightning followed each other so close that the sky seemed like a bug zapper ready to short-circuit after frying an army of dive-bombing moths. The sun had set, but its traces still dyed the thin cloud cover pink and threw the green cacti into black shadow.

The Range Rover rocked a bit as it passed first from asphalt to sand and then finally to hard caliche. The tires made a sound like a fat man taking a bite out of a hard shell taco as the treads gripped the ground.

"Can he talk?" I asked.

She watched me for a moment in the rearview, tapped the last of her Gauloises from the soft pack, and sparked it. "He's getting better than he was. That's all Luna told me."

Luna?

My Spanish was barely good enough to know that meant "moon."

We took the oxbow bend in what passed for the road and drove beneath a wooden entrance shaped like a massive horseshoe, on which someone had written "Ghost Gulch" in whitewash.

My uncle's house came into a view a short time later. It was mud brick, a Spanish Mission-style hacienda with red-tile roof and honey-colored stone slabs cladding its sides. The sashed windows were heavy leaded glass, clear but still somehow as somber as stained glass.

To the right of that was a tin-roofed awning propped by split rails palisading three sides of a concrete apron. Along one wall of the open-faced garage was an ancient horse trough and hitching post set in the gravel, looking as big as planter boxes compared to the massive fishtailed Caddie in the center of the concrete pad. The only other car was a late model silver coupe parked to the right of the sky-blue Cadillac.

Debbie put the car in park in front of the house and got out, ditching her half-smoked cigarette and crushing it under her box heel. She shifted her purse across her body bandoleer-style, pushed her sunglasses up the bridge of her nose reflexively. I hefted my bag and got out after her. We walked up the stone walkway to the front door.

She clutched the brass knocker fitted in a massive oak door but the door pulled inward before she could knock. A whiff of lilac-light perfume hit me. Standing there was a beautiful Mexican girl with thick dark eyebrows and cocoa-brown skin, black hair pulled into a ponytail that spilled down her back. She wore a white ruffled peasant blouse patterned with roses, and low-cut jeans that left a bit of midriff exposed, across which she'd strung a gypsy coin-bejeweled belt.

Her eyes were heavy-lidded, with a sensuous droop to them, as if she'd gotten stoned and was trying to hide it. She smiled and the brightness of her white teeth was almost fluorescent in the fading twilight, and the sleepy-sexy eyes became half-alert as she took us in.

"Michael?" Her smile was impersonal but not fake.

"Moon," I said, like a dumbass. I took her hand in mine and found her small fingers literally cold but somehow intimate. She grazed my hand as much as gripped it, and I went rigid in the hopes my blood would slow, not course toward my dick and embarrass me.

"Oh, 'Luna,'" she said, "*Sí, muy bien.*'" She blinked, curtly endured my lame attempt to impress her.

Her bushy eyebrow arched. Don't ask me why but I'd always found those caterpillar brows sexy on a girl.

She waved us in and then turned. My mother smiled, Luna's easy manner having apparently put her at ease. Or perhaps she was eyeing the antiques, the rosewood cabinets and mahogany-cased player piano.

I tried to keep my mind clear, my senses a blank slate on which I refused to let anything emerge. I could steal glances at Luna throughout my month here, work up the nerve to get out monosyllable answers before I risked my voice cracking, and each night I could exorcise my demons and purge my urges as I saw fit so my crush wouldn't be too obvious during the days when I had to deal with her, if I did.

But I knew immediately that I couldn't be comfortable around her, not really. I could barely relax around Anglo girls my age. And here with only the merest warning from my mother someone had thrown me in front of this Aztec princess.

"Mr. Reeves is just finishing up his dinner."

Luna's Birkenstocks slapped against the tiled floor as she moved. I noticed she had a small charm bracelet around her ankle, made of tiny dancing silver bells that looked like miniature candle snuffers. The shoes flopped as she walked, exposing the slightly paler flesh of her ball and arch, wrinkled and darkened with dirt.

I looked up at the cathedral high ceiling, where a coach wheel chandelier hung from chains that belonged in a dungeon. Fake candles in bell jars made the massive room glow like a gaslit 19th-century hotel.

On the walls were cattle brands, 10-gallon Stetsons and coiled lassoes settled on pegs. There were saddle blankets and sombreros and stretched rawhides and pegged buckskins. They were the antiques that theme restaurants tried to replicate, but these were original articles.

"Here we are."

Luna walked toward a doorway carved in the rock between the main room and the kitchen where a tin Pioche Railroad Pacific sign graced the entryway like a cowpoke's version of mistletoe.

"How are we doing, Champ?"

She pushed through the pair of wooden-shingled batwing doors that she held open behind her so they wouldn't flap in her wake and slap me or my mom. "They're easier for him to use than door handles." She smiled again. "Is the soup okay?"

I saw him from the back, his skin as worn by the sun as a lizard's hide after too much time perched on a hot rock. His shoulders hunched blade-like and time had tonsured the top of his head, leaving only the thinnest wisps of hair on either side of his head. It was the hair one imagines clinging to a corpse in a coffin after their soul's passed into the afterlife.

He turned toward Luna's voice but locked on my face. His eyes were cloudy, but they sharpened into something like focus as he took stock of me. Then he smiled, as if he recognized me, and I smiled back without knowing why.

I didn't smile much, and it startled me. I looked over at Debbie. She looked in a hurry to go. I had no desire to keep her.

"See if you can be a help," she said, still wearing her sunglasses.

"Oh," Luna said, and walked around to the front of the old man. "We've got this covered. He barely needs my help."

There wasn't the faintest trace of something patronizing in that voice, and I liked it. I got the sense that as foggy as the old man was, he might sense being treated like a plant that needed only occasional watering.

Regardless of where his mind was, though, his body clearly wasn't taking its orders.

His plastic spoon stopped mid-dip into the thermos where his tortilla soup swam, bits of corn and black bean floating to the top and creating a starchy tomato-scented skin. Luna took his liver-spotted hand in her own, held it tightly, and mimed the motion of bringing the spoon from the bowl up to the head twice. She let him go, like a parent training their child to ride a bike, and he finished the motion on his own.

Once he completed that, slurping the soup into his head, it was easy for him to do it again. It seemed she'd help establish his rhythm. She smiled as he ate.

Luna took up a seat across from him, in a wingback chair fixed with brass studs up and down its wooden body. I took my place in the third seat at the table made for four, lifting rather than dragging my chair legs so the sound wouldn't upset the old man eating his soup.

"We'll listen to music and have a bath after this."

My uncle nodded, accepting the offer the young woman had extended. My mother's hand appeared over his right shoulder, touched the fabric of his work shirt, rubbing the stitched epaulettes of his guayabera. The shirt was powder blue and open, revealing both easy-snap buttons and patches of Velcro on the inner seams so the man had the option of how to close the shirt, if and when the draft got to be too much and he covered up. Tufts of cotton-white hair popped from his chest, across which a faded India ink tattoo of an anchor and globe bled into the ancient skin. A scar that rose like a topographical feature on a treasure map traversed the space just below the tat. I wondered if the wound was from surgery or from a fight.

He regarded my mother's hand on his arm as an imposition on his soup-eating claw and shrugged it off. She huffed, shifted in place, squeezed him once on the shoulder as he spooned more picante broth into his mouth.

"Goodbye, Deborah," he said, his mouth full. The clarity of his voice goosed me, and I shifted on the burgundy chintz pad of the uncomfortable chair where I sat. She turned without a word, leaving their unspoken history to hover over the table. The lights glowed brighter, as night finally descended outside and painted the desert black as the background in a velvet painting.

My mother clogged her way across the room the same way she came in. The front door groaned as she tried to slam it shut behind her. The ancient oak refused to budge to her whim and moved in its own time, like the massive door to a vault groaning closed rather than dramatically clapping shut.

That left only silence aside from the sound of the man slurping, winding down in his repast. Luna seemed content with it, those black eyes watching from above a smattering of cinnamon-brown freckles. *Estos Ojos*…Or was it *Este Ojos*? Spellbound and spellbinding at once those eyes were, as if she were under the sway of some strange hypnotism but also had the power to draw in anyone who made eye contact for long. She wouldn't have to worry about that with me; only stolen glances.

I couldn't take the silence and shifted until my chair scraped the tiled floor. Thankfully, the old man saved me. "We go prospecting for gold tomorrow?"

We both laughed, she more openly, and I more guarded. She rearranged her face, screwed it up as if she'd just had a shot of whiskey, and said, "The gold in them thar hills done already been mined, Kit! Someone done jumped your claim."

"That's pretty good," I said.

Her eyes flitted to me. "I should hope so. I've read all the Zane Grey and L'Amour books in the house and I've gotten some practice watching those old cowboy movies with him." Luna paused. "He was in some, you know."

"Champ first and foremost," he said, weaving back into clarity for the moment. I looked over at him. I could tell it took some will to bring himself out of the past, or to at least make himself present enough to speak of bygone days. To think or talk was to test his mettle now, as much perhaps as boxing once had been.

It seemed almost to be a physical effort to think, and his body trembled so that his chair shook and the tiles below his chair legs rattled. His tremors caused him to tap his foot in time for a moment.

Luna's hand came out reflexively, as fast as if he was falling off a cliff and she'd caught him by his hand. He steadied, said, "Soldier, actor, greeter, but fighter foremost."

"That's right." Luna held him until the tremor sufficiently subsided, as if it were an electric current and she was the ground. When the last of his shakes had passed from him to her, when she had healed him with her steadying touch, she let go of him and stood. Her eyes caught mine, and I stood and followed without being asked.

She walked into another room on the other side of the kitchen, this one's doorway draped with a curtain of white dentalium shells interlaced with turquoise glass beads. The sheet rattled in our wake. We entered a den with a barrel-stave floor the color of an aged cognac cask, across which the golden pelt of a brown bear stretched, virtually camouflaged against the unvarnished wooden floor.

The stone fireplace was big enough for a tall man to stand in. It was sooty and blackened from a recent, roaring blaze someone had made in the river-stone hearth. Above the fireplace but below a set of massive steer's horns was a bejeweled belt. There was a diamond-studded buckle in its center that looked like an oversized scapular medallion, only rather than being tin or gold-dipped it boasted what looked like real precious stones that caught a prism's worth of light as I walked toward them.

Matted in the glass case on a black background was a sepia photo of a man in a ring, togged in boxing shorts and hand wraps. His face had swollen almost beyond recognition, his ear so engorged with blood it seemed like it might drop off the side of his head, unable to support the weight of the claret spilling from a busted blood vessel, with the red stuff swelling the lobe faster than a condom fitted over a water tap going at full-blast.

It was the old man in the room next door, in the flush of life. Maybe he had been suffering worse back then than he was now, though there was no way for me to know that for sure. I could have asked him, but men of his generation didn't bitch about such things.

"IBC screwed me." His voice echoed from the other room, and I shivered, not sure whether it was a draft from the desert that had broken into the old adobe house or if it was something else. "Redman Lopez clocked me on the break, the bastard."

Luna looked at me, beaming. I dropped my eyes, embarrassed by the trust I saw in her face, as if my respect for the old man's accomplishments could outweigh the electric charge of being this young and this close to her. I felt that the old warrior was worthy of her presence, or more worthy of it than me. But her beauty and manner made me ashamed to exist.

"So I didn't get the IBC belt, but the *Police Gazette* boys knew what was what and gimme that."

I looked up, not courageous enough to meet her eyes with my own, but at least graduating from keeping them on the floor and at my toes. I looked somewhere over her shoulder and said, "I'm guessing you've heard the story he's telling before?"

"Many times," she replied, glancing at me and then staring at the strapping young warrior drenched in blood in the old photo, smiling through the down-pouring veil of his red wounds and lifted on-high, chaired by cornerman, trainer, and whatever well-wishers had broken the police cordon to lay hands on the champ hoping some of his magic might rub off on them.

I wondered if Luna had lived back then and run into him in some hotel lobby or train station, if they might not have slept together. Maybe even gotten married and had babies.

She looked away from the mantle and spoke to my great-uncle still in the kitchen, sitting with his now-empty cup of soup. "Are you ready for your bath, Champ?"

"Yes." He tried to stand up from the table, writhed a bit. She padded quickly across the den, the open toe of her sandal kicking the Kodiak bearskin lightly on its nose as she walked over the rug. She leaned down to my uncle. "Beat the ten count, Champ!"

He looked in her direction, as if she was his cornerman and collodion dripping from a cut filled his eyes. "How about we say they paid me to swan dive and I stay down? I could nap right here."

She smiled, teeth creeping out of her mouth to bite the reddish bow of her bee-sting fat lip. "One, two…" Her muscles strained slightly, and he pushed off with a groan. The struggle had caused the rest of the buttons on his shirt to pop free and after he stood he walked now, unashamed and open-shirted, like a drug boss promenading at the beach.

Luna looked at me. "You follow us." She touched the air just next to his elbow in case he needed steadying. "Your room is on the left."

I followed them back through the den, stealing a last glance at the photo of the bloody man in his prime. Then I turned my attention back to Luna leading me deeper into the house. Her hips were narrow but her ass was ample, its teardrop shape causing each cheek to move in counterpoint to whatever motion she took, as if it had a mind of its own and was defying her. I stole a couple glances at the swaybacked booty and then looked back up, hopefully before she caught me.

"You'll be sleeping there." She pointed to the left as we entered a corridor.

I stepped into the guest room. The bedroom was silo-shaped, and the walls sloped up to a domed ceiling with crossbeam rafters made of creosote staves. I'd seen one of those red-tiled minarets on top of the house when we'd been driving up; now I was in that room.

There was only one window, carved into the deep slab of the far wall. The room was probably lit by a warm brown color during the day, but the light of the Hunter's Moon coming through the window bleached the quarters bone-white. In the center of the space was a double-bed covered in a straw-brown comforter, a couple Navajo blankets piled on a steamer trunk at its foot.

I took in the rest of the room: there was a kidney-shaped earthenware pan next to an old jug on the nightstand where a jade-colored lamp sat and two old burlap gunnysacks that may have once contained flour or potatoes sat stacked along the walls.

I set down my black bag next to the bed. And then I let my imagination do its thing.

Was I a bounty hunter who'd stopped at this outpost on my way to Carson City to find a snowbird on the lam, or was I monk sequestered in his friary, willing to go out and preach the Word of Christ to the heathens even if it cost me an ear or I ended up getting beaten to death with coup-counting sticks?

I hid my imagination from the kids at Redrock, and my penchant for storytelling from everyone but my English teacher, Mr. Granski, the same way I hid things from everyone but Mr. Hurley, the only person who knew my interest in history was deep enough for me to sit attentively in class while half the other kids snored and most of the others stared off into space.

I was alone now. That meant I'd not only let my imagination run free, but that I might have no other choice. There probably wasn't a town around for miles, and I doubted there was much I could do with my uncle, or that Luna was keen to spend much time around me.

I sat on the edge of the bed, let my weary body unwind a bit from its aches. I fought to push school and the Shrooms Incident out of my mind. Leaning down, I unzipped my bag, rummaged through a swirl of blue and red t-shirts, brown khakis and jeans, until I heard the soft crinkle of my Kush in its baggie.

Where to smoke it, and with what? And what would Luna do if she found out? Flush it, or maybe smoke it with me, probably. Worst-case scenario she'd call Deborah, but my mom was probably on her way back to her apartment in Paris, filled with its Lautrec reprints and a couple postmodern butt-ugly originals, along with a view overlooking Charles Eiffel's steel skeleton tower visible from the wrought-iron balcony.

I reached in the bag, the smell of the weed potent as fresh organic coffee, coming through in rich waves even though I'd taken pains to make sure the Ziploc bag was sealed.

"All settled?"

I looked up. Luna was standing in the doorway again, limned in the light spilling from the other rooms into the hallway.

I instantly regretted not paying more attention in Mr. Field's Spanish class. I thought if I was fluent or at least conversant, then maybe that would impress her, or show her I wasn't *un gringo feo*. But "*Yo quiero papas*" or some other basic sentence wouldn't get me very far.

"Thank you," I said.

"The laundry room is at the other end of the house." She took her arm from the doorway and pointed. Stubbly hair slightly whitened with flecks of roll-on deodorant was visible in her armpit.

"Thank you."

"*De nada.*"

She turned to go back to the bathroom where the sound of slowly running water echoed, like a distant babbling brook.

"Who's Caddy is that out there?"

She stopped and turned. "Oh, it's not a Caddy."

"Batmobile?"

"It's a Polara."

"Is it yours?" I didn't see her driving an American steel classic behemoth and him keeping current with the latest coupes.

She showed her teeth again in an open, unselfconscious smile. I think she knew she was pretty, but it didn't much interest her. It was something she acknowledged maybe once in passing, like a naturalist stopping on a trail to look at a specific butterfly fluttering on a leaf before it lighted away.

"No, it's his car. Or it *was* his." She lowered her voice and walked closer to me.

I stiffened, quickly zipped my bag closed, but either she didn't notice the gesture or thought nothing of it.

"He's not allowed to drive. The mechanic showed me how to take off the distributor cap so he thinks it's broken down." She looked back toward the bathroom and a raven bit of bang spilled from behind her ear, cradling the right half of her heart-shaped face. "If he complains about the car not working, just go along with him."

"Will do."

She walked away from me and ceased whispering as she spoke. "If you need a ride into town, let me know and I'll take you to Sonora Bend for provisions."

"That's what the prospectors call them way out here? Provisions?"

Luna giggled. If I'd had a diary, I would have marked that down in my moleskin notebook: the first time I'd made a female laugh intentionally. I wasn't ready to belly up to the green baize in Monaco and tell a spy-seductress that I liked my martinis shaken, not-stirred, but it was a start.

"Gotta go."

She turned from the door, and I exhaled as if I'd been holding my breath the whole time she'd been there. Then I bathed in the lingering scent of her perfume, deeply and with the same intensity I would have reserved for smelling another girl's panties.

The tightness left my chest, and I thought about ways to ingest the weed besides smoking it. Maybe if she took me to town, I could get some cocoa powder and bake the herb into some brownies. I bet the wood-fire stove or adobe kiln would make killer cookies, though I'd have to be careful about putting the leftovers in the fridge or leaving them out on the counter. Then again, I'd heard weed was good for all kinds of old people diseases like arthritis and glaucoma.

The shrieking of beasts on the prowl outside brought me out of my thoughts, the mewls echoing on a desert wind. I knew that sound from Redrock. It was the call of the coyotes. It wasn't like the bloodcurdling baying of a wolf, more like a scraping noise that was unsettling rather than terrifying, like the squelch of a caller's receiver when they phoned in to some radio show but forgot to turn down their own set. Coyotes always sounded wounded, pathetic, yet dangerous at the same time. Especially when they started whimpering to each other in the night.

"They don't hurt anyone," I remembered Adam telling me during one rock-climbing Outlook weekend expedition we went on, where we had set out with the goal to pursue natural highs and to conquer our fears, but we had barely rationed our toilet paper. "It's just the wolf-coyote hybrids that do the killing. And even then you just got to pick up a rock and throw it at them and then they run off like bitches."

Sure, I thought, *but what if you don't have a rock?*

I lay back on the bed, safe knowing that the animals were out there and I was in here, lodged in this peaceful place for about a month, with a beautiful young woman and an admirable old man, whose voices echoed in the bathroom out of which poured the sound of splashing water.

CHAPTER THREE
SOME MEN WEAR THEIR HATS TO BED

The ceiling came to life above me, brick backsplashes groaning until there was a circular portal in the center of the roof, like in an Indian sweat-house. Bright sunshine streamed in through the skylight. I covered my eyes with my hand and stood up, feeling like crap but having no drug or alcohol to blame it on.

"Not bad, hey?"

I looked across the room at Luna in the doorway. She held an oversized remote control in her hand. There was a slight mischievous grin on her face, as if she'd just done a barrel roll with her remote control plane over the family picnic blanket.

"Not bad."

She flicked a toggle, and the wall started moving back into place. When it was dark in my room again, I removed my hand from my eyes. I sat frozen on the bed, however, as my shirt was off and my morning wood was still at half-mast beneath the blanket.

"I'll let you get dressed."

"Thank you."

She wore a gold velour tracksuit, with vertical white piping up and down the legs and arms. The sweat suit showed her form without hugging it too tight.

"Let me know if you need any help in there." I tilted my head toward the other bedroom where my uncle slept.

"Thanks, but I've got it. Unless you want to help just to do something."

"Not a problem," I said. I could always search the scrub and chaparral outside for peyote buttons some other time. Might need gloves too, to avoid scorpion stingers.

She left the room, and I stood, waddled with my blanket around me until I closed the door to my bedroom, at which point I dropped the covers and went over to the black duffel bag.

I could get cleaned up later. For the time being I threw on a fresh green Izod shirt and a pair of pressed Wranglers, padded across the cold sandstone barefooted, out into the hallway.

Luna was visible through the doorway to the bedroom where my uncle slept, standing at the foot of his bed as if keeping vigil. She saw me, held a single shushing finger in front of her full lips, and mouthed something about the guest bathroom being down the hall.

A snore truncated in a grunt, like someone with apnea struggling for breath, and the old man stirred in his bed, fighting to break free of some demons in his sleep. A homburg perched on the crown of his head. The hat was brown, with a black satin band that held a red bird feather.

I kept my voice to a whisper as I came into the room. "He sleeps in his hat?"

"He won't sleep without it."

"Must make combing his hair hell." I stopped a few feet short of her, afraid to get any closer. It was as if there was a force field around the pair, some bond fused by time that I had no right to break.

He sat up as if something had bitten him in bed, which was a distinct possibility out here in the desert. "Nuh!" His eyes widened, full of life but also terror. He swallowed twice, looked first at Luna, which calmed him, and then at me, squinting.

"Marcus?"

I looked over at Luna. "Marcus is his son," she said.

I didn't have the heart to confuse him by telling him my real name, or that I was the son of his trophy wife of a niece, but I couldn't lie and tell him I was his son either, unless Luna told me to do that.

She knew more about this stuff than I did, and so I looked to her for confirmation, for something.

But we suddenly had bigger problems. "Agh…" I knew from the timbre of the moan that this was something in the guts, the bowels or kidneys.

"Uh-oh," Luna's voice was free of humor now, professional. "You should turn away."

"No," I said. "I can handle it."

She lost some of her sphinxlike bearing as she acknowledged me, maybe for the first time, as something besides a horny teenager. She recovered quickly and looked back at him. "Okay, you help steer his legs over the side, because this happens quickly."

I slowly gathered the old man's legs, which felt weightless, like the leaf-stuffed overalls of a scarecrow. His legs followed my guidance, and I turned away as Luna held something like a bedpan in front of him at the foot of the bed. The homburg fell off the back of his head and he moaned a sigh of relief as piss trickled out, spilling into the container.

It came to me then, that lie that everyone tells themselves, that they'll kill themselves when they get to be that age, but I knew that as much as I pretended otherwise, death scared me, just like it did almost everyone else. I'd had plenty of chances to check out and plenty of friends who'd already done so, but here I was, helping collect piss in a bucket and not even feeling too bad about it.

"Thank you" she said.

I couldn't say, "You're welcome," because I needed to help him as much as he may have needed the help. I'd been useless until this moment and now I felt more like a human. I wondered if this had been Debbie's plan from the jump. It was a character-building exercise, but not like the bullshit ones we did on retreat.

"I'll dispose of this." Luna stood from the old man's bedside, nodded her head toward the bathroom. "Why don't you wash up in his bathroom after I finish up in there, and then he'll do his breakfast and his morning writing exercise?"

"Sounds good." I didn't think he was in any condition to pen his memoirs, but I went along with it.

My uncle continued his business as if I wasn't there, sliding his feet into a pair of terrycloth slippers that had been hiding under the fringed edge of his bed's slipcover. He pulled on a pair of tube socks and adjusted the elastic waistband of his pants.

"You need anything?"

He shook his head, more to get rid of the sound of my voice than in answer. The young punk who might be his son had made a sound, and he didn't need to hear such sounds this early.

I held up my hands defensively, stood, walked into the bathroom as she was coming out. The porcelain bath was huge, like the shell of some monstrous clam dredged from the depths of Atlantis, as deeply berthed as a Catholic baptistry. A green plastic bath seat clung to the side of the tub. Nonstick decals and rubber mats made to look like cute cartoon frogs and lily pads covered the floor. I washed my hands in the sink, dried my hands on a towel on the rack. I returned to the bedroom, but the old man had left.

"Where d'you go?" My voice echoed through the empty stone rooms as I walked, still barefooted. I let my overlong jeans sag so I could use some dungaree fabric to cover my cold feet as I waddled.

Luna's laugh was a clarion bird titter. "Your uncle's fast when he wants to be."

I stepped through the kitchen where Luna hovered over a griddle on top of which several corn shells were grilling and a row of eggs fried. "Go into the main room, then veer right." She pointed the blackened spatula toward the room where I'd first entered with my mom.

I did as She-of-the-Spatula bade and entered the room, bright with the light of daybreak like all the others.

"Gay Blade of the Gillette Cavalcade!"

I followed the sound of his voice toward the right, though it was hard to locate the source the way all noise echoed around this cavern. I found him in a plush den, the footrest up on his Geri-Chair, his slip-on shoes kicked off. His posture said that he was the Alpha Male of a rest home, king of all bingo games and crochet-crafts tables he surveyed. A solid state radio, like the speaker in a fast-food joint from the fifties, sat on a wooden end table beneath a lamp topped with a cognac-colored shade. It wasn't as old as one of those sets where the label featured a dog listening to a gramophone horn with his ear perked up, but it was vintage.

Classical music came out of the thing and the man leaned back farther in his sofa-chair, letting the music of the ages wash over him and remove all earthly pains. He smiled with his eyes closed, seeing something pass before the canvas of his mind's eye. Whatever he saw there was none of my business.

I left him in peace and walked around the room, contented by the dull sizzle of the cooking sounds crackling from the kitchen and the frenetic violin music coming from the radio in front of me.

The room was all gingerbread brown gewgaws, like the quickie marriage roadside chapels they had in Vegas where a fat Elvis in sequined Kung-fu outfit officiated. There was some older stuff too, including a mahogany bar back, a relic from a Barbary Coast 19th-century brothel.

"Better not let Debbie see this place or she'll strip it for parts." I spoke more to myself than him.

His grin was sly, his face pulling into a smile against his will. I thought he'd not only heard me, but had understood me. I was convinced he would deny it if pressed. I knew that he was sick and old, and that some of that sickness had touched his mind or maybe even eaten parts of it, but I think he also knew how to pretend to be out of it when it was convenient for him.

I had a smart man in front of me I suddenly knew, and for reasons I didn't understand I somehow saw him now not as pitiful, but as an opponent in some conflict. But in what? A fight for Luna's love? I was sixteen and still (a little) pudgy, and this guy was on his way out. Neither one of us were getting anywhere with her.

And I still didn't know why I was so attracted to her. Sure, she was pretty and the only woman around, and I was sixteen, which was enough reason to stick my dick in anything short of a garbage disposal if given the green light. But there was something else, something abiding that kept making my double takes turn into lingering looks, which had turned into tossing in bed last night, clutching my pillow and pretending it was her.

Yet her presence, or even the ghost of her presence, had been there with me in the room, making it hard or more like downright impossible to whack off thinking about her. She wasn't just off-limits for me in reality; she even resisted incorporation into my fantasies. And I had a good imagination.

Maybe I would try again when stoned. Good weed got me horny, dropped inhibitions like drinking but without the undercurrent of violence.

"I like Luna too," he said.

"What?"

"Here we are," Luna suddenly said, her voice breaking the thick air that lingered between me and the old man in his chair. He opened his eyes, blinking rapidly like a lizard as he accepted a tray of pulped orange juice in a fluted glass and a stoneware plate topped with a Southwest omelet.

"He's at his most lucid in the morning," Luna said.

"I noticed that."

"So if you want to tell him something or ask him something…" Her voice trailed off.

"What is there to ask?" he asked and waved a fork where some green pepper and a fluff of egg dangled from the tines. "It's all here."

I looked around the room, at the framed photos on the walls, at the certificates of appreciation from this chamber-of-commerce or that hotel, "Thank You's" to him for opening a golf tournament or christening some ship. This was the only room that didn't have a desert décor, and the wainscoting showed at least one picture or medal per panel of antiqued wood.

A life well-lived.

Beneath a set of pica spears (either faintly stained with the blood of some long-dead bull or oxidized with rust), there was a picture of him on the cover of *Leatherneck* magazine. It was a black-and-white photo bleached to sepia by time. He stood in his fatigues with a set of cherry-red oversized boxing gloves on his fists, a cigarette dangling from his mouth. "The Best Fighting Marine since Gene Tunney."

I looked over at him. "Who's Gene Tunney?"

He snorted to beat a bull, almost to pull a wad of scrambled egg through the roof of his mouth and into his flaring nostrils. "Some pansy-ass who got lucky against Jack Dempsey."

I didn't know who that was, but at least the name sounded familiar. I would ask Mr. Hurley when I got back to Redrock. If I went back. My mind was already scrambling for excuses to stay in this stone mansion in the middle of nowhere. *Mom, I want to stay here, take care of him, get my nurse's certificate, like Luna.*

"There's more food in the kitchen, if you care to join me," Luna said.

The sound of her voice was soothing, but her words were unnerving. *Be something you've never been before*, I told myself. *Be cool.*

"Okay." The voice didn't squeak. My sebaceous glands were on my side for the moment. I stood up with Luna, and the old man was too busy eating to note our departure. The sound of his fork scraping against the stone dish played us out of the room.

She stopped in the doorway as we were walking, and the soft warmth of her form bumped me. Blood rushed from my head to toes and I breathed.

I thought her face twitched, but it was only the slightest change in her expression and I couldn't be sure. She spoke to him. "When you're done with that, we'll work on the writing, like we talked about, when Cliff comes."

He nodded to that, rocked a bit in his chair. The classic music went to a station break and a tranquil midmorning DJ's basso voice spoke from the golden radio, telling us which one of Verdi's Four Seasons we'd just heard.

The rest of the food in the kitchen lay displayed smorgasbord-style, the eggs and tortilla shells covered in still-hot tinfoil. A crystal pitcher of orange juice sat in the center of the table where we'd all met last night.

"You can help yourself," Luna said. "I already ate." She sat down at the table, and I heaped a plate for myself, taking a seat across from her. Sunrays broke through the windows and hit the pitcher, turning it into a prism of blues and blushes, like a soap bubble on a hot sidewalk.

I looked across the table at Luna, or where she should have been. There was a glossy academic text opened in front of her face. I read the title, which was in blood-red serif font and featured some grinning idol or totem done in woodwork on the cover. *Cannibalism among the Tribes of the Ancient Southwest.*

She somehow sensed my eyes on the book as I strained to read the subtitle. I gleaned "Ceremonial" and "Gustatory" and two other words, which wasn't bad for someone with eyes gummed in the dust of sleep.

"It's for an anthropology course."

"Online or is there a campus nearby?" I poured orange juice into one of those champagne glasses the old man had been sipping from.

"No, I…" She paused, lowered the text. "Okay, I'll come clean." She frowned for the first time since I'd met her, a pout that made her veer from sexy to cute. "I'm reading it for fun. But some people look at you weird if you tell them you're reading something like this for fun."

"Pellagra," I said, dumbly, or maybe not.

She had been ready to put the book to her nose again, but lowered it and said, "What?" flatly.

"People in America, or the United States used to get this disease from corn, that they didn't get from corn down in Mexico. Some doctor, I forget who, found out that the Mexicans ran their corn through lime-wash or something that gave them a source of vitamins that kept them from getting the disease."

Thank you, Mr. Hurley! Thank you, me, for not getting stoned or skipping class that day!

"Pellagra," she said, almost dreamily. I knew it was a disease, but it sounded like a wine request in her mouth.

It grew quiet enough that I could hear the radio from the den, the faint trill of a violin playing that Bumblebee piece that even the biggest philistine would recognize from old cartoons or TV ads.

Luna continued reading, but she had the book out in front of her set on the checked cloth over the table, scanning with the curve of her fingernail rather than holding the text up to her face.

"Who's Cliff?" I asked, remembering her words from the den, and mention of my uncle's notebook.

Luna reached toward a fruit bowl on the table, groping for it blindly since she wasn't willing to take her eyes off the page to get a hold of it. I took the wooden bowl in hand and slid it across the table toward her. She picked up an apple, and bit it hard enough that juices spilled and flecked her honey-colored skin. She spoke with her mouth full. "Cliff is Charlie's oldest and dearest friend."

She turned the page and I let it go at that, content to watch her read her book about cannibalism, wishing that the half-eaten apple in her hand was my heart.

CHAPTER FOUR
AN OLD TIMEY TEXACO

The den was an unlimited trove of memories, spitting out new wonders one after another like a nostalgist's version of a clown car.

"This is cool."

I held up a trinket I'd found in the room, heavy and made of metal, like an old vintage lunchbox. It was a massive oversized refrigerator magnet shaped like a gloved fist cocked and ready to swing.

"Pabst Blue Ribbon Wednesday Night Bouts give me that." My uncle rocked in the chair, softly and seemingly without worry. "Got some Christmas ornaments from them, too, one year."

I imagined an evergreen tree in some living room where a son in his cowboy outfit laid track for his model train on the carpet, while his sister used her new Chatty Cathy doll to derail the train.

A red and silver glowing object caught my eye from the nearest open cardboard box. I leaned down and brought up the Christmas ornament he was talking about, held it by its fishhook, and let it dangle.

"Speak of the devil," he said, grinning to make his ears twitch.

I put the shiny red ornament down and waded through the clutter that made the back of the room look like a packed storage locker. Near the rear wall there sat an old rosewood rolltop desk piled high with precariously perched boxes and stacked documents, an ancient piece of metal still catching a glint of light and serving as a paperweight for some loose files arrayed there.

"What do you call this?"

I picked up the piece of metal. He looked at it. "End-swell," he said. "It stops swelling. They didn't have that in my day."

I carefully set it back on the pile of papers, turned around. I saw a canvas drop cloth tacked to the left wall near the corner where it joined the rear wall. From the front of the room it had looked like the sheet was up there to keep a new coat of paint from getting on the floor a million years ago, nothing more, but viewed up this close I saw it was a matte painting or some kind of background from a theater production.

It was a watercolor small town, lain against the wainscoting so tightly it looked like a portal to another dimension. The time from which all these relics had come was now literally only a step away, like a magic mirror in some fairytale. The living painting reminded me of a Rockwell, only with a more impressionist stroke. In the center of the fake town there was a flatiron-shaped canopy over an old-timey Texaco filling station. A white-hatted attendant who looked like the Good Humor man stood next to a gas pump encased in red that resembled one of those old Coke vending machines.

"Careful there."

The voice wasn't my uncle's. It was deeper, much deeper, practically vibrating through my bones when it spoke.

I turned to the voice. Another older man was standing in the doorway, a Cuban cigar locked in the sausage-like fingers of his right hand. "You're standing in the same spot where Milton Berle used to stand to do his monologue."

My uncle grunted at that, stopped rocking. "Man could stop a seaplane's propellers with his hard-on."

"I heard the stories like everyone else."

Cliff bounded more than walked to reach the old man before he could try to stand up in an effort to greet his guest like a gentleman. They clasped arms rather than shaking hands, like old centurions surprised and pleased to find each other still alive on the scorched field after a rough battle.

"This whippersnapper breaking in here trying to steal your stuff?"

Cliff looked at me and winked to let me know it was a joke. His bushy eyebrow didn't budge as his eye closed. "How you doing, son?" Now that my uncle was steady on his feet, Cliff let go of him and took my hand in a sturdy grip.

"Michael," I said.

"Cutty or Cliff. I'd say my friends call me this or that, but I don't have enough friends to make those kinds of observations."

The smell of Aguardiente flowed from him to me. The liquor gave his face a flush but something told me he could handle a buzz, spent most of his days in that state, and had no intention of changing his ways.

His eyes were massive behind his tinted square-frame specs, as if he were looking at me through twin magnifying glasses. He had a face they didn't make anymore, tough-but-gentle, a reminder of more rugged times. It was a mug weatherbeaten from riding the rails or storming shores as ocean spray slapped his boat on D-Day, maybe both.

He could wear a fedora and not have it look like part of a costume, though he'd chosen to go hatless today. Shocks of white hair shot from either side of his head, complimented by tufts composed of hair thin as filament pouring out from his ears. That, along with his stocky barrel frame, short arms, and pitted face gave him the look of a loveable bulldog, ugly but dignified and hard not to like.

He stowed the unsmoked, unclipped cigar in one of the four pockets of a rayon shirt that showed a sunset bleeding red light over a palm-shaded lagoon. Then he went into another pocket and pulled out a pad and paper.

"You ready, Charlie?"

"I been practicing with the Señorita."

"Left and right-handed?"

"Just like in the ring, southpaw and orthodox."

"That's good, cause Doctor Parks is coming over here later today to make sure we've been doing the exercises like he told us."

"Nuts to that quack." His contempt was only halfhearted, and his old friend laughed with him.

"That 'quack' is the only reason you and I are talking. Remember how all you could do a few months ago was drool? Of course not, you might as well have had a lobotomy back then."

He looked behind him, at me still standing beneath the Texaco Theater backdrop. I moved, shifting under his stare, and as I did so I got tangled in the cloth a bit, lost in its folds like a jilted bride chasing her fiancé down the aisle and tripping on the trousseau.

"Careful," Cliff said, this time more seriously.

"Sorry." I let go of the cloth, seeing as I released it, that it wasn't tacked to the wall, but that someone had lodged the cloth above the wall, cinched to an architrave over a doorway to another room, probably a small closet.

Cliff shifted nervously, his wingtip alligator shoes clogging as he studied me with new eyes. I got the feeling he wanted me to leave while they discussed something. "You can stay," he said. "Just help me get some of these boxes down, clear a space."

He huffed as he removed the cardboard boxes from the desk where I'd just been nosing around. He wheezed as he worked. The liquor and cigar smell got stronger, washing over me like the comforting aftershave wafting from some childhood memory of a long-dead grandpa.

Cliff passed the final boxes to me and I set them down, taking care not to touch the Texaco cloth again.

"Alrighty, Charlie. Park your duff over there and let old Cliff work on your cuts." Cliff rapped his knuckles on the rolltop, but the soft leather was unresponsive, and his hand brushed the end-swell.

He looked at it like it was a soft grandkid complaining about having to walk to school in the snow. He didn't have to say, "You know, back in my day…" The look said it all.

My uncle moved around the desk which, uncovered now, showed its surface made of old saddle leather. Cliff fumbled around until a lamp came to life, its dragonfly-colored glass a mixture of amber and jade, filling the room with the warmth that only came from a real Tiffany.

"Yeah, definitely don't let Debbie in here."

Cliff looked at me. "Don't do what now?"

I shook my head. "Nothing."

Charlie sat down in a chair that was Louis the XIV, or maybe Chippendale (I'd learned more antiquing with Debbie and her Caballero in shining starburst spurs than I'd ever wanted to). The chair creaked, gave off a smell like mothballs, and the old man groaned in time with the protest of the thing's ancient wood.

"All right." Cliff walked back over to the Geri-Chair, where a square swatch of eggcrate-ribbed foam lay draped across the chair-back, still warm and indented from the impression of my uncle's body. "Let's do something about these tunes."

Cliff fiddled with a lacquered knob on the radio. Bach walking his fingers over pipe organ became the oom-pah-like fart of a Tejano oboe. Some singer wailed about a bandito's exploits with the gringos in some bygone border skirmish for Aztlan.

My uncle groaned theatrically. "Aye, Dios Mio, no, por favor."

"Quit trying to pretend you speak enough Spanish to do anything besides order a taco, you old borracho."

"I'm borracho porque los golpes, carnalito. Un borracho de Manos."

"Claro. Don't I know it. Your broken Spanish is making me feel like I took all those blows to the head."

Cliff's spatulate fingers stopped their twirling, and a pledge drive became classic rock became country & western. The croon of Marty Robbins echoed across the barren plains of FM radio, singing about the face of Jesus appearing in a jagged fissure of lightning over a stampeding drove of cattle a hundred head strong.

"I can live with that," my uncle said.

"You shit-kicking white boys and your hillbilly music," Cliff said, although he didn't seem to mind it all that much either.

Cliff went over to his old friend and they hovered over the open notebook together, like a coach and quarterback working out a play. "Here…" Cliff's voice dropped. He took my uncle's hand in his, sort of like Luna when she was working his grip on the soup spoon. Just like Luna, Cliff let the old man's hand go once he felt it had assumed the first stages of its motion on its own. My uncle's fingers trembled as they gripped a fountain pen, resolute but shaky, him versus his body, doing his best to hold Father Time to a draw in the fight for his nervous system.

"Good," Cliff said, all the ball-busting mirth out of his voice now. He watched my uncle write slowly, focusing so hard that his tongue crept out of his mouth and he bit it, concentrating on some finishing touch to a letter like a draughtsman slaving over blueprints.

"Again," Cliff said, sounding like a trainer punishing his fighter with extra laps for sneaking some chocolate mousse in camp.

"Your ass, 'again'."

"You can give me one more signature, Champ. Switch stance. Let's see that John Hancock southpaw style."

"We're not getting anywhere with this crap!" my uncle snapped.

"It ain't 'us.' It's 'you.' It's your mind and your life. It's your hand."

Cliff paused, inhaled deeply, patted his body to feel for the lump of the cigar he'd absently placed in one of the four dayglo marsupial pouches on the oversized fluorescent-painted print he wore. When he had the stogie secure again, he stuck it in his mouth and spoke around it, sounding like a gangster hamming it up for the press as his jaws accommodated the Cuban.

"Just like in the ring. I can be there in spirit. I can shout over the roar of the crowd, but I can't make you fight. You want to quit on me, go ahead and just tell me to stop wasting my time." He gazed around the roomful of memories, tempered a rich brown like the inside of a humidor, the dust so strong it was like an incense. "You can sit here feeling sorry for yourself, doing your best Brando for la muñeca allí en la cocina, or we can try to get that brain back. Then we can take care of some unfinished business."

The pep talk registered, the old man's hand trembled, stuck in place on the paper, like a bayonet dagger plunged obstinately between the ribs of an enemy soldier caught unawares in his trench. Cliff watched Charles Reeves, urging him with his mind, with his boring eyes, to become unstuck on his own, without a guiding hand around his own gnarled claw.

Charlie's hand and his mind broke through whatever obstacle had been there, but he over-corrected as he fought the disease or whatever it was and he made a massive scribble as his hand worked, moving seemingly on its own power like a Ouija planchette. "Shit on this." He pushed the stationary and pen away from him with greater finality than the first time. Pen and paper hit the cold sandstone floor, the sheets flapping as they caught a wind and buoyed for a moment.

Cliff leaned down, huffing from the exertion. "You don't want my help, fine, but that fountain pen cost me a pretty penny. I use her on my racing forms, you know."

"When are we going to the track?"

"Never again, if you have any sense. You got too much to get back to worry about throwing money away. I'm-"

He looked back at me again. I knew I was an unwanted interloper no matter what he'd said earlier probably just to be polite, a towheaded kid at the grownups' table during Thanksgiving Dinner eavesdropping on a dirty joke just as the punchline was inbound.

"I can dip," I said.

"Dip?" His bushy eyebrows stitched together into a gunmetal grey unibrow. "Hell, you can smoke if you want to smoke. I don't do chewing tobacco."

I'd meant "dip" as in leave, but it was stupid of me to use such current slang with him. The teachers and students at Redrock spent so much time around each other they had no choice but to pick up the slang themselves. It was normal these days to see some nebbish Algebra teacher wiping equations from the chalkboard and muttering, "My bad y'all" when he forgot to put some integer or an X in the right place as he diagramed a problem.

"'Go', I mean."

"No," Cliff said, giving a magnanimous wave with his wand of a cigar. "Nonsense, kid. I'm a good judge of character. You got a trustworthy face."

Patsy Cline's sweet voice came from the little box of a radio, plaintive but winsome, singing the soul of every grandma who'd once been an overworked waitress by day and a mistreated girlfriend the rest of the time. Someone had played Patsy for a fool but she was more focused on her own mistake than his deed. Her voice said he wasn't worth the anger, and he'd done some unwitting good by producing the heartache that birthed the song at least, and she knew it.

We all were silent for a moment, showing the woman some respect.

"Come 'ere," Cliff said, waving me over like a shoeshine boy. I had my problems with authority like most other kids my age at that "special" school I attended, but these two men struck me as big kids themselves, willful teenagers who'd stayed that way into their seventies or however old they were.

Whatever the conspiracy involved them, I wanted in.

I hopped over to the desk. Cliff held up the pad on which scribble-scrabble writing filled the page to the edges in the margins, cursive curlicues flourishing with a more controlled hand in the center of the college-ruled page. There were jagged, weird marks that for all I knew were diacritics from a foreign language filling the rest of the page, deeply inked impressions where someone drilled the pen into the paper, probably in frustration, the whole crosshatching of graffiti topped by that most recent big ink swirl my uncle had made in the pad before getting pissed and chucking the thing to the floor.

"Look at that." Cliff held the cigar out over one line, using the stogie like an old-school laser pointer. "Does that signature look better to you than this one?" He swirled his cigar with its outermost leaf peeling over to a less legible scribble in which nothing like a letter was discernible.

"Yes," I said. "Definitely."

"See?" Cliff looked at my uncle, who was surly but self-contained enough to not be snappish anymore. "He's a young buck with twenty-twenty vision. I'm an old fart who's got a case of wet brain, and you're a punch-drunk pug whose got Alzheim-"

"I'm not punch drunk!" My uncle went rigid, but he'd meant his screams for some internal voice that told him the same thing Cliff was saying, only more often than Cutty's gentle goading. The rage in my uncle's voice almost covered the doubt.

Cliff stuck the cigar in his mouth, bit, and said, "Good, get angry. Being angry beats giving up."

A female voice came from behind us, speaking laid-back Spanish, laconic and lingering on the vowels. It was Luna, a clear plastic tackle box in her hands. She adjusted a gold locket draped around her neck, whose tiny heart-shaped pendant dipped into the décolletage of her plunging neckline, where the literal gold nestled in the warm shadow of her bronze cleavage.

Cliff spoke to her in a Spanish that was fast and staccato, machine-gunning from his mouth like a wire report from a cub reporter. He didn't stick to his vowels like she did, or taste his words the way she lingered over hers.

Cutty's was city Spanish, and hers was countryside Spanish, I decided.

He looked over at me. "These non-Boricuas talk too slow for a boy from El Barrio."

I didn't know what that meant, anymore than I understood the Spanish before that, but he was smiling and so I smiled, too.

"Take that cigar out of your mouth," she said, "and lose a couple chins and it might be easier for me to understand you."

He reddened in pleasure. The spotlight had sought him out, and he'd gotten zinged in the front row by his favorite Borscht Belt comic.

Luna looked past Cutty, suppressing a smile meant for the cute old man who'd taken the insult in stride. Her eyes were blind to me and I felt like a ghost, absent and formless without her gaze. She looked toward my uncle sitting in the shadow of the massive desk on the other side of the room, alone in his mind. "Mr. Reeves, I'm going to sew some Velcro tape on your new shirts so you don't have to use the buttons." She held up the tackle box. "The doctor just called, and he said he'll be here in thirty minutes."

My uncle didn't speak, move, or acknowledge her words, or the rest of us in any way. She lowered her voice and spoke to Cliff, using English probably for my benefit. "How's the apraxia exercise going?"

"It's going." Cliff took a deep breath, one meant to remind him to be patient with both this process and with his old friend's mood swings. "Say," Cliff said, and switched into Spanish after that. He squinted as he spoke to Luna, as if it had been a long time since the mother tongue had touched his lips and he had to search for phrases locked up the cobwebbed vault of his mind.

Luna listened with increasing impatience, frowned as if she'd bitten into unripe fruit finally as she readied to reply. "I'm not a seamstress, Abuelo. I'm doing this as part of my nurse's duties. You mend your own shirts, you old goat."

"I'll pay you."

"I have my very own money, too, thank you. This is a nurse-patient situation, not a maquiladora."

She left us without another word, lugging the tackle box away from the den where country music softly played. Cliff beamed as he watched her go, shaking his head as he admired the controlled chaos of her hips swiveling as she moved, above that teardrop booty that could call down thunder easier than a whole tribe in a drum circle trying to draw rain from the angry heavens. Cliff made the sign of the cross over his person with the unlit cigar.

I knew how he felt.

***

The refrigerator was a giant black space-age slab that groaned low as I got close to it. Luna had said the apples were in the bottom crisper on the right, and I found one in the drawer, just where she said it would be.

I rinsed the apple in the sink. Her voice came to me from the other room. She said something that was indistinct, but repeated it as she walked into the room where I could hear her. "You don't have to wash those. They're fresh from market. No pesticides."

She had a new book in her hand, a bodice-ripper paperback with a die-cut cover, in the center of which was a swarthy musclebound man with a ponytail, cradling a damsel. Luna saw where my eye was and held the book up, no shame in her game. She flipped the pages quickly. "Sometimes I have to take a break from the heavy stuff and read trash."

"A lot of people don't even read trash these days. It's better than watching trash." I did that, too, but I didn't want to tell her.

"Have you seen the backyard?" Luna asked.

"No."

I got the feeling she wanted me or us out of the way when the doctor came.

"Come on. I'll show you where I live. But first…" She stepped around me and I held still, as if she were a magician performing a potentially dangerous trick and it was imperative I didn't move. The electric warmth of her being this close to me produced two contradictory sensations, a paralysis and a desire to jump out of my skin.

She held up the apple she'd gotten from the fridge and attacked it without first washing it. "Come on."

I took my unbitten apple in my hand and followed her down a tiled hallway toward the back of the house. She pushed aside a sliding glass door, and it was at that moment when I heard voices from the front foyer. The doctor had apparently arrived, though Cliff's rumbling voice was the only one that carried, or rather quaked, through the brick of the house's walls.

The heat of the day made it feel like we'd walked into an over-steamed sauna. The atmosphere was fraught with a warm pressure like we were just waiting for the back draft to kick in and scorch us, turn us to terracotta to match the rest of the baked desert landscape.

"You live out here? You pitch a tent or something?"

"No, I sleep in the swimming pool."

"I could believe you were a mermaid."

It was corny, but earnest, and she gave me an over-the-shoulder glance. "I wish I was a mermaid."

We passed under a narrow tunnel of shade, a pergola made of untreated mesquite wood, through whose lattice stunted pomegranates tried to grow. We came out into the pool area. Water dyed lagoon-green rippled in an amoeba-shaped swimming basin that quivered as if in anticipation of fusing with some other massive ameboid.

Luna walked to a Nissen hut-shaped house, where someone had stacked sandbags in pyramids on either side of the double doors in front of the building. Two flags flew on the roof, or rather slumped in the windless heat. One was the Mexican tricolor of Tenochtitlan, sporting a heraldic eagle with a snake in its talons. The other was the coiled "Don't Tread on Me" rattler. The latter flag faced the former, so that the old liberty snake seemed to root for his serpent companion to break free of the talons of the bird-of-prey.

"Your uncle's sapper buddies from the Marines set this up, and some electricians did the rest. I love it."

She walked with a mincing step, and I couldn't blame her. One false footfall and she'd be coming out of her sandals, and there were all kinds of cacti around here, barbed and nettled and hungry to sink their points into the pads her pretty brown feet. I did a quick scan like they taught us to do on weekend trips at Redrock before pitching camp, looking for jagged rocks, creepy crawlies, and cacti that might have made it hard to get a good night's sleep in my Sierra Designs mummy tent.

Large clumps of mountain ball cacti bunched together, looking like tumbleweed that had gotten stuck and forgotten its job was to roll through town on the heels of some desperado; there was some prickly pear resembling a sea-foam-green blowfish, along with a couple unidentified species that looked like they had enough spikes to hobble a shoed horse in mid-stride.

Luna disappeared into her house with her book.

I didn't ask her what she was doing. Instead, I got to work, walking over beneath a massive pebbled-glass table shaded by a beach umbrella. Next to that was a briquette-filled grille. The lingering smell of blackened fish and seared cilantro made my mouth water.

I set the apple down on the table in front of me and pulled out my pen tube, working the top of the apple free, first slicing and then ramming toward the core with my plastic tool. Once I'd made a hole, I wiped the apple juice that had spilled on me onto my jeans until my hand was dry, did the same with the pen tube until it was clear of juice and fruit flesh. Then I carved a chamber in the apple's side to compliment the other hole in the top.

An unwelcome memory of carving a jack-o'-lantern with Debbie when I was a child intruded on my mind. The weed would take care of that.

I pulled the herb from my pocket, feeling the bulge of the seedless, stemless good stuff, smelling like a potpourri of happy memories waiting to be reborn as soon as I fired it up. I'd fill the air with the smell of Christmas and clouds and the warmth of an opium den where I could sleep a thousand years like a teenaged Rip Van Winkle who didn't give a fuck about time, about the future, about working in my douchebag stepdad's Subway shop.

I unrolled the Ziploc, felt the clumps of weed there. I was an expert at eyeballing and feeling the bags to make sure none of my so-called friends pinched anything from me. I felt the bag again and there was no doubt this time. The bag was light. And I hadn't been smoking in my sleep.

I wasted no time in pulling out a thick bud, a glowing green sticky monster, part of a batch of a landrace strain they'd probably been cultivating since the Bering Strait land bridge had been in effect. I'd sampled it earlier. The weed was strong enough to let a Jamaican communicate with the ghost of Haile Selassie.

Buds were overflowing from the apple when Luna came outside with a towel draped about her body. I tucked the herb-stuffed hollow-bellied fruit in my pocket, where it made an inconvenient bulge hopefully hidden by the glass tabletop.

Luna thankfully didn't seem interested. I looked over at her. "You going for a swim?" I winced on my question, born more of panic than curiosity. *No, asshole, she's going to the moon in a bathing suit.*

"Something like that." Her eyes were downcast, studying the ripple of the water, as if it was enchanted and there was some kind of aquatic sprite resting there only she could see.

She dipped a toe into the warm green-blue surface, found it pleasing, and took off her pima cloth towel, tossing it onto a half-reclined beach chair.

Luna's swimsuit was tasteful, which somehow made her more stunning. Her body in the solid black halter with the frilled tennis skirt suggested all and revealed nothing.

I was sure she knew the effect it would have on me and I was sure she didn't care, either. I was incidental to her swim, and okay with that, as long as her sudden appearance hadn't surprised me to where stashing my weed caused me to lose any herb. Or any *more* herb, rather, since someone had already stolen some. I'd have to sleep with it under my pillow, like I was waiting for the Cannabis Fairy to heed my plea in slumber and refill my bag while I dreamed at night.

"Mind if I sit?"

Cliff's bearlike frame had somehow preceded his aguardiente and cigar smoke scent. I hadn't even seen his shadow as he crept up. I figured that he'd developed his nimble ways while working corners as a cut man, inserting himself into the mix of ring officials and referees to work his magic on a bleeding boxer.

"Please," I said.

He sat. "Mind if I smoke?"

I didn't move. I wondered if he'd seen me packing my apple. I didn't enjoy getting high around old people, period. It was too creepy, and the one or two teachers who got too close to students and smoked with them always made me feel uneasy, like they had hidden agendas and maybe a sexual interest in some kids at the school. One psychiatrist had already left the school under a cloud and I had my suspicions about a couple other faculty.

Old Cliff set my fears to rest, however, sparking his Cuban he'd been threatening to light all day. Sulfur rose on a waft of smoke, but the matchhead that just touched the striker plate couldn't compete with the heat of the day encroaching on us.

"My God," he said. "She's something." I looked over at Cliff, feeling like Luna's brother for the moment, like her honor needed defending, and her swim in this Edenic patch needed shielding from his eyes. But he wasn't looking at her, or even in her direction. And running the sound of his voice through my brain again I also heard nothing lecherous.

It was just a statement of fact. She *was* something, a marvel, and to not even acknowledge it would have been an offense.

"Your uncle's doing better." Cliff sucked his cigar, let the smoke flow from his nose like steam from a boiling kettle.

"Good, I'm glad to hear it."

"He used to write his name perfect with either hand."

"Hell, not even people who've never taken punches can do that."

"He could," Cliff said, nodding to himself and taking another draught of smoke, slow and at his leisure. He leaned back farther in his chair, looked off toward the red and brown horizon of stone and sand softening to vermillion at the line of the vanishing point. "That's how you know a guy's got equal power in his right or left. Your uncle's one of the few guys I knew besides Hagler who was a true two-hander. He could switch without you even seeing what he'd done, mid-combination."

"He sounds like he was something."

"He was," Cliff agreed, pursing his lips as he sampled the bitter aftertaste of the smoke he'd just drunk. "He will be again." He nodded emphatically. "He just has to keep working with the Doctor."

Cliff looked back toward the main house, toward the memorabilia-crammed den where presumably the doctor and my uncle were working on the man's handwriting.

I stole glances at the pool, saw no Luna, felt the panic of a child abandoned by its mother in the mall, saw her break through the surface of the green water in the next moment, body aerodynamically arced like that of a dolphin. The water had turned her brown hair black, the deep raven shade making her look like a witch from a time long-enough past when "witch" would have been a compliment that conferred power.

"La Brujeria de Agua," I said.

"Close," Cliff said. "Bruja is witch. Brujeria is just witchcraft."

I looked away. Soon I'd need to smoke my ganja and commune with that suburban white boy version of Jah who got me through my days.

CHAPTER FIVE
GOING THROUGH PHOTOS AND WALLS

This part of the desert looked like it was in a rain shadow, like where Redrock sat, but even if the rain couldn't reach it, the moon had no trouble pouring its beams over the hacienda.

I'd opened my window intending to blow smoke outside after putting a towel from the guest bathroom underneath the door's crack, but something about it didn't feel right. I could see Luna's compound behind the pool glowing with lamplight, and I didn't want her to get the impression I was spying on her when I was just trying to blow my smoke outside.

And the courtyard was just too creepy in the moonlight, looking like an old church's ancient graveyard. I shut the window slowly and left my room with my herb in the apple and my Bic lighter in hand.

The hallway was silent, bathed in the same blue light from the moon as the yard outside. My uncle's door was open, and I could hear the whipsaw sound of his snoring. It was loud enough that I figured I didn't have to creep around.

That left the problem of where to blaze up.

It hit me I could try the study where he and Cliff and the doctor had spent a good part of the day. The smells of Naugahyde, cigar smoke, and the slight formaldehyde scent of old age had soaked itself deep into that space, and I could probably get away with adding the perfume of my evergreen hydro weed with no one noticing.

I walked from the kitchen to the main sitting room. A buffalo head mounted on a wall above the hearthstone watched me with its black glassy eyes as a draft chilled my backside, pushing me onward. Other unlucky animals fallen to the gun sat mounted and stuffed, also pleading from their pedestals, the disembodied antlered buck staring the hardest as I passed him.

I tried the brass handle to my uncle's den. The door opened with a slight creak. The radio was on low, a twangy country ditty about a crash on the highway where whiskey and blood ran together, but nobody bothered to pray.

I closed the door behind me, walked toward the lamp, fumbled around until I turned it on. Warm golden light bathed the room. It looked like a good place to get stoned.

The hill country music gave way to a steel guitar whining, eerie enough in the night to sound like the redneck version of a Theremin. I sat down and plugged the carb on my apple and put torch to the top. I only had to drag once, since the apple had basically sunbaked in my pocket throughout the day while Cliff and I chilled poolside.

I drew a gulp of smoke into my lungs, felt a tickling in my ribs, and coughed in spasms as warmth flooded over my body.

The stuff was high-powered, and I already felt good. I knew that if I took one or two more tokes, my eyes would stay glued shut past noon tomorrow.

I drank the next hit, held my breath like I was in a contest, and let this one out much slower, a controlled yogic toke that left me high as hell before the last of the smoke left my lungs.

The smoke plumes curled, and I brushed them away from my face, cutting and karate chopping the air as the music from the radio came to me in rippling sound waves.

"Oh, shit." I heard my voice before I'd planned to speak, already at that peak crescendo of disembodied stoned. I struggled like a drunk trying to get his legs back.

Cliff had told me something earlier today, some advice about boxing I'd thought I'd never need.

"A lot of guys don't know this about the eight count." I'd tried my best to listen to him and ignore Luna swimming only a few feet away from us. "You get put down, you take the eight count, *if* it's a body shot."

"What about a headshot?"

"No, it's like being drunk. Your brain's like a computer. As soon as you stand up, it reboots."

I finally stood up, leaving the smoldering apple to sit beneath the lamp. There were still a couple more hits in the pipe until I cashed it, but I was baked for the evening. And I'd have to pitch the apple, since nothing smells as strong as the charred aftermath of a fruit-based smoke session.

I threw a few punches into the air. I saw myself in the ring, imagined the roar of a tuxedoed crowd in my head, women at ringside clutching their minks and pearls as I pummeled some man savagely on the turnbuckle. The Mob had paid me to dive, but Michael "Madman" Reeves didn't do the swan dive for no man.

I would beat this dude into submission and then flee town with my purse in one hand and my dame on my other arm, a peroxided blonde in a bullet-bra.

My windmill routine brought me across the room, over to the backcloth of the tiny town, a slice of Apple Pie Americana drawing me toward it like a tractor beam. The strain of weed I'd smoked was only a couple steps short of a hallucinogen. I touched the cloth as if expecting it to react like a magic mirror whose acrylic-painted surface might ripple and come to life, reveal itself to be the waters that would allow me to cross over into another dimension from which I might never return.

Hell, I might not want to return.

I looked at the gas station, coated in whitewash, the black Studebakers and green Packard's and cherry-red Comets all cruising through traffic down a Main Street in Anytown, America, with its storefront diners and hardware shops and bowling alleys.

I wondered if it had ever been real, any of it, I mean, the world in that painting. Men beat their wives back then, just like now; they didn't let black people share space with them in restaurants. Wars had come before and they'd come again. Even the dumbest kids at school who couldn't keep awake for a single class knew that much.

And still depression was blooming like a flower in my stomach, for something that the painted cloth awoke in me. If that world had once been, and was no more, then that made me sad. If it had never been, and it was only a lie and a dream of what should have been, then that was even sadder.

Those were my options, sad or sadder, stoned out of my mind, stoned out of my senses, on the verge of synesthesia as a mournful yodeler from the radio and the lament of his steel guitar almost become blue-green colors before my bloodshot eyes.

I touched the cloth again, and pulled it aside, revealing a door to another room. My sadness died as my curiosity came alive. I tried the doorknob. It was unlocked, so I turned it and stepped into another room in *La Casa del Peleador*.

All was dark. I felt with my hands along the wall, wondering if the lights were out just in the room or if I had somehow blacked out. I got my answer as my finger caught the end of a toggle on the wall. A neon saguaro cactus lit up, throwing a festive lime green over the room and pouring its tinted shine across the artifacts.

A lizard watched me, a scaly little chuckwalla with slit eyes, seeming to say with his saurian pea brain that if he were bigger, he'd basically be a Komodo dragon and I would be a midnight snack. I searched around the room for something to throw at him, wiped my dry hands on my pants and swallowed so that my mouth felt a little less like sandpaper and closer to cotton.

Squinting revealed that the lizard was a carving, convincing enough to scare me even if I'd been sober, done in intricate detail on a length of driftwood.

"Shit," I said. This time I had made the words come out of my mouth, rather than just feeling them as I stumbled through a head rush halfway between the adrenaline of parasailing and a flat-out panic attack.

I calmed down and looked at what the rest of the room offered, moving from a curio to a photograph as if I was in a museum, in a special velvet-roped section they rarely let the public enter.

There were photos of my uncle, post-prime, bloated a bit with that old fighter's face encased in a couple new layers of accreted flab and fat from the whiskey bottle. In one he wore a piebald leather coat that made him look like he'd skinned a moo-cow five minutes before taking the picture with a somewhat famous blonde I knew by sight but not name.

There was a framed photo with him next to an over-tanned man with a piled cockscomb of grey hair. He looked like a news anchor but his signature said "Burt Bacharach."

I'd been to Vegas enough with my mom and the Highroller to recognize the chorus line of lovely ladies surrounding my uncle in the next photo. The Folies Bergere gals wore massive peacock-plume feathered headdresses, their faces in tight, elegant smiles. Turquoise rhinestones covered their bras and feathered flamingo-pink boas draped seductively over the lone man in the middle of the posed still. My uncle flushed red and held up his fist.

I suspected he'd done all right with the ladies, maybe too good. I'd bet he had a couple kids he didn't know about floating around Sin City, changing lightbulbs on Vegas Vic down in Glitter Gulch or fixing arcade games at Circus-Circus, never suspecting their erstwhile sperm donor of a father had been a world beater a million years ago.

"Oh, crap!" I sounded like a kid, and rightly so. In front of me was a real relic, a classic one-armed bandit, not like the ones the slot junkies played at McCarran or the phony-gold ones at the upscale joints. This wasn't the Mega-Bucks where a million suckers got fleeced an hour and every once in a while some family from Peoria hit the jackpot and had their picture taken with a white Bengal tiger. This was a real nickel-plated slot machine from the days of Frank Sinatra and the Rat Pack, either refurbished or preserved by someone who'd kept the thing mint by packing it in a Lucite resin or something similar.

I couldn't bring myself to touch the gold box, though I let my hand hover close enough to bathe in the reflection of the champagne-colored light coming from the old cathode tube. Not a finish or a button was gimcrack. Three cherries showed from the last pull. A Jackpot.

Next to that machine was another big box draped in khaki-colored Oxford cloth. I guessed it was also another slot machine or maybe a jukebox, but I didn't want to pull the cloth off.

I stepped away from the slot machine, giving it the berth a bushman might give a crashed airplane that landed in his remote village. As I stepped back, my hands brushed a walnut desk where an open pad, a bunched accordion file, and some Post-Its and pens sat scattered, next to a brushed steel handheld recording device.

Whatever was going on here had a lot of moving parts, so many, it appeared, that it threatened to spiral out of control.

I picked up the pad and read.

"Luna has been adding turmeric to his tea and to some of his soups. This may also be helping with memory, but not to the same extent as the OCT axial projection, which continues to break the ganglia plaque even faster than previous transgenic experiments in lab showed. There is always the fear that replication will not hold when going from simian to human, so Charlie's progress has been heartening, to say the least."

I barely knew what photosynthesis was, so all of that would have been Greek to me even without a head full of Kush. I flipped the pages, landed on another page in which the doctor had written, his M.D. cipher a code nowhere near as bad or impossible to crack as the handwriting of your average doctor.

"Near-infrared will continue, OCT axial projection onto nerve tissue in Slot 1 (Charlie has said leave 2 alone, and I want to respect the patient's wishes, as I know my father would have).

"But it is important to remember that even though we are on the verge of a breakthrough, and perhaps have already crossed the Rubicon, a breakthrough should not be considered nor conflated with a miracle. A solid punch to the head from a professional heavyweight produces a force of 520 m/s^2. His white matter has more spots than a leopard, and the grey is the most scarred and lesioned I've seen in my eighteen years of practice. I understand, now, my father's guilt, and why it's important that I continue in my mission, for his sake, for mine, and for Charlie's. Clifford continues assisting me when asked and has been a Rock for his friend through these difficult times. We are not out of the woods yet, but-"

It continued on. I could have turned the page, but I knew that I shouldn't have even started reading it, or passed through the drop cloth to this secret chamber of wonders. Hell, I shouldn't even have come into the den without permission.

I did my best to leave the book on top of the walnut escritoire as I'd first found it, walked backwards. Then I turned the light off and watched the green cactus and the chorus girls go dim and return to darkness.

I closed the door on my way out, readjusted the cloth, like a mother tugging laundry on the line in the backyard. I went for my apple on the end table and walked out of the room, closing the den door behind me and leaving all as it had been when I'd first intruded.

Guilt hit me. I thought about when me and Adam had been toking and my little brother had barged in my bedroom to show me a new trick he'd pulled off in his PlayStation wrestling game, and he had seen me and my friend powwowing around the ceramic wizard bong, smoke trailing from our mouths and no sense in lying about it.

Adam had done proper damage control, a true bro and friend to the end, by getting up and showing enough enthusiasm to distract my little brother from his confusion at what he'd just seen there on the carpet where we'd sat together, kissing-close as we smoked.

"Whoa, man!" Adam had said, spurring my little brother on, as he sat next to him on the leather sofa in the media room watching him play his game on the massive big screen where Jim sometimes watched football. "That's a kick-ass pile-driver! Yokozuna ain't getting up from that one."

Adam had looked back at me and shot me a wink, not a conspiratorial one, but more one to say that he had this under control and there was nothing to worry about.

But maybe there was. A kid like my baby brother Lance was the type to keep things to himself. He got dragged from city to city, from child custody hearings to weekends with our dad (before he got busted), lost in a world of bright animated video games and Ritalin and his own secret thoughts that he never let me in on; I never knew how he felt about our mom, our dad, his own life, girls, what he wanted to do with his life. Anything.

I loved him, but that didn't help or explain or solve anything. And by the time he was thirteen he'd probably be smoking weed. And by fifteen my mom would find some of his insulin needles stashed beneath his bed, hidden maybe in that closed and locked Soviet chess set she'd bought him on a trip to Sochi. He'd be smart enough to padlock the thing, but Debbie was a determined individual when she wanted to be, and would pop the lock with a screwdriver, and find a spoon and cotton balls, both stained with blood, hidden beneath that hand-carved Bishop, whittled to look like a Greek Orthodox priest made of Riga softwood.

My brother would have a habit obviously, but the monkey on his back wouldn't have grown to gorilla size yet because he hadn't bothered to pawn the set. That day would come, though, and once the Highroller saw track marks on his veins Debbie would send his ass to join me out in Redrock just to keep the peace in Death Valley between her and her meal ticket.

Lance would smoke weed because he'd seen me smoke. And from there it would continue to be monkey-see, monkey-do all the way to the big leagues, where people died, the rich and the poor and everyone in between dropping like flies with blue lips and eyes rolled into the backs of their heads.

I decided that I would take my apple, pitch it somewhere (maybe out my window, where the scorpions and spiders and lizards could eat it and maybe catch a buzz from the resin) and then I would flush the rest of my very expensive weed down the toilet. I'd curse myself as a numb nuts fool even as I did it, but it was the right move to make.

I left the den, closing the door softly behind me, knowing that the weed had me too blitzed and I needed to take every precaution to make things look as if I'd never been there. They would know that I'd been snooping around (but not that I was searching more for a place to smoke than for any other reason). The only question was whether I would lie if confronted directly.

"Luh!"

My uncle's voice, in pain and terror, untethered from his mind in the fever of dream, echoed through the house like a gong pealing in a belfry.

"I'm coming!" I shouted. Getting rid of the apple would have to wait for now.

***

"Nuh!"

I wondered what he was thrashing against in his sleep, what he was denying or fighting. He could have been wrestling the Grim Reaper who told him he was coming soon, hellhound on his trail, with a scroll's worth of sins unfurling from birth to this very moment.

I figured the fear of losing one's mind was greater than of death, though ageing had to be the hardest thing in the world, since that was the slow process of both losing the mind and walking off into death.

"La!"

"Nah!"

The panicked grunts were getting closer together, like contractions of birth.

But I knew what the words were, or rather what the word was, as I padded across the hall, through the kitchen, at the threshold of his bedroom where she was standing, already one step ahead of me and moving toward her charge where he flailed on the bed.

Luh! Nuh!

Luna.

She stood over him, wearing a raglan sweatshirt she'd thrown on, with the hood up so she looked like some nun interrupted during evening prayers.

My uncle spoke in a rush and he writhed until the hat he wore to bed fell off and hit the ground. I picked it from the sandstone, while Luna sat next to him on the bed and held his arms in a way meant more to comfort than constrain him.

"The ski-," he said. "It's the skimming that's the end of…"

He stopped screaming, breathing heavy, saw Luna and myself. His eyes narrowed from saucers to slits. He looked sheepish, pursing his lips in embarrassment.

"The skimming?" I asked.

Luna shot me a sidelong glance, rage causing her eyes to grow radiant with the shining reflection of some poison I'd injected into this house just by showing up, now made worse by my pesky question.

"The War," my uncle said, and I immediately realized my mistake. "The skimming" must have had something to do with a round or a plane (maybe a kamikaze) skimming its way onto a deck or across the water and maybe shearing off the head of his friend who'd been smoking a Lucky Strike and manning his station in a life vest a second before.

"I'm sorry." I meant my words for him and for her. I handed him his hat and looked at Luna with an apology written across my face. I had screwed up, I knew, and I walked backwards as I edged toward the doorway, like a servant too frightened to take his eyes off his wrathful master who'd just booted his backside.

"You can stay." Luna's soft voice had a mesmeric effect. I stopped backpedaling and walked forward, toward her.

How, I asked myself, could I be horny at this instant? Why couldn't I be a human, be sympathetic, stop thinking about her and try thinking about him? Using his illness as an excuse to get close to her, show her I wasn't a POS (when I was) was about as low as hitting on someone's widow at their funeral.

But I was desperate to lose my virginity so that I could tell the truth when I went back to school, rather than lying about my luck after the Sadie Hawkins dance with some girls from a sister institute we'd invited to Redrock. I knew Luna wouldn't screw me (and that she shouldn't) but my body wouldn't accept the truth of our age difference or of anything else real.

Luna pulled down the hood on the track jacket, which had accidentally flopped up when she'd come running into the room. She rubbed my uncle's back in comforting clockwise circles. She looked at me. "I will make some tea. Can you stay with him?"

"Sure." I sidled up to him, sitting on the bed next to him. The mattress was memory foam or Posturepedic and my butt barely made a dent as I plopped down.

Luna walked out of the room, and I did the human thing by not even glancing at her posterior and looking at my uncle instead. He regarded his hat, holding its brim by the outer edges of the felt. He tossed it like a disc across the room. "I'm not senile." He frowned so that twin lines appeared on either side of his face. "Who the hell let me wear a hat to bed?"

"You did."

He regarded me, awake now, though still shaken and clammy. "Who the hell are you?" His brow furrowed into a knitted mass.

"I'm your great-nephew."

"Cynthia's kid?" There was a lilt in his voice suggesting he hoped I was. I shook my head. I dashed the hope. "Deborah?" he asked.

"Yes."

The frown was back.

I felt like apologizing for being my mother's son. From the kitchen I could hear the opening of heavy wooden cabinets and the clatter of glass, the rumble of crockery rattling on its hooks above the stovetop.

"What the hell are you doing here?"

"I don't know." I put my head in my hands.

"What did Deborah name you?"

"Michael."

He grunted, amused. "Well, I didn't mean to ride herd on you. Just, it's strange to be me again."

"Who were you before?"

"Me, but without…" He paused and his tongue darted out between his lips. He looked parched, like he needed a sip of something caffeinated, and a glance he gave over my shoulder toward the kitchen only confirmed my suspicion. "I was me, sort of. I had my memories, but nothing else. And my body wouldn't do what I told it to do."

"You're getting better?"

He nodded, slowly first and then more emphatically. "I'm getting better." He looked around the room, toward the crossbeams on the rafters above, at the walls with tchotchkes pegged in place on old tenpenny nails. "I'm not as healthy as I want to be. Or as I will be." He eyed me and smiled, and neither the eyes nor the smile were reassuring. "You've got to help me."

"Sure, you need help getting up or you got to pee?"

He waved off my patronizing rap like it was an irritating gnat buzzing in pesky haloes around his head. "No, *real* help."

"Okay."

The soft hiss of a kettle simmered from the kitchen where Luna hummed a song. Its sound made me feel like I could curl up right there on my uncle's bed and doze in the depths of a peace I hadn't known since my days with the needle.

"Doctor Parks can't know how fast I'm coming along." He waved his hands that were gnarled and nubby with arthritis when the fingers were open, but assumed the form of anvils when he closed his fists and got resolute. "Neither can Luna. You never tip your hand in poker. And in boxing, it's…" He cast about for words, stunned by all the options dancing in his previously battered brain. There was too much to choose from and the ability to speak was almost as terrifying as being stricken and without words, trapped in his mind and frozen behind the wall of his glassy eyes.

"It's like Jose Torres said. You know him?"

"He a flamenco guitarist or something?"

He looked at me like I was trying to run a con on him now, playing dumb. Only I wasn't playing. I was still only half-sobered by the panic that had brought me running down the hall.

"Jose Torres, light-heavyweight. Said the best boxer is the best liar. Make 'em think you're going to do one thing and then do another. Wars aren't won by warriors. They're won by the guy who knows how to use the warrior's pride against him."

"What happens when you get two warriors fighting, and no lying?"

His smile was cocked now, slanted as if he recognized something in me for the first time, as if I might not be dead weight. "Then you get more blood's than necessary. The crowd loves it, eats it up. Your promoters make money, but you and your friend sit there in a hospital room with bags of ice on your eyes and passing blood for a couple a weeks. And in the end, people forget."

I looked around at his plush digs. "They didn't forget you."

"No," he said, agreeing, shaking his head first and then nodding once. "They didn't, and that might be a problem."

"What-"

"Tea is ready," Luna said, brightly, either unaware of what had happened between us, or playing her own brand of poker.

"Thank you." My uncle gave a gracious bow with the upper half of his body, stood in his bedclothes and smoothed some wrinkles from the silk PJs. "Come on, kid." He tapped me on the shoulder with a hand I hadn't seen move, and my head turned instinctively toward it, where his hand now no longer was.

I looked forward, confused, feeling like a fool, and followed the old man who'd gotten the jump on me and was ambling down the hall. The lucid uncle who'd been sitting there with me on the bed a moment before disappeared again, and he hunched, spine worn by time and pain, toward the guest bathroom.

Luna craned her neck past me, warm breath smelling like cinnamon. "Mr. Reeves, do you need help?"

"No, thank you. I can go on my own."

She looked at me, eyes wide with joy and her smile causing dimples to form in the soft skin of her cheeks. "That's the first time he hasn't needed the night commode."

"I guess he's making a little progress."

I would not tell her the extent of said-progress. I'd already agreed to be part of his conspiracy. All the same, I wasn't up to anything worse than a lie of omission, not with her, and I dropped my eyes.

Lying usually came easy to me, but the lies were mostly told to avoid getting in trouble at school or to avoid getting my ass kicked in the hallway between classes. This was a lie, or at least a withholding of the whole truth, whose revelation would have made her happier than she already was.

I didn't see why he was eager to keep it a secret that he was getting better. I thought that was the point of this whole endeavor. Her, the doctor, Cliff. I thought most about him, now, Cutty the clay-faced old rugged bulldog with his ever-present cigar stink. No doubt he was on our team, and I could trust him with whatever secret my uncle had. Because whatever the former boxer asked me to do, I wasn't sure I could handle it alone.

"Ah!" The sigh of a man relieving himself came from the bathroom and carried down the hall. Luna suppressed a smile, not wanting to reveal that she found something so simple and vulgar funny. So much of her work had to do with bodily functions, and the helpless patient might misinterpret any kind of laughter.

The sound of water came from the faucet in the hallway. I'd already half-made that bathroom my own, stocking it with toiletries, conditioner, and a couple seashell-shaped lavender soap bars.

Charles Reeves stepped from the bathroom, shuffling with a lumbering gait, hobbling as if one leg was shorter than the other. "Come on, Son." His voice was hoarser than it had been when we were together sitting on his bed, as if each word cost him a great effort.

I looked to Luna, seeking her permission. She nodded and then dropped her eyes, a meek yet-sad warmth radiating from her. "Go," she said.

I obeyed, and followed a couple paces behind him, unsure of myself like a dog trailing a man who might not want him around. He drank his tea from a baby's plastic sippy cup, manic clowns in white face paint patterned on the sides of the thermos.

He turned into the living room, taking in all the artifacts of his past, seemingly for the first time, looking at the mounted and stuffed heads as if the dead deer and buffalo might be secretly passing messages to him that only he could hear. He even nodded, either in agreement with something he'd thought or a signal he was getting from the animal heads frozen in regal poses.

The moon waxed full outside, and stars in the sky glowed like diamonds to make a jeweler weep. "Come on, son," my uncle croaked, limping his way toward the den with an uneven gait.

He tippled the plastic cup into his head, held the door open until I'd passed through, and then closed it behind him.

"All right." His fake hunchbacked posture was no more and his voice no longer sounded like his vocal cords were crumbling.

"What did I say when I woke up?"

I hesitated. I didn't want to make him think of the War again.

He went over to his Gerichair, set down the clown-covered cup with a look of disgust on his face, as if Luna had mocked him by giving him the child's plastic trinket and the clowns themselves were laughing at him.

"Come on," he said, leaning over to the radio, impatient with me and with it. He fiddled with the knob until the country became classical again. It was a Granados toccata, which I knew because I'd been in a rehab with a music prodigy who was the only one to take advantage of the Steinway in the sunlit dayroom, while the rest of us played cards or killed time with junk food and daytime TV.

He turned the music up, and Granados tickled out Andalusian airs over the ivory, hopefully well enough to cover our voices.

My uncle looked at me with a look that said *Don't bullshit me*. That was usually my cue to turn on the sewage hose with adults, but I respected him, which was a first with grownups. Was I selling out? Would I be telling Mr. Granski and Mr. Hurley who was copying homework from whom, sneaking glances at the tests and bubbling their scantrons based on what they could glean from the handful of Asians and Jews at Redrock?

"You said something about skimming."

I might as well have hit him with a cattle prod. He went bolt upright, rigor rigid, and I was afraid he'd had a heart attack.

He recovered, gripping the Naugahyde of the Gerichair's armrests so that the fabric emitted a leathery groan. "Yes, it's the War. The skimming of the Amtracs across the water."

"Amtrak? Like the train?" I'd been to the station in Vegas once or twice. It was a historical landmark, a part of old Vegas that looked more like the Alamo Chapel Mission in ole San Antone than something you'd expect to see thrown in with the tacky glitter and glass-skinned buildings and light pollution that passed for a skyline in Sin City.

"Amtrac," he said, bringing me back to the moment. "Like an amphibious vehicle."

He stood up fast enough for the recliner to transform into a rocker in his wake. He moved around the room, groping as if blind, searching high and low in panic, like he was late for a date and still couldn't find his keys.

"Ah ha!" He held up his right pointer finger, which trembled. A moment before it had been steady. I wondered if this clearheaded state would last, or if the mind would fog over again and the nerves would break and he would be as old and shattered as I'd found him when I'd first met him.

Or maybe he was just excited, and that's why he shook.

"Old Cutty kept this stuff hidden for me. And hidden *from* me."

"What?"

He leaned down, came up out of his half-crouch holding a white three-ringed binder he'd stumbled across where it had been protruding from a box, the coat battered pleather. "You may not want to see this."

That made me want to see it, whatever it was.

My uncle dropped the album open on the desk and flipped through the laminated sleeves where old photos from the Second World War sat. In one set he and another man in green fatigues and helmets covered in fishnet stood on an open ship's deck navigating dark waters, smoking cigarettes and leaning over a massive mounted machine gun. The perforated shroud of the barrel pointed into a wake of foaming water that looked a ghostly gray in the old picture.

"That's me and Kassel. They teased him for his Kraut name."

"Kraut?"

He looked back at me as if I was incidental, less real than the photos. "Sprechen sie Deutsch?"

"Nein."

His irritation increased a little. "You know how to say 'No' in German."

"'Oui.' Just like I know how to say 'yes' in French. But two words do not make fluency. Just reading the labels on the stuff Debbie brings back from Les Galeries LaFayette taught me a lot."

He suppressed the smile, singeing a bit as if I'd scorched him when he didn't expect any pushback. "Touché."

I looked down at the photo with him. "You guys keep in touch?"

He shook his head. "He died at Betio. Can't even visit his grave."

"Too painful?"

My uncle looked at me. "'Too painful?' No such thing as too painful. Pain is just the body struggling not to succumb to death. Pain's good news. If a car motor could feel anything, it'd feel pain the whole time it's running."

"I meant, going to see his grave would be painful for you."

"He doesn't have a grave." My uncle gave a gruff laugh pitched only slightly closer to human than the bark of a chained dog. "What was painful is getting stabbed a couple hundred times by the Garamond soldiers. They were like Samurai. Could slice you all day and keep you alive. They threw him in the water while he was bleeding and hoped the sharks would get him."

"Did they?" I thought about Luna, knowing it would fill her eyes with rage if she were here, laser beams burning into me for encouraging him to talk about the War.

"Sharks got him but he'd already been chopped to chum by the LST motor and probably some friendly fire by that time. He went from friend to food quite quick."

He turned the page in his book of memories before I could digest that, with no time for my horror, pity, or even his own emotions or thoughts. These were things that had happened to him or things he'd seen and that was all there was to it.

My uncle smiled. There was another photo of him with the same guy, their shirts off and their chests concave and emaciated from a lot of fighting and probably not much food. They stood at the foot of a volcano's black tufa, looking so weak that I couldn't believe their dog-tag chains draped around their necks didn't drag them down like ship anchors. But they smiled through the sunburn.

"We cleared that island pretty quick, found a couple cases of Kirin." He flipped to a page that showed him and several other marines in various states of khaki, squinting against the sun or suffering under wads of bandages that were thick as rolls of toilet paper but were still soaked clean through with blood.

The next page in the series was a spread that showed a Japanese man well over six feet tall, dead but standing on account of a bayonet on the end of a Browning rifle being rammed through the shocked "O" of his mouth; his eyes were open. The bayonet blade jammed in and through the man's head, exiting the back and going all the way through the heartwood of the coconut seawall behind his head, two scraggly screw pines doing nothing to shade him as the sun mummified him where the skewer impaled him through his open mouth.

It was the worst thing I'd ever seen outside the internet or while on LSD, but it was just another photo to my uncle. The only difference was that the smile from before when recalling his friend disappeared, got replaced with a new smile, one that was ear-to-ear and beyond something as simple as sadism. I could have judged him, but I figured a man who had seen his friend chopped apart by a boat's blades and then torn apart by fighting schools of sharks had at some point lost the ability to care what the warless ignorant thought about anything.

Who was I? A soft mass of suburbia floating through the warm medium of a poisonous prosperity, given to me by a mother who looked through me to the dinners and theater showings and shoes awaiting her once I was out of the way, and a stepfather who couldn't stand me. Those were problems, but they weren't friend-eaten-by-shark problems.

And he'd been a boxer, too, beaten and probably killed men with his hands while taking punishment himself.

Shit.

I looked at him reminiscing, ignoring himself in all the pictures and soaking up all the other details. I was glad I was on his team, in whatever new war we were waging together.

The slap of the laminate sheets was loud as a flyswatter, as his enthusiasm for the good and bad, brotherhood and blood, caused him to move through the pages as if it was a flipbook before him and he might reveal some secret animation in the album if he rifled through the leaves fast enough.

He stopped on a page, one that I think he'd been searching for, in which there was a single sheet of rice paper covered with Nihongo characters inserted in a mylar sleeve. I recognized the Japanese language because of some Baccarat players who'd visit Big Jim's ranch and would humor the Gaijin on the outdoor patio over Asahi and swordfish near a red-hot brazier, and there were a few Japanese kids at Redrock, wayward sons of black-suited businessmen.

"What does it say?" I asked.

"Hell, you telling me you don't read Japanese?"

"About as well as I speak German and French."

"Verständlich," he said, which sounded more like German than either French or Japanese to me. He dragged his fingers over the letters carefully. "This is a personal communique composed by the Emperor himself, from Hirohito to the Garamond, telling them they fought gallantly, and Bonsai!" He shouted the last word, not in the bucktoothed broad imitation of a Japanese man I'd have expected from an American of his generation, but properly inflected and with that half-constipated grunting sound of a real Shogun.

I was certain he had killed quite a few of them, though I didn't get the impression he hated them, or if he had, the blood spilled on both sides had caused respect for their fighting spirit to shade its way into the War's ambiguous blood-soaked color wheel probably by the end, when the blades and bullets had drenched everything Nippon red.

"I imagine it's worth something," my uncle said, and slammed the photo album shut. He glanced around the room, whose walls reverberated with the sound of Segovia strumming his own *Recuerdas*, though of the Alhambra and not the South Pacific. "Some stuff I have is probably worth a lot."

A knock at the door startled us. "Hello?" It was Luna, her voice lilting as if she didn't want to interrupt the boys while they were watching football but it really was time to act civilized and eat dinner.

"Coming!" My uncle's voice had gone seamlessly back into its hoarse decrepitude, and he hit me with a wink one more time before the eyes went half-vacant and stricken again.

CHAPTER SIX
SONORA AIN'T THE ONLY THING BENT

My uncle crept into my room like a coconspirator in a crime a couple hours later. It was barely dawn, the sun just touching the cloudless sky and dyeing it pink. "Wake up, get dressed."

I looked at him. He was already way ahead of me, both wide-awake and dressed. He'd made his peace with his clown sippy cup, but there was coffee instead of tea in there, or at least that's what it smelled like.

"Why? What's up?"

I was still groggy from a nightmare whose details I could barely remember.

"We're going for a little ride."

"Sonora…" I tried to remember the name of the little tank town Luna had mentioned.

"No, not Sonora Bend."

"Don't tell me Vegas?" I asked, sitting up. I hated the place.

"No," he said. "Not yet, at least." He turned to leave the room and give me time to wake up and get dressed. "I'll be out front."

I did what I could in the time he gave me. I snuck my bag of weed from inside my cotton pillow case, springing to life, putting on some khakis and a grey crewneck, slipping my watch on my wrist as I went to the bathroom. I hit my face with a couple splashes of cold water, gargled with some

Colgate mouthwash and maced my chest with body spray and hit both pits for good measure.

He was outside in the two-car garage waiting for me, watching a thin welter of cloud un-spool in the sky and then dissolve as the sun continued its ascent. "You ready?"

"Yes." I wiped the last sleep from my eyes and yawned.

"You don't look ready."

I definitely wasn't as duded up as him. He wore a silk Bat Masterson vest, like a croupier in a themed gambling saloon, boiled hounds tooth shirt and elbow garters. A leather thong tipped in brass caps cinched the mini steer skull on his bolo tie.

"Let's go."

The motor on his Polara was already purring, causing the hardtop to hum. It looked even better this close, its sky-blue topcoat catching the early morning rays that outlined its sleek Batmobile angles. She looked aerodynamic enough to take flight.

"How d'you get it started?"

"Luna thinks she's clever. I fixed the distributor cap, and the rest was quick jimmying with a flathead. I was learning to hot-wire from the older kids in juvie probably half a century before you were a mote in your father's balls."

He got in on the driver's side.

I slid into the soft ribbed leather of the passenger seat. I had never been this close to a car this cool or classic, not even at auto shows. "Luna will kill us."

"I love her," he said, pulling out, "but she's my caretaker, not our mother."

He pulled out and pointed the car's bullnose toward the desert. The rocky soil might as well have been new asphalt under the smooth grace of my uncle's hand; his alleged hotrod escapades were probably as real as he hinted.

I cranked the manual roll down on my window. It whined, but it worked.

"What year is this?" he asked.

I looked over at him, still tired. "You serious?"

"I've been out of it a long time."

I shook my head and stared out the window. "Alzheimer's is not something you recover from."

"I told you I wasn't senile."

"Okay, pugilistic…" I fumbled for words.

"Pugilistic Dementia. Punchy." He took a sip of his coffee and hissed with satisfaction as it went down.

"You don't recover from that."

"First time for everything. Thank Dr. Parks."

I leaned back in my expansive seat, at ease and with my arms stretched out like I had a movie theater to myself at a midday matinee. "What are you guys up to?"

"You can ask him yourself the next time he comes to the house."

It relieved me he was at least thinking of coming back, that there were no high-speed police chases on the itinerary.

"We robbing a bank?"

"Don't be ridiculous." He wagged his head. "We're going to a cathouse."

My heart leapt in fear. "I'm too young."

"We're not going there to get laid."

"Great," I said. "Next we can go to the bank and not get money."

"Fine, don't tell me what year it is," he said, steering, at one with the desert road unfurling before us. "Just tell me if we're driving Nucleon hovercraft to our moon colonies yet."

I hated to be the bearer of bad news but gave it to him straight. "I don't know what a Nucleon is, and there's no hovercraft or moon colonies. On the bright side, the Jetsons are still on in reruns."

"What the hell has humanity been up to since I've been asleep?"

"Not progress," I shrugged. "The usual."

He pulled onto a two-lane road. A lizard with a plump dewlap and horned green pompadour of spines lay split in half on the road in front of us. I took it as an ill omen.

"Any wars since Vietnam?"

"A couple."

He looked over at me, sizing me up. "You enlisted?"

"Too young." I didn't mention that I wouldn't have enlisted even if I was of age. Back in his day war might have been something everyone did, but these days it was just background noise unless you had someone in your family personally in the service, and I didn't. Plus the Army piss-tested, which meant I was assed-out.

"You playing tennis today?"

That seemed pretty leftfield. I looked at him like a dog encountering a new noise. He shot a glance at my feet. "You're wearing tennis shoes. Plimsolls, as my old man called them."

"Everyone wears them now."

"Not me." He tapped the leather of his cowboy boots, handstitched with roses and high as Wellingtons.

The desert expanded all around us, a massive red bedrock the color of the crust on a pie left in an oven set on "high" and then forgotten. I didn't know at what temperature sand became glass, but the sun had gone from a mild suggestion of light and heat into an inescapable force dominating the sky and pressing down on the Earth between the time he'd roused me and now. Someday they'd conduct one too many underground nuclear tests (or the aliens would just drop a payload to put us out of our multiple miseries) and we'd all end up sealed under a massive half-geode of brown glass that would preserve us like mosquitos in amber.

We'd make great specimens for some alien's collection, as they happened on our burnt rock still floating on its course through the solar system a couple billion years hence. I was looking forward to being pinned, matted, and labeled in some alien scientist's file drawer.

"Keep your head in the game."

My uncle's voice brought me back to the moment. "Can I hit this?" I reached for the coffee cup where it sat between us.

"Hit it with an uppercut for all I care."

I took a pull on the strong coffee, a bracing gulp that woke me up more than that splash of water to the face first-thing this morning.

"I figure Luna's waking up right about now," he said.

"She will feel worried."

"I'm an adult."

I knew better than to argue with an old person. He pulled off at the exit, blazing a path through what was a hell of convincing replica for tourists or a real ghost town, complete with puncheon walkways, false front saloons and general stores with batwing doors.

He turned into the lot of a place that sat catty-corner to the main strip, whose rusted tin shingle informed us it was "The Pony Pitstop." An unlit bullseye lantern hung from the signage, untouched by the slightest wind and with glass panes so fogged from dirt and dust it wouldn't have been any help even had it been lit at night.

He eased in front of the shop, parking but leaving the motor running.

"You got money?" I asked.

"More than you know, boy." He looked back at me before closing the door. "You need anything?"

"Rolling papers."

He walked toward the old-timey building, where a Cigar Store Indian chieftain tall enough to be a totem pole hovered over old pine crates that once held vanilla sarsaparilla bottles along with ancient branding irons, and horseshoes set down to keep a breeze from scattering piled gunnysacks and burlap bags.

My uncle shadowboxed the air, milling to an invisible opponent's body and finishing up top with a short uppercut before he reached the porch. He muttered something to himself like "Still got it" and disappeared into the shop, the door's chime following him in.

I waited, watching the rearview for a sheriff's cruiser or the flashing blue Mars light of a local cop car, maybe the dogcatcher or whoever they sent after you with a butterfly net when you were old and they were trying to keep you corralled.

My uncle came back carrying a brown paper bag made to look like a haversack that said, "Pony Pitstop."

He set the bag in my lap and started the car again. "Got some provisions, little food items. Got your papers, too. You got any Bugler?"

I shook my head, looked at the bag.

"I only smoke Bugler."

His hands beat mine into the sack, and he came out with a plug of pink saltwater taffy that he unwrapped from a wad of wrinkled wax paper. He threw that in his mouth and chewed the clump like cud while studying a laminated square on an atlas he spread open on the steering wheel.

"I called the Sawdust in there. Vick still works there, but she's the madame of some museum instead of a working girl."

"So we *are* going to Vegas." I pulled out the golden packet of rolling papers, extracted the first leaf.

"Sawdust, not Stardust."

"Oh."

He spun the wheel, and we drifted back through the ghost town the way we came in, and eased back onto the highway.

The day was bright through the windshield, though the blue of the literal sky couldn't beat the sky-blue topcoat on the classic ride. The sun hit it and made its metal shine, but the air-conditioning kept the sun from doing much of anything to us. My uncle drove, and I rolled my weed, his eyes narrowing like an owl's scouting the ground for a sign of a field mouse.

"So what's the boxing scene like now?"

"I wouldn't know. I don't watch it."

He looked at me like I'd said I was a communist, back when that was still a thing. "What do you watch?"

I shrugged as I crumbled the weed. "Movies, pornos."

"You go to peepshows?"

"No, on the computer."

It felt like a bit of a sacrilege to crumble such weed, a waste of good bud and THC crystals, but my hollow apple was probably already home to a colony of fire ants out there in the desert where I'd chucked it yesterday.

The car lurched as if it was between gears. "You trying to get us ten years!" My uncle shouted.

I looked over at him, pissed that he'd make me spill my herb and almost catch a case of whiplash. It wasn't coke, but it was too expensive to be smoking, let alone losing to his erratic driving.

"Ten years?" I said. "You sure you didn't kill Luna this morning or hit someone with the car when I wasn't looking?"

He took his eyes from the road long enough to nod at my weed, which I was collecting from where it spilled onto my pant legs. "Your reefer."

I laughed. I'd only heard it called that in old movies. "We won't get ten years for some bud."

"I'll take your word for it, Future Boy."

"This is the present," I said, recovering most of my weed and re-rolling a tight one with what I'd salvaged. I didn't have my buddy Adam's skill (he could roll them so they looked as perfect as on the antidrug posters), but it would smoke and burn at a steady rate.

"It might be the present for you," he said. "But I've been somewhere else the last few years."

Yeah, I thought, *somewhere that people don't come back from. So why are you back?*

I'd leave others to ponder the mystery. I had weed to smoke.

"We had computers, but we didn't have any skin flicks on them."

I decided not to tell him that the "skin flicks" weren't on the computers, per se, bukkake and blowjobs being fed into punch cards on mainframes the size of filing cabinets, but that they stored everything on the internet. I figured that would lead to too many questions, like *What's the internet*, and I'd already gotten enough old people over that hurdle on a field trip at Redrock to the Sunrise Nursing Home.

I sparked the joint, took a deep pull, and sent a stream out the window. I held the small burning wand out to him, and he shook his head.

"Yeah," I said, taking another pull, straining to hold in the smoke and speak. "It screws up your short-term memory, but it's good for other things."

"I once got hopped with Sammy Davis."

"No shit?" I let out smoke, and the world outside the window, just dry desert a moment before, became as fascinating as an aquarium filled with exotic fish.

"Shame the way they treated him."

"You didn't get the…" I checked myself before I could say "senility." It seemed a sore point for him, and I didn't know enough about the various diseases to know the differences. "You didn't start getting ill until the late eighties, early nineties."

"What's your point?"

My fingers warmed as the paper smoldered and the cherry burnt, heating my hands and staining my nails with smoke. "It's not like segregation was in effect. You were lucid well after MLK and all that."

"Yes, but…" He winced, prideful and obviously not wanting to allow where the weaknesses were in his mind, or where the great legend of his life was swiss-cheesed and time and fists had punched holes in his trove of memories. "The further past, the clearer it is. I feel like I've been in a coma.

Or at least I got caught with Marciano's Susie-Q, zigging when I should have zagged. I've just woken up from a Sunday punch."

A couple more tokes and my joint would be ready for a roach clip, and since I didn't have one, it would be out the window where hopefully some guy on work detail from the local prison doing litter pickup in an orange jumpsuit would find himself a nice surprise on the ground.

Even as my uncle looked at the road ahead of him, his eyes were really gazing inward, at some past playing before the mind's eye he'd recently reacquired thanks to a doctor I knew nothing about and a regimen he hadn't seen fit to let me in on.

"I remember they made an exception, let Lena Horne stay at the Copa." He gripped the steering wheel with his meat-hook hands so that the leather or vinyl groaned in protest. "Because it was a whites'-only establishment, after she checked out the concierge gave the staff instruction to burn her sheets rather than launder them."

"Not like that anymore," I said. "They're too greedy to be racist. You got dough in Vegas, hotel dicks will help you dump the escort's body in the Hoover Dam. If you're a black man and the girl you iced is white, maybe they charge you a couple more g's or mean mug you, but that's the extent of it. You're not getting lynched."

He eyed me sidelong, hunched up in a defensive posture that would have been a crouch if he'd been standing instead of sitting, and boxing instead of driving. "Lot of 'suicides' at that Dam."

I didn't press him. "I never towed a color line," he added, after a short silence.

"What does that mean?"

"Some white guys wouldn't fight black fighters. Not me." He shook his head. "I hated no one. I'd fight everyone."

"What about the Japanese?"

His lips curled into a tight smile, as if there were secrets that wanted to pass his lips but he wasn't letting them out, not to me. Finally he said, "As long as they were dead, I could always live with the Japs."

I thought of Luna, her eyes boring into me when I asked him about the War, rounds skimming the surface of the water as he awoke from his dream. That had been as much emotion as she'd shown toward me. It was anger, but she had flushed from it and looked at me like I was someone, even if it was someone she hated.

I pictured her waiting for us back at the hacienda, standing in the driveway with a rolling pin snatched from a kitchen drawer that she tapped it into her open fist, ready to beat our brains out whenever we got back.

Stunted Joshua trees stood lame sentry on either side of the road, looking about as imposing as old drifters trying to hitch rides with no luck. The sun had no more mercy for trees than for men, and poured lemon yellow light over them, putting the yuccas in deep shadow. They looked like crosses dotting some Southwestern version of the Appian Way, along which they had crucified Spartacus and fellow slaves for their mutiny against the pseudo-Roman Empire headquartered in Caesar's Palace on the Strip.

A second sun appeared on the horizon, this one smaller and lower, an incandescent cloudburst staked to a pylon in front of a series of low boulders within the perimeter of double-stranded cyclone fence. A guard came from within a thicket of sagebrush latticed like desert vines around a cinderblock shack.

The man kicked up dust with his spurs as he walked toward the car. He wore a wide-brimmed hat big enough to bale water from a sinking ship by the gallon and a boiled shirt soaked clean through with sweat so sticky it looked like it would take a crowbar to yank it from his grit- and sand-encrusted person.

"Howdy," he said, automatically, like a cowboy toy in an old junk shop whose sensor let him know someone had crossed his path and it was time for his one line.

"Tell Victoria Walt Disney's here."

The man nodded, so he almost bowed, a sign of respect, that, with his pointing toward the homestead, allowed us a peek at the twin Patterson Colts holstered in rawhide leather. "She's up that a way, Charlie. You can tell her."

My uncle shot the man a two-finger salute, and we rolled along the final leg of our desert journey, toward the Sawdust.

***

A caravan of RVs kicked up dust on the horizon, the retiree version of the Hell's Angels, only instead of cooking meth they were on the warpath for low-roller resorts and somewhere to hook their Big Berthas up to water and electricity lines.

I looked over at my uncle as we approached the front of the bordello. "You going to tell me what's going on?"

He squinted. "The less you know, the safer you'll be."

"So I guess because you're in the know, you're in danger."

"Now, you're figuring it out."

The flagstone path leading to the front door of the cathouse ended, two straw bales stacked on either side of the pueblo-style home causing my nose to run. A girl opened the front door. She wore a black leotard and had pale skin, a white forehead, and red lips. She'd pulled her chestnut hair into a bun knotted on top of her head and her widow's peak was an inverted chevron to match her arched eyebrows. "Here for Victoria?" The girl popped a pink gum bubble and wrangled it back into her mouth with a tongue that was all wet muscle. She looked like she'd been bored before she saw us, but taking us in seemed to put her on the verge of a coma, as if we'd brought a fatal lameness with us like a foul wind.

"Yes."

"Come in, please." The *please* she added made me think maybe she wasn't being rude, that maybe it was just a bad day.

She turned around, favoring us with her rear cleaved by a glorious lycra wedgie she didn't bother to dig free.

The room was bright pink, "cyclamen" as the jeweler at Harry Winston had told my mother one day when she asked him about the color of a piece she selected from the glass case.

"Hey now!" The voice was that of an older woman, middle Tennessee twang, sandpapery from a lifetime of smoking but still sultry and deep enough to sing torch.

"Vicky!"

A stately older woman crossed the room toward my uncle. A sleepy Pekinese with a golden coat was half-lost in the billows of her floor-length chiffon, scurrying against the silk as if it was quicksand. Vicki's dress looked like a curtain pulled down from a massive window in a banquet hall, as if she'd been running around some king's castle naked but the unexpected arrival of company had forced her to throw on the first thing handy.

"Welcome back to the land of the living." She shifted the dog from one arm to another, and he snuggled up in the folds of her ample bosom as if it was doggie bed. She looked like Dolly Parton down to the twin mounded endowments and I figured the dog would be warm and fast go to sleep.

She took my uncle's hand, and he leaned down to kiss hers, puckering his lips over a finger bejeweled with a scarab with a green sapphire carapace. His lips lingered, and her chest heaved, moving the dog a few inches deeper into the cleavage. I knew without asking that they had kissed before, and it hadn't all been introductory pecks on the knuckles.

"A gentleman." She smiled at him. The mole on her cheek and her eyes were the same chocolate-chip brown. The eyes held a lifetime of secrets about men but no judgement. Men were devils and pigs and dogs to be tolerated on bad days, and when they were paying, they were to be loved and appreciated for their moral shortcomings, since it kept cathouses in business and the collection basket full in the church on Sundays.

"You don't get many gentlemen here?" My uncle asked.

"They better pretend or they get bounced on their ear."

I didn't see any heavies, but Vegas was the same way, that sense of hidden power and men in the wings so muscled that their heads and necks joined into one cinderblock, and not even the most skilled tailor could hide the bulge of biceps or Barretta.

Her eyes moved from him to me, blinking with her Betty Boop eyelashes so long and black they looked like spider legs. Her look said *Who the hell is this and what's he doing here,* but she kept the smile braced on her regal face. I figured in her line of work she'd learned that the thoughts in her head should rarely leave her mouth.

"My nephew," my uncle said. "Michael."

She recovered as he said my name, as that gave her a bit of distance, something formal and not real. Pleasantries. "Hello, Michael." Her eyelashes fluttered rapidly, wincing now just in case I said something stupid that would require her to wince later.

"Hello."

That didn't give her much to work with, so she pointed to the bar on the other side of the room. "Why don't you head over to the bar, son? Clark County inspectors wouldn't much like it if you knocked back whiskey, especially at your age, but there's a Coke dispenser back there."

Doing some freelance soda jerking didn't appeal to me, but I smiled as if I were eager as a puppy to play with the bar gun.

As soon as they turned from me, my fake eagerness dissolved, and I kept an eye and ear on them as they moved toward the other half of the room.

My uncle and the madame walked over to a plush red sectional curved like one half of a broken heart pendant. A painting of a cowpoke dominated the wall behind them. The cowboy sat on his bedroll and cooked brook trout and coffee over a griddle fire; what looked like Yellowstone National Park was in the backdrop.

They sat down. "How's business?" he asked. "Still getting airmen?"

"More construction workers than soldiers these days. The state bird round these parts is the construction crane. Their cup runneth over and we catch the runoff. We're doing well. But I think you can still help me do better, if you think you can, that is."

"Memory needs jogging."

I couldn't tell if he was hinting for a bribe, a free roll in the hay, or if he was talking about the punch-drunk fog out of which he'd just emerged.

My uncle shifted on a throw pillow upon which he'd accidentally sat, sailed it across the couch toward a red-furred footrest. "Good help hard to find?"

"Hardly." She shook her head, set the dog down. "Gotta turn girls away. No one wants to sit next to a slot machine like it's a lamppost. Harry Reid's riding herd and the girls are getting thirty days like it's going out of style." The dog's ID tags on his collar rattled as he shook his head side to side, working off the humiliation of being a lapdog, staggering now, a shaggy lost little soul looking for someone else to pay him mind.

"The girls get tired of hopping from Caesars to the Trop to Sands. Security catches them, it's either a blowjob or a trip to Clark County

Detention. Then you got to worry about getting pulled into some psycho's room, buying your own drinks to keep from getting bounced. Here the girls keep a part of every bottle the customers uncork."

"I miss the Boys, the way they did things. They kept the lid on the pot."

The dog came sniffing my way, looking like a feather duster come to life and ready to shake off a lifetime of accumulated dust. He grimaced up at me, his face having that tortured expression all toy dogs seemed to have, as if he knew they had created him for someone else's amusement and it pissed him off a bit. Between him and the straw bales outside, my nose was tingling and my eyes watered like I'd hit my nostrils with a couple squirts of Tabasco nasal spray.

But I didn't want to offend the fur ball, and a mild allergic reaction was far from leprosy.

"Can I pet him?" I looked down, smiling the first genuine smile I'd felt cross my face in a long time.

His owner looked at me from the couch. "As long as your fingers ain't made of liver snaps, you'll be okay."

I stroked his silky coat, and he snorted, circling my legs to make sure this wasn't a trap of some sort.

"He gets hump-happy but in a couple weeks those two nuts will be Rocky Mountain oysters at Harrah's buffet."

"Don't think a dog's balls are that big, Vi," my uncle said. "More like Swedish meatballs, poor guy, and you shouldn't do that to him."

"The mailman will thank me. So will the girls. They're all on the same cycle, as happens, so he's a madman for a few days per month, almost as crazy as they are."

I followed the dog as he shuffled toward the wraparound bar, oblivious to all the talk about his poor little stones. He went through the legs of the high barstools as if they were an obstacle course, weaving his way pretty deftly for a beast with such stubby legs and schnauzer-esque dimensions. He looked up at me after he made his circuit, a little spittle dripping from his bulldog overbite as he huffed from the exertion. His look invited appraisal of his performance.

If he'd understood numbers I would have given him a perfect ten for his navigational skills.

"He wants for you to pick him up," Vicki said.

I figured she knew her baby better than I did, so I leaned down and lifted the little critter into my hands, sat him on the red vinyl of a bar seat.

They continued talking on the couch, only now in lower tones. I played with the dog's ears, lifted them out to the sides so he looked like a furry pygmy Dumbo who might take flight toward the pressed tin ceiling above. He endured it with good humor. I felt like hugging him, cradling him in my arms.

I let his ears go, gave his coat one last stroke, and leaned over the bar. A packet of matches sat on the scarred surface of the walnut bar next to a cut-glass ashtray. There was a fantail the color of an orchid in bloom patterned across the matchbook above the striker plate, the same pattern repeated ad infinitum on everything from the cocktail napkins to the mini-straw holder to the wallpaper fleurs, even the frosting on the ashtray, like the lettering on the door of a PI's office. The logo carried the legend "Sawdust" above the outspread feathers.

I pocketed the pack of matches, figuring I might not have time to stop at a gas station soon if I needed a lighter. Plus, if I brought them back to Redrock and lit a cigarette with them and someone asked what "Sawdust" was, I could offhandedly mention that I'd laid pipe in a bordello on a day trip with a world champion boxer.

"What's your name?" I asked the dog. He didn't answer me. "That's all right, 'cause I don't feel like telling you my name, either."

He placed his paw out, keeping it in midair as if wounded and he needed me to take a thorn from the pad.

"Manny wants to shake," Vicki's voice came from my right.

I took his paw in my hand, felt the warmth of his little life there. We exchanged greetings and his golden-brown eyes shined as if he wanted to cry. "Manny's his name?"

"Short for Manticore," Vicki said, "Like Siegfried and Roy's tiger."

The decibel on the conversation behind me rose, no longer pitched at the level of a call between a kidnapper and a loved one of the ransomed. They sounded more like they were eating brunch and were on their third round of Mimosas with the ratio of champagne to citrus deliberately botched.

"And Moe?" My uncle asked.

"Down in San Miguel Allende. Those social security dollars stretch when you convert 'em to Pesos."

"Yeah, but you got to learn Spanish," my uncle protested.

"So learn, why don't you, Charlie? You got your brain back. Or at least most of it."

"I'm working on getting the rest back." His protest sounded strained, as if he owed her money and she was a shylock running out of patience. I didn't like to see him on the hook, for whatever it was. He'd just gotten his mind back and with that some pride, and now it sounded like he was a couple point-counterpoints in this conversation away from begging to have more time to get the rest of his brain back, jumpstart that septum in the center of his head and learn Spanish just for starters.

A princess phone on an end-table rang, which brought Vicky to her feet (assuming she had any beneath the dress). The lady of the house floated across the room like a medium playing conduit to a dead loved one whose ghost had entered her body hard all at once. My uncle stood, letting me know with a stern look that we were to go, with no delay, and much more importantly *No questions.*

I gave the Pekingese one last stroke from his head that felt soft and warm as a newborn's fontanel down to his wagging tail.

I followed my uncle across the pink carpet. He stopped just at the door, blew Vicky a kiss she caught with the hand that wasn't holding the candlestick receiver of the phone.

When we were outside again, I spoke. "Everything okay?"

My uncle pulled his screwdriver from a pocket on his denim jeans, we got in the car and he put his old juvie education to good use on the steering column. The motor kicked over, and he stared through the windshield, caked now in the dust clouds the desert had kicked up.

"It's not that I don't trust you. It's your mother."

He turned around in the lot, cutting the wheel and leaving an overwide figure eight in the red soil. Gravel crunched beneath the tires and the cowboy with two sidearms returned the salute my uncle had first given him on the way in.

"I don't trust her, either," I said. *But I also don't blame her*, I thought to myself but didn't say to him. I didn't have much of a desire to defend her, even though I understood her well enough to do so, but I also felt I had no right to tell him how he should feel about her. Their relationship predated my birth by decades, and whatever slights or backstabbing had gone on between them was something I didn't know about, and something I probably would not learn about since secrets seemed to be the coin of the realm with him. We weren't in Vegas, but the *What happens in-* clause was still in effect as far as most things went with this old man.

At least he'd let me come with him, though, and that was something.

He loosened his bolo tie and unbuttoned his Bat Masterson vest, one-handing the steering wheel while he did that.

"Back about a million years ago, Vicki was helping some Combination boys with a skim."

"Combination?"

He shot me a look I figured a bug saw right before the lizard's forked tongue snatched it up and devoured it. "I'm already telling you too much. I'm not getting into those kinds of details."

"I got it."

Once his vest was open, and he had the steer skull cinch of his bolo undone, he continued. "Anyway, this guy who was our mutual friend had to do some time, but before he could turn himself in, he died." He paused, waiting to see if I was stupid enough to press him on cause of death. I was learning though and shut up.

"Old Jimmy didn't want his friends and family wanting for anything while he was in the can, and he knew the Feds were hell for leather on asset forfeiture, so he handed the scratch off to someone he trusted."

I didn't ask who. I could guess. Still my uncle said, "Me."

"And?"

His head shook so hard now he might as well have been a ventriloquist's dummy working all the tables in a crowded room. "I can't remember where it is."

"Do you remember how much it was?"

"I'd forgotten," he said. "But Vicki refreshed my memory."

"To the tune of…?"

He looked sheepish, as if I were the taxman during an audit and there might be something he hadn't declared. "Little over a couple million."

My uncle watched me for a reaction. When he didn't get one, he said, "I guess inflation's been going through the roof while my memory's been going to hell. They dinged me pretty bad at that Pony Post all for some rolling papers and jerky."

"Two million's still a lot," I said.

"Enough to get me killed."

"By her?" I wasn't sure whether I meant my mom or Vicki, or both. And he didn't press me. There were probably a lot of "hers" in his past, and if they knew he had a couple million there might be more hers in his future.

And in my future, too, if they thought I knew anything.

I cursed myself, curiosity, cats, the whole enchilada.

We drove past a low cluster of boulders that looked like one of those ancient Puebloan Anasazi villages, looming from the left-hand side of the road stretching across the flat wasteland in all four directions.

I felt around in my pocket. I still had the matches and some weed.

"You want to smoke some weed?"

The car lurched again, my neck swiveling bobble-head style.

"You trying to get us sent up for ten years!"

I thought we'd covered this.

The car stopped on the shoulder of the road, sand rising in hard and granular flecks, making a *ping!* sound as it slapped the windshield, like we'd hit a silica deposit.

He looked at me like I was a long-lost friend. "Kassel?" His confusion gave way to fear. "The Nips killed you. Chopped you up and fed you into the ship's blades and then watched the sharks eat you."

My fear bloomed, blossomed and exploded in my stomach like a mini-mushroom cloud my body could barely contain. "I'm not Kassel."

The roar of a semi barreling down the road beside us caused the ground to rumble, the dashboard to tremble. "No need to be ashamed of your Kraut name. You're aces with the leathernecks. We were just ribbing you. It happens on the ship."

The truck passed us on our left, slapping the side of the classic car with a wind that made me forget it wasn't a ragtop, and I wondered if we might flip into a ditch.

"Maybe," I said, stuttering, trying to control myself, my voice. "Maybe I should drive home, Uncle Charlie."

Those last two words worked like a charm, or more like a command, not causing him to snap out of the fog but to at least accept my trusting hand as we navigated the impenetrable haze together.

"Okay," he said, stared at the steering column. He looked back up at me, seeing neither his old dead friend from WW2 nor a nephew, his perplexity too total for him to take in anything more than the confusing scene before him lodged in the steering column.

"What the Sam Hill is a screwdriver doing in there?"

***

The strange, endless stream of words didn't stop coming out of his mouth at any point after he woke up from his nap and got going. And I couldn't keep up because I had one eye on the road and one on the glossy panel of the atlas that would carry us home.

"I got saddle sores."

"You can't get saddle sores," I said. "We're in a car, not riding a horse."

"Yeah, but Solomons still offered me some blackout fights. I mean, they're smokers 'cause not even the RAF can keep the Luftwaffe from dropping bombs on London, but a fight's a fight even if it don't go in the record books."

"Uncle Charlie," I said, "You should try to go back to sleep."

"Good idea." He closed his eyes compliantly and his chin promptly hit the steer skull of the bolo on his sternum.

The rich smell of grilled steak was in the air, entered the car even with the windows up, but I rolled mine down just to get more of the scent in my lungs, anyway. A cool breeze presaging night carried the mouthwatering musk of blackened meat to my nostrils.

A half-mile later on the highway I saw the culprit, advertising itself on a massive roadside pylon arm. Conestoga Steakhouse. The signage was kitschy as a Christmas Village or a fireworks outlet and more inviting for it. On the billboard there was a dude in angora chaps and spurs about as subtle as Chinese throwing stars, his lasso snaking off of the sign and coming toward the driver like a 3D optical illusion trying to rope us toward the exit.

I thought about getting off the highway, since dinner was tempting, until I remembered how Luna had to finger-feed my uncle or give him soft near-liquids like soup. Steak might be fun for me but an ordeal for him.

He saw and smelled what I did, and it opened his eyes. "You know Archie Moore used to chew raw steak before fights. He learned it in the Australian outback."

"Oh," I said. I didn't want to be disrespectful, but I had to stay noncommittal and keep my eyes on the road.

"They say Ray Robinson drank cow's blood from a tall glass, pressed straight from the raw steak, but that was just a publicity stunt to scare Jake. Who can scare Jake?"

"No one can scare Jake," I said, nodding my head and getting into this hype man role.

"Damn right!"

I'd heard the stories of old people losing their marbles and talking about no one being able to "scare Jake" wasn't any weirder than talking about the death of childhood horses on the farm.

We were getting close to the old homestead. The image of Luna and the rolling pin flashed again in my mind. Maybe Cliff was waiting, too, ready to put a cigar out on my forehead and leave a big Ash Wednesday-style smear there.

"Look, I talked to my shyster." My uncle's tone was confidential, low. To the right I saw the massive fake Conestoga wagon that sat above the restaurant, rising from the little exit town at the next offramp, bowed like a gondola but floating over sand instead of swimming over water.

"What'd the shyster say?" I asked. I didn't know why I was trying to keep him conscious and speaking, as if he might otherwise die and go into shock. The worst that could happen was that he might drift off to sleep, which he probably needed. I definitely needed it.

"He's going to try to get me re-classed as primary financial support so I don't got to join the Army, 'but what's the use'? I keep telling myself. The title's on ice as long as the War lasts, which might be forever. Brown Bomber's got to do his part for Uncle Sam. Why not Charlie 'Grim Reaper' Reeves?"

"Make your country proud."

"Give Tojo and Hitler a taste."

"Don't forget Mussolini."

We'd stopped for gas earlier and I'd checked all the levels and it looked good, but for the last thirty miles a noise had been coming from the tailpipe, soft at first and now growling from the exhaust manifold so it sounded like a coatimundi with its foot caught in the sharp jaws of a bear trap.

"The hell is that?" My uncle asked.

"I don't know," I said, "but we're almost home."

And we were, unfortunately.

Luna stood in the driveway, her eyes red from crying and cheeks puffy from tears already fallen. She kept her arms crossed above her mauve hippy blouse, but when our car was close enough, she undid her arms from over her chest and stalked forward.

I eased the ride to a stop to take my medicine. "Uh-oh," my uncle said from the passenger seat. "That señorita your little lady?"

"I wish," I whispered, and I did, even as she was coming toward us, a wrathful whirlwind balanced on two Birkenstocks. She clutched the keys to her silver coupe in her hand and stood in front of the car so I couldn't drive any farther toward the overhang where it had first been when we left.

I rolled down my window. She walked around to my side of the car and leaned in, the smell of a real woman flooding the ride, earthy but cocoa-buttery and overpowering. "Get out now."

"Just drop me off at my place," my uncle muttered, not wanting to get into the middle of our domestic row.

I got out of the car. Luna jabbed the sharp metal grooves of her car keys toward me, stopping just short of stabbing me with the blunt end. "What you did is beyond irresponsible." She clenched her teeth as she spoke, seething, her jaw squaring from the exertion of keeping her rage under control so it could remain measured, not devolve into insults.

"It was a betrayal of my trust, because now I could be fired for what you did. This could affect my career. End it!" She stopped pointing her keys at me, jabbed them in the air toward the passenger seat where my uncle, the starter of all this shit, sat looking placid, happy, and just a little tired.

"And taking him out in his condition."

"I didn't take him out," I said. "He made me-"

Her face came within an inch of mine and her eyes were liquid fire. "A seventy-five-year-old man with dementia cannot force a healthy young man to do anything. Or talk you into it."

I stood there silent, dropped my eyes as her voice continued washing over me. "And if he forced you, then you're the most pathetic excuse for a young man I've ever met. And if he talked you into it, then you're not just a horrible nephew, you're a stupid fool!"

The questioning of my nascent manhood hurt more than the insult about being a fool. *Fool* had sounded so colorful in her mouth, one syllable but stretched as she tried to imbue it with the strength of whatever better word she was thinking of in Spanish while she berated me in English.

I kept my mouth shut. When I spoke again, it was as lame as I thought it would be. "I'm sorry."

"You're sorry." She nodded her head, listening to my weak defense, a gutless couple of words that would erase none of the damage of the day. She sniffed before her nose could start running. "Sorry." She turned, or more like spun in a single twirl, a rush of purple fabric like a bloodstained bullfighter's cape, back toward her silver coupe.

"Where are you going?" I asked.

"I don't know. Maybe to tender my resignation. Maybe to report you to the police for elder abuse."

"Hey!"

That pissed me off. I walked toward her, stopped en route. I wanted to confess, telling her he'd had some super-lucid moments, and interesting words for both me and the Madame at the Sawdust. But I knew that I had to be a man, or try to be one, even if she didn't think possible. I had doubts.

And I needed to be careful about what I let fly if the exchange of words got heated. A couple million was floating around out there somewhere, and as much as I liked her and found it fun to pretend love was possible, there was no way I would blab about the loot to her.

Then it hit me: I was as greedy as everyone else. No, I wouldn't ever try to screw my uncle over, not even for a couple million, just on general principle, but I was definitely more interested in his welfare now that I knew about the money, and I had a newborn desire to follow him around like a conjoined twin fused to his hip. Maybe if he recovered that missing hole in the perforated fabric of his mind, he might also recover that money, and he might give me a finder's fee.

What was the standard commission? Ten percent?

Luna got in her car, slamming the door for effect. She pulled out, heedless of whether I bothered to get out of the way. Clouds of dust shot skyward and I stepped aside as she drove passed me. I saw her face through the windshield of her car as she went, the last of the sunlight splashing through the glass. She blew her nose in a balled wad of tissues as she drove away from the compound.

I walked over to my uncle's side of the car, opened his door for him like a valet. "Okay, shit starter."

"Shit kicker," he said, correcting me. He struggled to get out, beat the count, and I helped him out, or got him started at least by reaching over him to pop his seatbelt free. One of his arms strayed toward me as I leaned over. I didn't fight his grip, rather bowing under his weight as I struggled to pull him up with me.

He wrapped his arms around me, like a baby koala clutching its mother and hiding its face from the gawkers at the zoo. He didn't want to see something, some movie playing in his head, maybe a replaying loop of a bloody night in the ring or some battle in Betio, and perhaps if he pressed his face close enough to my chest, got lost in the dark fabric, it might keep the light of bad dreams from entering his skull and showing him those nightmare visions he didn't want to see.

"Help me," he said, faintly.

"I am." I leaned, let him throw his arm around my neck and we limped toward the front door like it would lead to a casualty clearing station instead of just an old house made of stone, where he would wait out his days until he died, hopefully in peace.

"No, really help me," he said. "Help me remember."

"How?"

"Him," my uncle said.

"Who?"

Gravel crunched again beneath car tires behind us, and I turned expecting to see Luna, got an eyeful of another car instead. It was a blue Volvo, formidable as a panzer tank, as much a piece of a certain class's accessories as tickets to the opera and conversations about Tuvan throat singing carried on in low tones on NPR.

"Him," my uncle said. "He can help me."

The Volvo came to a slow and sensible halt, the first car at Casa de Luna not to kick up dust clouds as it came or went. Cliff got out first, on the passenger side. He wore a pair of pressed bark-brown slacks with a knife crease in either leg and a gabardine long-sleeved shirt, a gambler's good luck charm with sewn dice cascading in patterns across the shirt, showing only sevens or elevens on the fabric.

Another man got out on the driver's side, holding a vulcanized doctor's bag, the old school kind, in one hand, and a clipboard in the other. The man wore a coarse wool sweater despite the heat, from which stray bits of fabric shot here and there because of the garment's being thrown in the wash instead of properly treated. The wrinkled shirttail of a blue Oxford that probably started the day tucked into his pants crept out below the sweater, coming down so far below the shrunk-in-the-wash sweater it looked like a skirt. He had the panel over his fly pulled back, but at least the zipper itself wasn't down.

The man was not so much a doctor as a doctor's handwriting made flesh. And yet, if this was the man I thought he was, his hand had been more legible than most of the MDs who'd written my mom scripts for Percocet and me ones for Ritalin and Adderall.

The twosome walked toward me, the doctor wide-eyed and inquisitive, friendly, Cliff a little more suspicious, although I sensed most of his ill-feeling was for his friend and not for his no-good nephew, who shouldn't have even been here.

"Doctor Graydon Parks," the doctor said, trust etched into his smile. He had the face of someone who was happy but at pains to conceal it, wincing like a nebbish whose wife henpecked him hardest in those rare moments he let his guard down and smiled. He was beetle-browed and his two furry eyebrows looked like one caterpillar some sadistic kid had sliced in half as it shimmied across a sidewalk crack. His bald spot glowed with what light the sun still cast over us, its rays soft gold and relenting.

"Nice to meet you, Doctor."

He extended his hand. Cliff spoke, interrupting the shake. "Everything okay?" He jabbed a thumb thick and short like an overboiled cocktail weenie toward Luna's silver coupe disappearing over the horizon, hopefully not toward a police station.

"Yeah," I said, sighing.

The doctor looked over at Cliff. "He knows, then?"

"I know," I said, though I didn't know what they thought I knew, or what they themselves knew. Sure, they were working on helping my uncle get his memory back, but did they know about the money? And if so, was that the only reason they were here, deep down?

It didn't seem like it to me. Cliff had that loyalty that didn't die, that quality common in dogs and rare in men. The doctor also seemed like he was a Hippocratic Oath guy down to his last fiber. His clothes bespoke his lack of materialism. The only one who might have halfway been here for money was me, but I definitely wasn't here only for that and my alibi was that I'd had shit role models, besides.

"Let's go inside shall we?" The doctor was still all smiles. Cliff gave more sideways looks, sparing some for me but still mostly stink-eyeing my uncle. I think he'd been so used to it being he and Charlie against the world for so long that he wasn't sure how or if I fit into this. Neither did I, though, so I endured the occasional scrutiny for as long as it lasted, which was until the front door opened and we went inside.

I'd usually seen this part of the house either when it was dark and I was tiptoeing or beneath the soft glow of lamplight, but because the lights in the house were off and the sun was the main source of light, different things showed now in long-slanting shadows and others became deemphasized under the gaze of a new and natural glow.

Acoma pottery pieces sat lined up in rows along the edges of the room, painted with glazed zigzags and ziggurats, half-men, half-birds dancing for fertility or war in ochre and vermillion. Wooden holy Santos prayed and lamented from their alcoves spread throughout the room, somber and locked in the prayers offered late in the day, matins and vespers, when everything slowed down and the Fallen World at least plummeted at a slower rate, until midnight, which brought with it new chances for fresh sin.

We went into the den where the radio had been on and as constant in its workings as a well-made clock. Tennessee Ernie Ford blew that bass instrument known as his voice for all it was worth, letting people know how the company store rewarded a man of flesh and bone for hauling sixteen tons.

The song was so good that Cliff and my uncle had to join in. Whatever they punched out of my uncle's head, it wasn't the music.

"This way," the doctor said, parting the old Texaco backdrop and bringing us into the other room. "I should start by saying that I have very strong and personal reasons for wanting to help your uncle here…" The doctor paused, and pointed at the old man, who meandered around the tight quarters as if all the relics of his life were new to him. "But I also have a touch of undiagnosed Asperger's, so if I step on your toes or cause you offense, please do not take it personally."

He looked at me, waiting for a reaction, a response, but I wasn't sure what kind his spiel merited. "Okay," I finally said. "I can handle whatever. I'm here to help him." I pointed toward my uncle, who was studying a photograph of himself taking a playful chuck on the chin from Muhammad Ali. Punch-drunkenness glazed the Champ's eyes, but a fire in the gaze that reminded me of Luna's own eyes let the world know that he was alive and thinking behind the disease, and maybe even happy despite everything that had happened to him.

"Tauopathy," the doctor said, "is the neurodegenerative disease to which your uncle's unclassified and perhaps unclassifiable trauma is most similar."

"Why is it unclassifiable?" I asked.

"Because it's reversible in his case," Cliff said. "It's been responsive to experimental therapy." He looked over at my uncle, who was wordless and near-catatonic in front of the Ali picture. "Sort of."

"It comes and goes," I said, nodding. I'd seen it firsthand today. It had come and went, or it had come and *gone*, not *went* (I needed to get back to Redrock to bone up on grammar and see how Adam was getting along).

"Where did you guys go?" Cliff asked me, his eyes slits, holding a look in intensity somewhere between hearty scrutiny and seething.

"For steak," I said.

"Yes, it smells quite good," the doctor allowed. "But to return to the disease. Some of my father's work helped pave the way for us, but we are in uncharted territory."

I liked the way he'd said "Us." I'd never been a part of anything before, or at least not anything good. He walked to the front of the glowing golden slot machine, rounded at the top just like my uncle's old Philco but much larger and alive with neon light and shiny precious metal plating.

"We've found a way, or a tool, rather, to help break the aggregation of tau in the neurofibrillary and gliofibrillary tangles in your uncle's brain." He paused in the presentation, smiled, not from the warming pride of his own ego, but for what the device could mean for my uncle and others like him. He popped open the face of the slot machine cabinet by yanking the lever of the one-armed bandit specially rigged not to pay out but to open forward. He had the common sense to say, "Patent pending."

A device that was half VR headset and half DMV eye test machine sat there, hiding in the machine's belly. The doctor flipped a toggle inside and the eye cradles of the frogman goggles glowed. He waved his hand proudly over his design, like Vanna White flipping a couple vowels on Wheel-of-Fortune.

"Mr. Reeves?" The doctor said. My uncle didn't budge, still looking at Ali, a kindred sufferer in the maze.

"Champ?" Cliff said.

That did the trick. My uncle turned toward Cliff, who had his Cuban slid between the second and third fingers of his right hand, as if it was a brace or Chinese finger trap instead of a stogie.

"Right," my uncle said, nodding. He walked over to the device and took a seat on the barstool offered him, happy to set his face in the cradle and comply if only because it would allow him to rest for a moment and pop a squat, two of any old person's greatest joys, especially after a long day like this one.

Light flickered in the device, a click as if family home slides were being cycled through one at a time. *Here we are trying Aunt Jeanine's famous mustard potato salad.* Click. *And here we are at the Gorge.* Click. *Park staff will only let you get so close, ever since that dumbass got drunk and died up here.* Click.

The doctor spoke as the images clicked faster, speeded through their cycle quicker than a slot machine gone haywire.

"This device is not entirely mine," the doctor said.

"Then how are you going to patent it?"

The doctor winced. "Let me finish," he said. "Nothing is ex nihilo. All must come from some previous source. I don't dispute either that I stand on the back of giants nor that others must follow me. But let it also be clear that this is my moment, both as a scientist, and as someone who is trying to explain something to you for your own benefit."

I ignored the provocative tone, reminded myself he had warned me, and that it wasn't personal. "My modifications are added to an already-existing machine used to assess retinal abnormalities *in vivo.*" He'd stressed that last bit of Latin as if hinting that he was fluent but just favoring me with a smattering as a foretaste. "Optical coherence tomography and so forth." He paused, seeing if that registered. It did not ring any bells for me. He continued, "It would be too hard to explain to a layman, but what was set for 'receive data' from his brain was used for that end, as intended, but once that data was collected and the trouble regions in the brain mapped, the flow went back from machine to man, instead of man to machine, with especial attention devoted to breaking up the plaques."

"I understand," I said.

The doctor smiled and nodded. I couldn't quite bring myself to do either, since he'd stunned me.

Cliff's voice was as deep and booming as a dropped microphone, causing us both to look over at him at once, and forcing my uncle to bump his head on the low ceiling of the headset in the slot machine as the cut man spoke. "Your eyes are made of the same central nervous tissue as your brain. It's like…" He paused, bit his cigar, which made him look less menacing, more gregarious, like a new father celebrating in the maternity ward. "Your eyes are part of your brain."

He looked over at the doctor for confirmation, as if he were being tested in med school and it was up to Dr. Parks to pass or fail him. The doctor looked at me, wanting, I supposed to make sure he played cleanup and undid any misconceptions the cut man held and tried to pass on to me like some ignorance virus.

"That's a glib interpretation," the doctor said, "but not entirely wide of the mark."

Cliff sensed he was only getting a minor concession, backhanded and overloaded with caveats at that, but the cigar in his mouth made him happy enough to ignore it, and I'm sure the Good Doctor had given him preliminary warnings similar to the one he gave me; someone wasn't really an asshole if they couldn't help it and you didn't take a swing on a guy who was doing everything in his power to save your best friend's mind.

Cliff focused on me, and not the Doc. I felt his eyes on me before I met them, the stare I tried to ignore becoming like a physical weight, a gravity pressing my chest and not letting me draw enough breath until I agreed to meet his gaze. He glared at me, no longer suspicious but pissed.

"Lot a ladies at the Conestoga?"

"Some," I said. "Why?"

"You smell more like a cathouse than a steakhouse."

"Mr. Reeves?" The doctor's voice edged toward panic, as if he had a patient code bluing. It brought Cliff and I out of our stare-down. We expected to see my uncle, his friend, dead perhaps of a heart attack with his face in the cradle.

Instead, however, he was only snoring, and a thin string of drool fell from his lips, the thread no larger than the fattest weaved strand on a spiderweb.

Cliff spoke to me in a tone that was both low and friendly, and my muscles relaxed, defenses going down. "This happens sometimes." The cut man watched his old boxing buddy with the eyes a proud mother reserves for her child asleep in his cradle, with the *don't-wake-the-baby* tone to match. "Usually we let him cop the Z's and go from visual stuff to sounds at that point."

"Auditory feedback and reinforcement," the doctor added.

"What he said." Cliff stabbed his cigar in the doctor's direction, as if he wished the Cuban was lit and he could give the doctor an eyeful of smoke.

I said nothing. I was speechless, in the mystery's presence emanating from this slot machine. It was like a music box found beneath a dusty rafter in an attic that had once belonged to a young girl who was now an ancient woman and could no longer dance, but merely rock in her wooden chair.

CHAPTER SEVEN
GRIM REAPER ON THE CAVALCADE

It was movie night in the media room. Cliff had herded us all in there to sit on ponderosa pine furniture to watch a surprise he had planned for my uncle. Luna was banking on a cowboy movie if her outfit was any clue. She wore calfskin boots that hugged the strong curves of her legs up to just below the knee where after a couple of inches of naked skin a denim skirt started and served as a place for her to tuck the excess cotton of her flannel shirt. Her pigtails were visible coming out the back of her straw cowboy hat. She was eating popcorn and sitting as far away from me on the large couch as she could, next to my uncle. I didn't know if he was in one of his lucid moments or if he was out of it, but if he was in his haze, I envied him. At least there one didn't have to deal with awkwardness or tension. You just sat alone on your cloud with thoughts of your past. I figured it couldn't be all unpleasant. The phrase "punch drunk" had "drunk" in there.

"You guys ready?" Cliff looked back at us. Dr. Parks, seated next to me, gave both thumbs up, all systems go.

Cliff picked up the remote and aimed it at the big-screen fitted inside a tooled leather case that made it look like a saloon mirror frame. Luna stood up and sashayed over to the corner of the room, where she adjusted the dimmer until the movie theater effect was complete. The painting above the mantel that showed braves building a signal fire on the open mesa disappeared into darkness, the Indian forms now ill-defined shadows looking like scouts at the edge of a cowboy camp.

An announcer spoke from the TV. "Tonight, our featured bout of the evening, Herbie 'the Assassin' Alonzo versus Charles 'Grim Reaper' Reeves. And if you don't know why they saddled him with the sobriquet of 'Reaper,' ladies and gents, I invite you to stay seated and pay attention, as you may well find out tonight."

A lusty round of applause broke out on the couch, drowning out the tail end of the announcer's spiel delivered in that clipped transcontinental accent that everyone from movie stars to newspapermen once spoke in.

Luna was more excited than the rest of us. A light pang of jealousy hit me flush in the chest as I looked over and saw her hug my uncle, as the ringside announcer rattled off his impressive string of victories.

"He donated all of tonight's purse to the Widows and Orphans Relief Fund, doing his part now for Uncle Sam's extended family as a civilian, just as he once had as a soldier."

"Very sweet of you." Luna pecked him on the cheek, and the old man flushed, grinned.

Her kiss infused him with life, wakening him more perhaps than Dr. Clark's strange little device hidden in the slot machine.

"*To look sharp, every day…*"

Cliff hummed and my uncle sang along with a ditty being squawked out by a cartoon parrot gripping the strands of the boxing ring, crooning about the wonders of Gillette Razors.

The parrot dissolved and a metal microphone dropped from a black cord in the ceiling, and the ref in his bowtie corralled the two fighters. "And now, without further ado, center ring with the principles and chief seconds."

The footage was black and white, but the beauty of my uncle's silk robe made it impossible not to sense the richness of its color in the old transfer being broadcast on ESPN2, something burgundy or blood-red.

"You can't see me yet," Cliff said, "but you'll spot me between rounds."

"You won't see my father tonight," Dr Parks said, "thankfully."

I was about to ask him what he meant, but the striking of a bell interrupted me. All eyes were on the white screen, all our silent mouths closed.

"Reeves is not known as a cautious fighter nor a dandy, though he is not bereft of science or lacking in ring craft."

My uncle was gaunt, tall, hollowed where fat was on most men, all sinew and ropy muscle, thin and strong like a whippet greyhound. I figured his lean and menacing figure got him the nickname of "Reaper", the way he couldn't help but loom and suggest inevitable destruction, but I reconsidered as his scything left hook rocketed back the head of Herbie Alonzo shortly after the bell rang. He threshed the man like wheat with a flailing hook. The punch was so hard that the man's marcelled waves bounced around and came unglued, even though they shined as if held in place by five pounds of pomade.

"Alonzo blows hot and cold, but when the spirit moves him, he's hell in short pants."

"Of course he blew hot and cold!" My uncle shouted at the long-dead announcer. "You think he'd tell Carbo and those other hoods to kick rocks when they told him to take a dive?" He shook his head. "You either swan dive in the ring or you swim in the Hudson."

Dr. Parks looked over at Cliff with a queasy look on his face. Luna, free-spirited cowgirl a moment before, now looked confused at what she'd just heard.

"Look," Cliff said, his voice genial but edged in panic. "You were the only guy I seen could get away with that leaping left hook where both feet was off the ground, at least before Patterson came on the scene."

My uncle's previous train of thought, bitter and veering toward something poisonous, now broke in another direction, the direction in which Cliff steered him. "Ray Arcel said, 'If he leaps, he sleeps,' but that never applied to me. Called it the 'Gazelle Punch.' Got it from Goldman. D'Amato claimed it as his own, like he never seen Rocky fight."

The doctor smiled, and Luna settled back into her seat, rubbing my uncle's back in a circular motion, as she sometimes did when he awakened from nightmares or was having trouble concentrating on a meal.

The footage crinkled, a dusty worm-shaped bit of some particle writhing across the old footage, so that the whiteness of the ring and the paleness of the two opponents brightened to a weirdly angelic light that threatened to blind the viewer or at least make the screen go blank. The hot flashbulbs popping in the crowd were just sensation-hungry and bloodthirsty orbs hunting for freeze-frames of faces punched, eyes swollen closed and cheeks rippling like water from the force of fists, but the snapping cameras still twinkled like stars in the firmament, and the crowd's shouting for hurt men also took on a strangely angelic quality as the screams blended, until the voices shouting for action and pain melted into something like a harmonized choir's rejoicing.

I had never enjoyed boxing, but I at least saw for the first time why some people did. Like an old Bela Lugosi movie, that everyone (or almost everyone) on screen was dead didn't lessen the power of it but seemed to enhance it.

"He hit me with so many jabs in the next round I was practically begging for a right hand." My uncle shook his head, leaned forward. His pride was no more, edged out by a perfectionism as he held his head poised in his hand like Rodin's *The Thinker*. He didn't so much watch himself as study the performance for mistakes, as if he maybe had another fight coming up in a couple months and needed to prepare, sew up some holes in his game lest his opponent also get hold of this footage and study his flaws.

"I zee zomefink," my uncle said.

Luna laughed, hanging from his shoulder. "Vat do you see, dear?"

"It's what Max Schmeling said," Dr. Parks said to her. "He was supposed to lose big to Joe Louis, but he watched tape on the Brown Bomber day and night. People laughed at him when he said he was going to win because Joe Louis kept making a mistake."

"What mistake?" Luna asked the doctor. She was still leaning on my uncle, who while probably not ungrateful for her touch wouldn't notice it while the fight lasted.

Cliff picked up the thread of boxing lore. "I von't tell you vat it is now. You vill have to vait for the night ov da fight." His German accent wasn't pitch-perfect like the doctor's, but I figured the good doc was probably a polyglot. For all I knew he was a German who'd just learned English so well that no trace of his original accent remained.

"There you are!" My uncle bolted upright. Luna's arm that perched on his shoulder fell into the empty air. She stood with him, massaging his shoulders rather than stroking his back, leaning down toward the couch as she did so, hoping with her movement to nudge him back toward his seat.

"There I am," Cliff said, more wistful than excited, nowhere near as amped up as my uncle, whose face glowed with the reflected black-and-white light from the TV in the room's darkness.

Young Cliff wore a satin jacket whose waist-tie and lettering were the same maroon trim as the cloth that made up my uncle's robe. They sewed individual letters into the fabric, which said "Team Reeves" across the cut man's back. Another cut man stood by in a fisherman's sweater, holding water in what looked like an empty chianti bottle swaddled in gauze bandaging coming unraveled from the green glass. Cliff stuck a stool through the second and third ropes and went to work on a minor cut above Grim Reaper Reeves' eye with a long-stem Q-Tip, with another one clenched in his jaws for backup just in case more blood squirted out of a slice in the flesh the size of the slit in a piggy bank. Cliff's head was nowhere near as bald then as it was now, but the glare of the hot lights searing through the thin strands of hair in his comb-over made it look worse, scrutinizing the silky strands with the force of x-ray.

"I was born bald as a baby and stayed that way through the rest of my life," Cliff said, his voice dragging. It seemed like the kind of thing a lot of guys found hard to handle. There was one kid at Redrock who was prematurely grey with shocks of white in his hair, and another who had a hairline so receded you could see the shape of his skull from forehead to occipital lobe.

"Think I could stand with some of that popcorn, Luna," Cliff said, turning to her. "Any left?"

"Sure." She held out the wooden bowl and shook it so that the cooked kernels rattled. Cliff showed her a staying hand. "Better get my own. I become a ravenous wolf when that stuff's around." He looked over at me. "Want a help me?"

"No problem." I stood and followed him. My back was to Luna, but I felt her eyes on us as we went.

Our sight adjusted as we walked into a room where brass dome lights hung from the ceiling and threw off enough wattage for an interrogation room. Cliff searched his person, his pants and his work shirt's slash pockets for his Cuban.

"Think you left your stogie in the media room."

"Shit." He gave a gruff cough, as if the slightly sore throat he had from a lifetime of smoking would have to suffice until he got his paws on another Cuban to smoke and make the throat a little sorer.

We came into the kitchen, the granite countertops and slate floor along with the brushed steel fixtures making it look like the cantina in an underground cave complex where some top secret government project was underway.

He opened a cabinet, pulled down a box of popcorn, took out a package of Redenbacher. "It's a good thing your uncle's getting better."

I thought of my uncle seated there on the couch, hands reflexively bunching and releasing, him jumping quick enough to startle Luna. She was all vital life force and still found herself surprised by the old man's motion, fluid as the water of which Bruce Lee had once spoken.

"But some people might not be happy to hear about your uncle getting his memory back. Don't get me wrong. Everybody loved him." Cliff threw his popcorn in the microwave, set the timer, and pressed the button. The bag rotated on the plate. The noise of the microwave that sounded like a hairdryer on full blast made him more comfortable as he spoke, as if maybe he suspected a wiretap in the room or that there might even be people in the house he didn't want to hear his words.

"A lot of people confided in your uncle, some of them powerful, some of them bad boys. He knows where the bodies are buried."

I was more worried about where the money was. Cliff eyed me, sensing my thoughts, if not specifically then at least that the gears were working in my mind. He watched me as if over a chessboard where he considered the diagonals of the bishops and the L-shaped leaps either of the two horses might make.

"Where did you go the other day?"

"Steakhouse," I said.

"Don't bullshit me."

"I'm not a snitch."

He took a step toward me, a steer with its rage barely contained. The kitchen overflowed with things that could make it easy for him to burn me, bash me, cut me if he had a mind to do so. I wasn't a total pussy, but I'd lost most of the fights I'd had in high-school, so it was a foregone conclusion that I would get my ass kicked or killed by messing with this bear of a man from Brooklyn. He knew mobsters and boxers the way I knew video games and weed.

He stopped where he was, looked down at his slip-on loafers. When his pulse was steady, and he trusted himself to talk and not act, he said, "I think you've got your uncle's best interest at heart."

"I think you do, too," I said, wanting to step back but forcing myself to stay in place, even as my knees started quaking and my balls retracted toward my stomach.

"But I don't know you do."

"You're right. You don't know that and you should be suspicious," I said. "And I don't know how I feel about any of them, either." I pointed toward the media room where the shrillness of the crowd and the manic staccato blow-by-blow of the announcer made me think someone had gotten knocked down or maybe even out. And I guessed that person wasn't my uncle.

Cliff nodded and closed his eyes slowly, letting me know by his grave and silent gestures that I was right again, that no one had earned enough trust for me to spill what I knew, or thought I knew, without seeing them lay their own cards on the table first. Regardless of whether those bodies Cliff was talking about were literal or figurative, he wasn't hearing about Vicki or the Sawdust until he told me something.

The microwave dinged, announcing the end of its cycle, and the smell of hot cooked butter flowed on wavering tendrils. Cliff turned around, our little talk at its end.

He pushed the latch that sprung the microwave door open and pulled out the popcorn, opening it so that salty steam wafted upwards and made our mouths water. "Movie theater style popcorn," Cliff said. "Nothing like it." He threw a couple hot kernels into the air and caught them in his open and upturned mouth as they came down, having barely missed the blades of the ceiling fan on their ascent.

"Still got it," he said, as he smiled and chewed. "Though this stuff's hell on a fella's dentures."

***

The sound the coyotes made that night was more complaint than lament, like they were baying about having bad backs but I just didn't quite have ears to hear them. A barking dog on a nearby homestead picked up the call, and it became a constant bark that didn't sound like it was ending soon.

I stood up from my bed, walked over to the window, looked outside. I hoped to spot one coyote but knew I wouldn't. They had mastered the shadows after long ago learning they were weaker than almost every other animal out here and would only survive by slinking and behaving like beasts a mere step up the evolutionary chain from rats, and maybe a rung or two below turkey buzzards.

A jaundiced eye of a moon hung in the far corner of the black sky. It threw down a lot of light, but it was a rancid-butter yellow that made me wish for some clouds or, barring that, a waning rather than waxing moon. I saw no Chupacabra stalking the naked desert, but maybe the goatsuckers moved too fast or kept to the shadows as the coyotes did; maybe the prairie dogs suckled at the cryptids' teats like Grendel at his mother's.

The front door to Luna's place opened. Her robed form stood shrouded in darkness until she shuffled into the light of the moon. The light that had been ugly and yellow a moment before was now a sainted orangish candle glow, first tinctured and then transformed by her arrival.

She shed her bathrobe on a patio chair and stood in a dove-white one-piece swimsuit that hugged the pendulous curves of her body. Gravity got us all eventually, but its work on her was a thing of beauty, giving her heart-shaped breasts and thighs a bountiful weight that meant every step sent a small aftershock through her body, which became a tremor in my body as her rippling movements reached my eye.

I knew I shouldn't be looking, that this was her time for herself, an unwinding after a night of babysitting my uncle as he watched fights. Nightmares of island-hopping the archipelagos around Betio would also probably be waking him in a couple of hours, and she would have to sit bedside and calm him through his terrors.

She didn't deserve to endure this, to have me looking at her in the dark, but the blood was pounding in my temples and in the rest of my body, and as long as it was dark and she didn't see me I didn't see any way to escape the hold of what had come over me.

I had done so well until this point, too, but that was the story of every addict and every sinner, and part of what made falling back into the trap so sweet. I'd engaged in a gentleman's agreement with a couple guys in the dorm back at Redrock and managed to not masturbate for two whole weeks, but there had been no beautiful women at school. Pretty teachers, sure, but they were never in their bathing suits, never one-on-one sitting across from you in the breakfast nook with their warm cinnamon breath and ever-present amber eyes and bowed lips.

Luna bent down, flipped a toggle lodged in the granite apron that ran around the pool. The blue water became radiant, softening the light of the full moon to a sheen of gold like an open treasure chest whose latch the saltwater had finally eaten through, casting doubloons outward from the sea trench where the coins caught rays of light from the sun breaking the ocean's surface.

She dived, sleek as a dolphin, glowed with the gold and blue reflection of the water. Her arms spread out as she performed the backstroke, whipping her way through the water and pulling herself along, her breasts bobbing hard enough to fight an ocean current at high tide.

She turned around mid-stroke and went underwater, headfirst and disappearing down to her toes, leaving only a small pocket of bubbles in her wake that were there one moment, and dissolved without a trace in the next. The surface was undisturbed, and if I hadn't seen her go down in the first place, I might not have even known someone was in the pool.

I waited, my breath bated as her breath was held, as if I feared she might not emerge but might drown down there. Or maybe her secret that had kept me enthralled, turned fascination to an obsession, was that she lived in a coral cavern down there but had to wait until midnight to shed the lies of day, grow gills and webbed feet become once again what she really was.

She broke the surface, gasping a bit for air and sending a spray of water upward in her wake. Her long black hair streamed behind her wet and shining, lustered as if she'd been swimming in the yolk of a rare bird. She pushed her hair back from her face, gave one small cough that made her features cute as long as it lasted, but then her mien calmed and she sunk back into the sleepy sultriness that defined her.

She looked toward the house and I dropped below the window's sash, my panic getting the best of me until I reminded myself that this house had many rooms, all of them equally dark, and there was no way for her to know I was watching.

Crouching made me aware of my dick, pulsing and warm and straining toward her heedless of what reality said about the likelihood that it would ever happen, that I could pierce her soft warmth, sheathe the conquistador's sword in the soft contours of the bruja's font of limitless hot honey.

My penis tried to break through the fabric of my boxers and snuck its way through the slit in the front of the checked flannel, like a drunk maneuvering around a bouncer. My dick strayed upward in salute as I worked up the nerve to peer above the half-foot thick stone wall of my room and out the window again, where the light of the pool and the moon and Luna reflected back at me.

The blood rushed in my head until it sounded like mission bells clanging and I gave in, hating myself as I stroked and imagined myself there with her in the pool, not in my own teenaged and still-slightly chunky body, but as a man of whatever kind she needed and hadn't found yet or might never discover, or maybe didn't even want.

I imagined myself as a Telenovela doctor, the center of a hospital intrigue where an heiress in and out of a coma and several nurses in white dresses all vied cattily for my eye and strong touch.

But that was no good, and I didn't want to imagine myself powerful before her. For the first time in fantasy I wanted to be me as I was, so that rather than being experienced she could lead me over the threshold of my fear into something like manhood, give me what only she had the right to pass in the consecrated ritual between woman and boy. It would have been illegal but our love would exist where the law was irrelevant, and the beauty of our secret would be strong enough that, unlike any of the other kids at Redrock or most boys my age, I wouldn't feel the need to boast and it would never become some lame scandal that gave me boasting rights while she found herself forced to leave the school under a cloud of scandal.

Luna, give me a chance. I can keep my mouth shut, or open it only to lick the diamond facet-like beads of sweat and water that taste like nectar dripping off you, lick your pussy as gently as a cat velvet-tonguing a saucer of milk in a moonlit alley.

I composed poetry with what part of my mind hadn't completely shut down by the throbbing of my cock and all the blood rushing to it and away from my heart and brain, my arm flailing as I whacked off so it became sore in the shoulder from the repetitive motion. I beat like I'd never stopped or started, was just part of some pneumatic Luna-worshipping machine, a drone producing some nectar I didn't understand whose real purpose was part of the Queen Bee's secret plan. And if I was not just a slave, but one among many who were nameless in her worshipful army, then I was cool with that, too. It was easier to worship that which was not aware of you, and it was a masochistic ecstasy to pretend that she expected as her birthright that which I gave vainly hoping she'd be grateful.

Behind the prison of my castle wall only a few feet from her I willed myself, astral-projected until I was poolside there with her. I used my teeth to pull the rubbery fabric of her swimsuit from where it had bunched in her ass, bit her gluteus, and just to give a soft pleasured coda to that I kissed her thighs and pecked each half-heart of her pendant-shaped ass in supplication. I kissed out a pattern on her ass and repeated it, dropping on my belly, serpent robbed of legs, but there was nothing to regret and there was plenty of work needing attending even on my belly and cast this low. I sucked her toes, licked the spaces between them with a frantic tongue programmed to seek her crevices and taste her dirt.

I stopped just short of coming, took my hand from my cock burning with pleasured nerves, a single tear of pre-cum promising a geyser if I rubbed any harder, or so much as touched my vein-shrouded screaming dick.

I turned from the window, pulled my erection up and used the elastic band of my boxers to cinch it in place as best I could, but it was a half-assed restraint like two weak guys holding back a third intent on fighting another hardhead. Then I waddled over to the pillow, took my bag of weed out of the pillowcase, and stuffed it in my pocket.

I knew this all needed to get done before I could think twice about it, so I pushed myself, taking deep breaths and hoping that would do the trick that I might eventually need cold water to achieve, get my erection to wilt and allow my mind to make some decisions my cock had been handling for me up to this point. Some guys at Redrock who'd had to deal with embarrassing, constant erections had taught me to wear a couple pair of boxers rather than one, when the unwanted boners kept coming in waves, and I made a note to myself to wear two sets of underwear tomorrow to give myself a fighting chance in front of Luna.

The guest bathroom was empty when I waddled in there, and I closed the door behind me, turning on the lights and the fan as I did so. A mica lampshade softened the overhead light to earth tones, throwing the Moorish tiles of the floor into a radiant liquid brown that gave the room the feel of being preserved in amber.

It had the opposite effect of fluorescence, contouring all my flaws in the mirror into something that I could live with, especially if I squinted watching myself there in profile.

I made sure the bathroom door was closed and locked. Then I pulled down my pants, lifted my shirt, squeezed my stomach until a slab of abdominal wall halfway peeked through the rippling gelatin of my gut I'd worked so hard to get by snacking, smoking weed, and staying as sedentary as possible with video games on my beanbag chair. Whacking off and weekend paintball had been about the only exercise I'd gotten up to this point in my life, aside from whatever bitch-work Big Jim could concoct for me on the ranch while he and my mom went about their ritual of gambling, traveling, and antiquing.

My straining with my stomach muscles caused my erection to bounce like a tweaked door stop spring and I slapped it as if I thought that might force it to go down, relax and sleep rather than having the opposite effect. It was obstinate and the purplish lips grinned in mockery, a one-eyed monster cyclopean and blind to all but its pleasure and not caring about STDs or pregnancy, stupid fleshy Venus Flytrap whose hunger could never achieve satiation.

What a nightmare it was to have a dick, pumped with an insistent and barely dammed flood of semen trapped in full balls and always looking for a way out. I wished I was a woman for the moment, not knowing what that might entail, what risks and pains that brought that may have been a greater hardship that being a man, or at least a male, a boy.

But how to become a man, aside from waiting?

"Shit, go away," I said, as if I could reason with my dick and it didn't have a mind of its own, or at least the cunning to strip me of whatever mind I had whenever the whim struck it, and it needed me out of the way to sink its way toward its goal like a drill seeking a subsurface oil patch.

I flipped the toilet seat up and dumped my weed into the bowl where the evergreen buds turned a dull sage color on contact with the water, the herbs floating around the porcelain and soaking up liquid as they swirled in a circle. I flushed the toilet and watched the weed disappear, stood and moved around the confines of the bathroom with my erection, as if I could walk it off like a strained muscle after a rough play on the soccer field.

It was still with me, slapping my legs as I walked, bouncing between them like a pinball between two flipper arms. From a recessed nook carved in the stucco mudstone of the wall a Lady Guadalupe or Virgin Mary (were they the same thing?) watched me with a disapproving look. She held her expression with lips pursed, bemused, and shaming like a Mona Lisa whose eyes followed but whose thoughts never became known, only I think I knew what Mary was thinking and that was, *Flush all the weed you want; you're still going to hell for whacking off to Luna when she didn't know you were there.* The Christ child in her arms thankfully had his eyes downcast before my sin and weakness. His hair kinked like lamb's wool and his mother held him with the arm not cradling a relic of a heart double-stranded with thorns that looked like a blend between barbed wire and prickly pear barbs.

I wasn't religious, but crossed myself reflexively with the hand I hadn't been using to whack. My act was somewhere between empty gesture and ritual, like mobster going to Mass on Sunday or that guy who'd stepped out for the bell at the twelfth round to fight my uncle at Ogden Outdoor Arena earlier tonight, but hadn't made it through the next three minutes, his imprecations to God notwithstanding.

I turned off the light on the way out of the bathroom and returned to my room, fighting the impulse to go to the window and see if Luna was still there, swimming beneath the light of the moon, perhaps now feeling safe enough to have shed her swimsuit and swim Eve-naked, doing backstroke laps from one end of the pool to the other, a creature of the water at home and alone with her aquatic gods who somehow weren't a heresy against that Mary in the other room, since they somehow complimented the Mother of God (or the Lady Guadalupe) in the weird pantheon of deities (but mostly goddesses) that made up Luna's universe.

No sooner was my head on the pillow than my was hand on my dick again, flagellating head and shaft down to the root so quickly and hard that my public hair rustled like a disturbed forest. I punished myself with my unlubricated stroke and choking grip, saying "Luna," a litany of pained-pleasure that made me weak and strong with each whack as I clutched, squeezed, pumped, apologized for the last sheet of flab I promised to shed from my stomach if it cost me my life.

I came, ashamed and enraptured in the same moment, wishing I hadn't flushed my weed away, wishing now that Luna was in bed with me, not for another round of sex but as a wife, someone I didn't take for granted but whose presence I'd grown to expect, a warmth coiled against my body and fitting my form, us interlocking like two puzzle pieces that hadn't solved the world's problems but at least solved this small patch that granted us the peace of a marriage bed.

"I love you, Luna," I said to her, even though she wasn't in the room and even though I knew that I did not understand what love was, knowing that whatever it might be, it was not what I shared with Luna, which was more some tenuous thread kept intact only by my uncle's presence and my own delusions.

And I shouldn't forget for a moment that this was temporary, a suspension from that half-juvie, half-rehab hellhole waiting for me among the red rocks. I hadn't been counting the days, but I'd already served out a good chunk of my suspension here, and it would end sooner rather than later.

"Lo siento, Maria," I said to the stucco whorls in the ceiling looking like fingerprints left in a plaster cast rather than in ink, a million glyphs scrimshawed on the ceiling above me, outnumbering the stars in the sky's canopy to which the coyotes and that lone mangy dog still cried.

***

The day and Luna were both unavoidable. She was waiting for me in the kitchen where she busied herself setting my uncle's meals and snacks out in Tupperware, covered in tape labeled with a black Sharpie to help him along through his courses for the day.

Sleep still had me half-concussed and with a mouth that tasted like halitosis, and I felt like I was moving in slo-mo underwater as I watched her work so quickly.

Her bamboo bead necklace and bracelet both rattled as she flitted around the room. She'd coordinated the jewelry with a brown knee-length linen dress that smelled of patchouli. It was an odor I usually found overpowering, but the amount was just right, whether she'd dabbed it on or the cloth itself just carried the smell.

"I don't appreciate what you did."

She hadn't looked at me and did not show that she had even seen me in the room. *Crap*. Fear rocketed around in my chest and travelled down to the pit of my stomach, where it felt like half a tray of ice cubes leaked out, freezing my organs.

I looked up at her, unable to speak. "I didn't start out thinking I would do that," I faltered. "That hadn't been the plan."

She shook her head softly, spoke in an even softer voice. "You could have cost me my job by letting your uncle leave here that day."

I inwardly let go a massive sigh of relief. "I'm sorry," I said. "I was wrong. I apologize."

My words didn't quite stun her, but they caused something tense in her to loosen. She smiled, seemingly proud of me, as if I'd rejoined humanity.

"You see?" Luna said, bushy brown eyebrow arching. "It's not so hard is it, to take responsibility?"

"I'm trying to be a man," I said. "Trying to learn."

"That's more than most boys your age do." She stacked the Tupperware containers, set them in the fridge. "It's more than a lot of men my age do. I can attest to that firsthand."

I wanted to ask her if she was seeing someone, but killed the words before they could leave my lips. I'd just gained some ground, become something halfway human again in her eyes. It was too early to screw that up and undo all the good work.

"It wasn't just me you jeopardized." Luna walked over to the French press and poured two glazed clay mugs near to the brim with Chiapas brew. "Think of Dr. Parks, and all the effort he's put into this project."

"Why?" I asked.

She shot me a venomous look, misunderstanding my *Why*, not meant to ask *Why* I should think of the effort he'd put in (that would be a real shitheel question), but what was motivating him. I clarified. "Why is the Doctor so committed to him, this project? Did his dad have dementia?"

"No." Luna lifted the cup and took a sip and absently played with the links in her necklace with the fingers of her other hand. I went to retrieve my coffee from the counter, thanking her in a low tone as she continued. "He was a ringside physician. He saw a lot of other men end up like your uncle, or… how your uncle was until a few days ago. He was improving and then backsliding, but when you got here he got much better, much faster."

I blushed, dropped my eyes to my coffee, shy and unable to meet her stare. I could feel her eyes boring through me as I averted my gaze. She was drinking in my timidity, which I enjoyed. When I worked up the balls to make eye contact with her again, she was grinning ear-to-ear, the only subtlety in her expression now the ever-arched eyebrow silently inquiring what kind of mischief I'd been up to with him.

"Coincidence," I said, smiling with her. "My showing up here and him getting better."

"Maybe," she allowed, drank more coffee. I had my first sip, the java's caffeine kicking like a mule's hind legs as I reseated myself at the kitchen table across from her.

She took a gulp big enough to cause her jaw to pulse and her throat to contract. I counted the scores in the table's woodgrain catching light from the ancient sun pouring warm morning rays through the kitchen window.

"I have to go into town," Luna said, "to get some supplies for us and some medications for your uncle."

"I'll watch him."

She stood, carried her empty coffee mug over to the sink. "Don't take offense, but I've put a club on the steering wheel, just in case he gets any ideas." Luna turned on the water and rinsed out her cup. "He can hot-wire her all he wants, but he's not steering."

"Not unless he has a blowtorch handy."

"Don't give him any ideas. Oh, before I forget." She left the room, walking on sandaled feet across the stone floor. When she returned, she'd crowned her head in a chapleted chain of desert blooms, flowers plucked from plants that were poisonous or stickered, but which she had charmed with her soft touch into harmlessly yielding up fruits they would have defended to their deaths if any hand besides hers had approached.

"What do you think?" She asked. "It took me an hour to braid it up. Some ladies who do beadwork in town will have to judge my workmanship." She made do with the reflective surface of a tin teakettle's funhouse reflection of her, then moved on to the black polarized glass of the microwave.

Most women's features were sharper in profile, but hers were as gently sloping from the side as from the front, the only slight juts the button of her nose and light curve of her chin.

"Queen," I said.

She took a step back, slapped by the open and candid force of my undisguised worship. "Michael…" It was the first time she'd said my name. I didn't answer. I was waiting for a command to follow, and to carry it out.

But she didn't speak, and I realized she was waiting for me to answer her. I fought around the dryness in my throat, the thrum of my heart, and did my best, which was, "What?"

"I'm flattered, but I really wish you wouldn't say things like that."

"Queen?" Her defenses broke again, even though I didn't intend to praise her this time around, but just to clear the air. She took another half-step back from my words, but this time when she recovered her eyes were less stunned, and sterner. She walked closer to me.

"Yes, I think you need to use this time to get your mind ready to go back to school." She drummed the soft fingers of her right hand on the tabletop.

"Look, I enjoy your company, and not just because one gets starved for any contact out here. And I'm impressed by how you've taken to helping your uncle, when you're not enabling him."

I nodded, kept my fool mouth shut.

"But if you say inappropriate things like that… or if you *do* anything inappropriate. Anything *else* inappropriate, I should say, it will disappoint me and you'll be letting yourself down, too."

"I heard the coyotes, and I went to the window. That was my only-"

"It might not have been your intention to do it, but no one told you to bring marijuana here, or to smoke it."

My heart stabilized again. We still weren't talking about me spying on her, behaving like a creepy peeping tom. And the saddest, most pathetic part of it all was that if I thought she didn't know about what I'd done, then I might try to do it again. If she was in town long enough, and I couldn't fight my body's passion and poison, I would eventually find myself drawn to her house out there, the "Bunker" where the flags flew. And I'd search out her panties the way a pilgrim sought a saint's reliquary, a couple trace dots of her menstrual blood stained on white lace or black satin potent as the ever-bleeding heart of some holy man that refused to burn even after the Indians tore the missionary's heart out and tried to scorch it on the pyre with his body.

I nodded my head. I had problems, but I also had at least some good news to report, something that might make her happy that wasn't a lie. "I flushed the rest of my weed down the toilet last night."

"That means a lot to me. I know it couldn't have been easy for you."

"Don't want the old man getting reefer madness." I regretted the joke as it spilled from my mouth, since it could lead in other directions that could get me in trouble with her again.

"Did you smoke with him?"

I shook my head. "No." I had smoked in his presence, but that wasn't what she was asking, was it? Or was this a lie of omission? I didn't care. I wanted her to love me, and barring that, to respect me even if I had to trick her into it.

"This is important, Michael." She walked toward me, forgot her own part of the bargain to respect boundaries, came close enough that I could see myself reflected in the warmth of her large brown eyes, consuming me, her lips parted as if we'd already kissed and they were re-assuming their natural, supple and full form after I'd bit them and the flushness returned to her mouth as we broke apart and I released the grip of my teeth. My erection tried to fight through both layers of boxers as I remained seated and her hand grazed my leg.

"Doctor Parks wanted a sample of the marijuana, after I told him I'd taken a little from you."

"That was you?"

"I've heard they use it for medical research sometimes, especially with the elderly."

She backed up.

I stood. For the first time with her, hell, for the first time, I was in the right and had the right to be angry, too. I'd milk this for whatever self-righteous rage I could get out of it. "You went through my things." Just saying the sentence with feigned anger brought some real anger to the surface, bubbling up. Just because she was beautiful didn't mean she could do whatever she wanted. I mean, it meant that, but my goal was to deny that as long as I could, to not let slip again that she was my secret queen.

"Your mother asked me to."

"Debbie." I spit the name out, tasted it, hated it, hating her.

I hated the way she went through boyfriends before bagging Big Jim. I didn't begrudge her trying to find love in bars, online, or at work but I hated her for being willing to roll the dice by bringing strange men into the house, men who could have been ultra-creeps for all she knew, men who could have molested my brother, which would have required me to kill her.

Im my darkest moments I wanted to plunge a knife in her chest, hard into the sternum or whatever part of the breast was toughest and had the least give, so that the knife bent and warped and maybe broke at the tang. I wanted to stab her and shout "Cunt!" until the tears flowed from my eyes, and I didn't care what that made me. Yes, my father was a failure, but he wasn't bringing his cellmates around the house to get drunk around my little dog or my younger brother.

That was what it had finally come down to: a choice between the knife or the needle, and I had chosen the latter. I couldn't blame anyone else for what I did with my veins, but dammit if Debbie could have just kept men away from the house maybe it wouldn't have come to that.

I had to keep reminding myself it had been my choice to do heroin, because even though I knew it was the blame game they cautioned us against at Redrock, I still felt she had helped put that needle in my arm, as sure as one of Big Jim's many debit cards with easy-to-guess pins had helped me make withdrawals at ATMs, until every piece of plastic got cancelled and it all came crashing down.

"I'm sorry," Luna said.

I waved my hand. "It's her and me, not you. You didn't know me then."

"No," she said, walking away from me, over to the sink, looking into the stainless steel basin as if the answer for any of life's complicated problems might be there, swirling down the drain.

I wanted petty revenge against her too, though, Luna and not my mother, because she had made herself my mother's lackey. My princess- no, my queen- who betrayed me. Or even better than a queen. I searched for something, a title or honorific, some superlative to alienate her permanently from me and let her know the depth of my loyalty to her, notwithstanding the dagger she'd just lodged in my back.

"I forgive you," I said. "My goddess."

She put her head in her hands, closed her eyes, exasperated with my foolishness and her own mistake of trying to treat me like an adult, and confide in me. She took the chaplet from her head, opened her eyes and looked at it, as if it instead of me or she or my mother had caused all this confusion, whatever was unfolding now.

And who knew, maybe the wreath was at fault. Maybe in the same way that a dumb falcon got tricked by a hood into thinking it was night, I had seen that wreath on her head and mistaken her for something semidivine, instead of just another struggling girl trying to make enough money to get a better car, find a stupid-but-strong-man to fuck in the short term, and later a weak-but-rich-man to marry.

"I have to go to town now," Luna said, her back to me as she headed toward the front door. "If the geriatric psychiatrist calls, please take a message."

"Yes, ma'am."

"'Luna' is fine," she said, primly, afraid of the sexual undercurrent to any obeisance I might throw her way.

She stopped halfway to the door and turned. "I would very much appreciate it if you didn't spend time around me, unless it was in your uncle's presence, or one of his friend's or the doctor's."

"Get some mace when you go into town, just as insurance."

She turned, eyes brimming with scorn, chest rising. "Well, considering I can't even go for a swim after a long day's work without you ogling me from your window like a monkey in a cage, mace might be a good investment."

My face dropped, her sadism evaporated, and pity caused her eyes to well. I had thought for a moment that I was the resident doctor in our little Telenovela and she was the demure nurse who was but putty in my hands. I'd forgotten that I was a boy, and she was a woman.

She left without another word. I waited for the sound of the door closing and then ran into my bedroom. I collapsed on the bed and put my face into the pillow, weeping and wishing my weed was still there sleeved in the pillowcase. I hated her and myself, but even as inexperienced as I was I knew that this agony was the normal state between adults, only worse and more amplified, so even if this wasn't love (and it wasn't) at least it was a preparation of sorts for the hell to come should I ever be lucky enough to find that special someone and dumb enough to trust them with my heart.

The phone rang from the kitchen. I stood from the bed, broke off my pity party early, and ran across the hallway.

The phone was a heavy wall-mounted green rotary job that looked like an instrument used to measure pressure in a World War II submarine. The ringer was so loud that the handset rumbled in the cradle and threatened to come loose of its moorings. Maybe it was President Eisenhower calling to tell us the status of the nuclear football.

I picked up the phone. "Reeves' Residence."

"Michael." It was my mother. I breathed, told myself to stay civil. I would make no sarcastic quips about thanking her for having the girl I obsessed over shake down my gear and search for dope, like Casa de Reeves was Redrock all over again.

"How are you enjoying yourself?"

"Good," I said.

"Is Luna there?"

"No." I put my right arm beneath my left armpit, as if it had a mind of its own, a hand from a horror movie just itching to go for the butcher knife. "She went into Sonora Bend to restock on supplies."

"How's your uncle?"

"Good," I said. "We watched some of his old fights last night." I struggled to find a small talk subject. "So are you in Arizona or Nevada or…" I faltered. I thought my politeness would make her suspicious if I kept it up much longer. I would have to get off the phone soon or risk maybe making her come back here earlier than planned.

"I'm back in Paris."

"And how are *Le Perroquet* in the Eight Arrondissement?"

"Don't begrudge me my happiness It's small of you. I've worked very hard my whole life, as has Jim. And there's no reason if you don't work hard enough that you can't enjoy the finer things in life yourself, or find someone with whom to share those things."

That last bit sounded like someone had told her I'd barnacled myself to Luna, or maybe she knew it would happen before she even brought me here.

I leaned my head down so I could cradle the receiver between shoulder and the gray cotton of my Polo shirt. "That Subway summer gig still on offer?"

"Maybe," she said. "Jim says it depends on your weight and your grades."

As if everyone in Glitter Gulch or even on the Strip had a perfect waistline or the best pedigree. It was the Wild West out there. Benny Binion himself once said something like, "I never learned how to read but I know how to count."

One could say the opposite for me, but that didn't get you very far in America, unless you stayed hiding in academia, and if professors were half as depressed as the high-school teachers I knew, then that wasn't a road I wanted to go down, either.

"I'll tell Luna you called. I'd like to stay on the phone, but I'm waiting for another call from the-"

"Geriatric Psychiatrist." She completed the sentence for me.

"You, Jackie Stallone, and LaToya Jackson should team up. You'd make beaucoup bucks running a psychic hotline."

I hung up. As I turned I saw my uncle standing there, an open pajama jacket over a torn Gleeson's gym shirt hanging loose on his ropey thews of muscle, hard-won probably as a stevedore or longshoreman, so rocklike that the remains of the formerly chiseled slabs had never entirely gone away and remained solid as knotholes down to their testosterone taproots. Arthritis had eaten some edge from the tissue and gave the flesh a liquid-like, liver-spotted look on the surface, but there was still a solid undergirding to the man's body that the youngsters juicing and bench-pressing in the gym could never replicate with their over-inflated and veiny pecs and biceps.

He wore grey cotton drawstring sweats bloused into his kicks, which were boxing shoes.

"Screw your ma and screw the headshrinker."

A towel concealed a moment before behind his back appeared and whipped toward me, leaving a red imprint on the exposed skin of my neck that had me hopping and laughing from the whipcord recoil.

"Let's go beat the bag or something," my uncle said, retracting his towel after snapping me.

"As long as we don't take the car. Luna will have my ass."

He clutched his towel around his neck, gripping the ends so that the cloth was bent into a horseshoe shape over his shoulders. "Who?"

***

Neither babysitting nor hospice was something I'd ever done, but now it looked like I might need to do a bit of both to keep this thing from getting out of control, and to maintain the probationary respect Luna had for me. The fort needed holding down til she came back.

"You want to go lay back down for a while, or maybe watch one of your fights?" I asked.

My uncle fidgeted with some pieces of lint caught in the Velcro lining of his striped pajamas. "You the applesauce man?" His mouth hung open after he asked, an expectant "O," as if he was waiting for me to spoon it directly into his mouth, which wasn't happening.

"Let's see if she left some in here." I turned toward the massive black coffin of a refrigerator, stopped halfway in my motion when his mocking laughter interrupted me. I turned back around toward him.

His face creased from laughter, age lines and scar tissue fusing together across his sandpapery patchwork skin. "I'm just messing with you. I'm back now, hopefully for good."

I turned away from the fridge, walked past him, feeling like a fool. I pulled out a chair and sat down at the breakfast table. "But you don't know that you won't slip back into it?"

"I don't know." His voice was somber, and he had to sit down, too, just to process what he'd said and what it might mean. "I'm still pretty much helpless. It was horrible before, though, when I really was helpless."

He shook his head. However, it felt to be him was something he couldn't communicate to me, not with words at least; maybe by expression but I didn't have the heart to meet the horror in his stricken eyes. "I could feel my mind slipping away when we were coming back from the cathouse. I was watching myself from inside my head. Helpless as a newborn, but with this old body."

He held up his hands, studied the liver spots and white hairs growing from the knuckles, examined the fungal yellow, calcified deposits at the tips of his fingernails he hadn't cleaned or trimmed in some time.

"Luna help you with your nails at all?"

He waved his hands, still examining them as if he'd been twenty yesterday and woken up seventy-something this morning. "No, she tries but I tell her it's not in her jurisdiction. It's hard enough having to piss in front of her." His pleading eyes looked into my own, that mouth open but calling for something more substantial than applesauce.

"I need my body back."

"Do you want to talk to the doctor?" I figured Doctor Parks could help him with this. I knew I couldn't.

"He can handle the brainbox stuff. This isn't neurologic. It's my body. It's old."

"I..." Shit. "It's not just your body that's old. You *are* old. Whatever he's doing with you in that den is revolutionary, but he doesn't have a time machine or the Fountain of Youth or something."

His expression was that of a whipped animal whose master had once been kind but had betrayed him for reasons he couldn't fathom. I reminded myself of my general plan for dealing with ageing. I'd die of an overdose or in a car wreck sometime between now and the age of twenty-five.

Fuck Redrock. What was the point of living life right, if your body would only be betray you, anyway? Suicide and self-destruction were just the smart man's way of beating nature to the punch. Or God. Whoever or whatever it was.

Science? Shit, look at what it did to him. Healing was temporary and made everything worse in the end.

I kept these thoughts to myself, but he was no dummy, and had to know that being given his mind back may have been a bullshit door prize on his way out of the dancehall of life, one last bit of mockery and a parting glance at an eternity he could never really behold with both eyes for any length of time.

"Kill me, then."

"I can't kill you." I shook my head, sipped my coffee. "Luna would love that. First time she leaves me alone with you, we go to a bordello. Second time she takes a chance and trusts me, I… what? Shoot you?"

"I've got guns all over." He searched around the confines of the kitchen, the only room in the house not filled with bric-à-brac.

"You want to risk it with an antique, try to blow your own brains out with a gun that hasn't been cleaned, much less fired, in decades?"

He stared at me, mouth still agape. I softened. "I'm sorry. I don't know much about guns. Paintball is the extent of my firearms experience. I don't know what to tell you. I'm having enough trouble not killing myself. I don't have a right to tell you not to do it."

"How would you do it?" He gripped the table as a tremor hit his body, like it was a time-released quake his nervous system had saved up for him and dispensed on the hour.

"Dope," I said.

"Marijuana?" He squinted. "I know it's gotten stronger since I've been out of it, but not that much-"

"No one calls that dope anymore." I tried to hide my laughter, but when it caught on with him I decided not to disguise it. His dentures were almost as stained as his fingernails but it was still a smile, and a relief to see. "No, heroin," I said. "Mama Heroin. Let her carry me away to a big white cloud in the sky."

"Hell, that doesn't sound so bad. I had pleurisy in the merchant marine. I got TB from a cow on a vessel and they had to go in through my ribs, gave me morphine and it was a dream come true." The soothing memory of that good pharmaceutical dope calmed him, the peace flowing out from his brain to the branching network of all his veins.

Say what you want about dope, but it was magic while it lasted, a crystal blue wave that imparted perfection that I couldn't explain, and was barely explainable even when the plunger was down. But it abandoned you quickly, and that's why only a real asshole would give a man his first shot, especially an old man confused and looking to get euthanized by deliberate hotshot.

I thought of something, or remembered it, rather. "How about the geriatric psychiatrist? He could talk to you about what you're going through."

"No." My uncle's resolve was strong enough for him to let go of the table. Rage gave him new strength, so he didn't have to worry about the shakes taking possession of him again.

"Why not?" I asked.

"First off, I couldn't talk to him about all this." He waved his hands around the sun-dappled confines of the breakfast nook, but I knew that he meant that little lab they had in that room hidden behind the backcloth painting. "I'd have to convince him of Dr. Parks' breakthrough, and he's the only one with a right to talk about that. And besides that, no one would believe me." He fidgeted with the Velcro of his pajama shirt. "They'd probably bring out the butterfly net."

He stood up from the table, walked over to the fridge, opened the right-side door. Then he selected a plastic container from the Jenga tower of balancing food boxes, taking it from the middle and not even wobbling the rest of the stack.

"That's impressive," I said.

"Played a lot of pickup sticks as a kid. I was once very dexterous, and aim to be again, someday."

Someday? "Someday" was somewhere far in his rearview.

He brought the container over to the table and its rubberized top belched as he pulled it off and started picking at the open-face Southwest Omelet.

"What's the other reason we can't talk to the shrink?"

"He's in cahoots with your mom, I think, or could be."

"Cahoots?" I knew what the phrase meant thanks to Turner Classic Movies, but I didn't know the nature of the conspiracy. I could guess, though.

He rolled the omelet in the tortilla shell like it was a fat White Owl cigar filled with weed, said, "Your mom hired the shrink which makes me think something's up." He bit the end of his makeshift burrito, chewed with one side of his mouth and spoke with the other. "She wants my money." He gulped down that first bite and tore another length off the shell and kept chewing.

"She knows about the two mil?"

He waved the remaining half of the burrito around. "I got money all over the place." He pointed the burrito over the right shoulder of his striped cotton PJs, at a stack of mail sitting on a linoleum counter below the big green phone. "Just the other day taxman sent me a bunch of money. Refund for the time I got scammed on amusement taxes at Silver Fox Theme Park."

"What the hell is that?"

"It *is* nothing," he said, licking low-fat sour cream from his fingers. "It *was* a money pit and a scam." He waved his hand in the air dismissively, as if he'd covered this ground a million times, probably even in a courtroom, and would not rehash any but the barest details for this young punk sitting across from him, me I mean.

"Silver Foxes were a minor league team, triple A, so we named our theme park after that. Only thing is, the shyster I went halves with was embezzling and he just kicked the bucket." He burped, waited for a wave of indigestion to pass. "His son cleaned out the old codger's place, found the books, and did the right thing. Had them audited, and now I'm supposed to get a piece of the estate."

"That was good of him," I said. "The son, I mean. He could have swept that under the rug."

"Mormons." He gazed off into the distance, spacing out, as if this show of kindness in a life that hadn't exactly been one streak of kind acts had thrown him for a loop. "Weird religion, but if Howard Hughes trusted them to conduct his business, they should be good enough for an old pug."

I was thinking of the squat, mashed-faced little dog with the overbite and Shar-Pei wrinkles on its face. "'Pugilist," he said, and pulled at the material of his shirt, the little acrylic silhouette of a shadowboxing man on his yellow Gleeson's training tee beneath the PJ top.

The muscles on the shadow man drawn there brought him back to his earlier thoughts, his idea that I had been hoping he'd leave well enough alone. "I have to get my body back."

He stood up. I stood with him. I wanted to help him as he went, but I sensed his desire for independence as much as his need to depend on someone, literally if his leaning posture and hobbled shuffle were any sign.

I settled for walking just outside the force-field of his personal space that I sensed as I got close to him, delimited by that weird formaldehyde and aftershave funk that all such old men carry around with them.

"Maybe, some step aerobics classes, mall walking," I said. "Then we can get you back in good shape."

"I'm a fighter."

I knew how it felt for someone to patronize you, to endure a shadowing by someone whose very presence was an insult, and it felt weird that Luna forced me into the role of patronizing caretaker. The problem was that I wasn't being paid, and that I was coming close to caring. I had no way of knowing the exact nature or name of the sensation overcoming me, though, since it was new.

"Why can't you kill me?" He asked, meandering through the living room where the dead heads of all the animals mounted on plaques watched us, their russet and brown pelts lit by the light of the sun streaming in.

"Why can't you kill yourself?"

"Fair question." He nodded at me even as he walked away from me, toward the backyard.

"Feel free to answer it."

"Catholic," he said, which more than sufficed. He struggled with the glass door, gripping it and pulling as if it was a pair of shut elevator doors and he stood there ready to get out of some department store where he found himself trapped even if it meant a hernia.

I stopped a couple paces away from him, knowing he needed help and that he wouldn't accept it or ask for it.

I tried being mean, or at least a little gruff, since that might go over better than pity. I took a chance, said, "Come on, old fart. We ain't got all day."

He stowed his smile. "You try it then, you little prick. It's stuck."

"I know," I said, walking around him. "Luna showed me the trick. You got to jimmy it a bit." I made a show of struggling, twisting as if I were lock-picking. Then I pulled the door aside, and it glided open on its runners. The smell of the pomegranate pergola filled the air, the desert bloom potpourri instantly reminding me of Luna, whose house with the flags out front (and drawers no doubt filled with panties) was waiting for us, or for me, rather.

My uncle had other plans, dropped his PJ top, and shed the pants in the next instant, half-taking them off and half-walking out of them so I feared he might become tangled, trip, and crack his head on the concrete apron surrounding the pool.

"It's not the fountain of youth," he said, walking toward the blue rippling wellspring. "But it's water."

He was naked, covered in a hirsute peach fuzz, a snowy down that was heaviest on his back and shoulders, thinnest at his shanks, the thighs and buttocks, where (unlike with the upper body) the pouches that once held muscle hung like deflated balloons of loose and flaccid flesh where nothing could grow again, no matter what kind of training he did. Unless Doctor Parks came up with some complimentary magical physical regimen to go with whatever the hell he was doing to my uncle's brain. And no one got that lucky twice, or was that brilliant. Thomas Edison, maybe.

"Ah!"

He smiled, face-up and afloat in the water, letting the bubbles of a false current take him, soothe him along the surface with his eyes closed, submerged except for a nose and chin scaly with scar tissue, left ear a lump of cauliflower flesh, all pain melting into the cool revivifying life waters.

"Does Luna let you swim?" I cursed myself for phrasing it that way. I knew what the stubborn, pigheaded wooly old bastard would say to that, or exactly at which of my words he'd take umbrage.

I don't need her permission, I thought he'd say, or words along that line. Instead, though, and to my surprise, the smile stayed on his face, or grew in size, and the eyes remained closed, preparing for the tranquil depths of an unfathomable sleep that would last an uncountable number of hours.

He spoke in a voice pitched just above a whisper, something on the order of a faint birdcall at dawn. "Tell Luna 'thank you' and 'I'm sorry.'"

I felt it pass from him then, that thing I didn't believe in and denied even in myself, felt his presence enter me as a ghostly residue even as he left his own body, which sunk now as quickly as a rock wrapped in a chain and weighted with a heavy anchor.

I was a bad babysitter, a horrible hospice worker, and all-around general worthless sack of shit. I missed Mama Heroin and regretted that I hadn't let the old man try it once, since he was going to the other side anyway, and it might have helped him on the journey I knew we'd all eventually make. Me included, thank God.

We could have pawned some of his Tojo swag and copped a bag.

I put dreams of dope aside and rushed toward the water and jumped in, fully clothed and crying, plunging below the surface to rescue him, or rather to retrieve the limp and naked body of the dead old man.

***

The weight of my wet clothes only added to the feeling of slogging in slow-motion through a nightmare with an end that was a foregone conclusion. My uncle was dead, and I was in trouble. I dragged him to the edge of the pool, moving toward the steps leading out of the water at the shallow end. His heels were dug in, obstinately dragging, and as I pulled him I appreciated fully for the first time the phrase "dead weight." I'd been in closed-unit (51-50) involuntary commission rehab facilities before, but this was the first time I was in the orderly role, fighting against something like the limpness of an OD case, or the even deader weight of a literal corpse.

"Why is this door open? You're going to let bugs in and out, not to mention the AC is on and it's a waste of-"

I turned from dragging the wet body from the water, saw Luna standing there in the doorway. She was holding some baskets woven from sumac or willow that she'd picked up while in town from one of the Navajo women running a roadside shop. The baskets had patterns that reminded me of the hides of corn snakes and even looked like serpents in that flashing second when she dropped them to the pool apron and rushed over.

"What did you do to him!" She shoved me so I fell back into the water hard enough to plunge, as if I'd done a cannonball from a diving board, to the very bottom of the deep end. That left her and my uncle at the edge of the pool and me going under. Water rushed in my ears, muffling the sounds of her screaming for my uncle to breathe. The chlorine burned deep into my eyes since I hadn't had time to close them before Luna pushed me in.

I waded now, walking across the floor of the pool, tired, enraged, slower still as the dunk in the water had soaked my clothes clean through. When I broke through the surface, she was already applying CPR, pumping my uncle's naked chest covered in white hair, checking for the faintest sign of breath from his airway. Her nose was runny with translucent strands of snot, and tears flowed from her eyes as if from a spigot.

She stopped going through the medical motions with him, looked up at me, holding her body over his own dead form, as if I'd not only killed him but had a mind to desecrate his corpse.

"He was old!" I shouted, my rage so strong that I forgot my former attraction to her, hated myself for ever having it.

As angry as I was, she was angrier. She stood, leaving the body for the first time since claiming her place at its side.

"I didn't do anything," I said, holding up my hands defensively, ready to block whatever she threw as she came toward me, storming with her fists balled and jaw clenched. Her under-bite gave her face the raging cast of a demigoddess.

She grabbed me by the wrists, squeezing tight, and water poured from the cargo pockets of my shorts as if from a busted canteen. I felt the weight and warmth of her body pressed against me, as the soaking wetness from my body became moisture on hers, causing her dress to stick to my shirt as we struggled.

I cursed myself for the erection, but I also imagined that my uncle had experienced something similar in the War, that heightened sense of horniness, the need to make life even as the threat of losing your own loomed.

"You crazy bitch!" I ground my teeth together, finding a new level of rage in myself. Occasionally I could get pissed enough to snap on a bully at school if he wouldn't leave me alone, but that was more a matter of dangerous hysterics than something like this.

My words only made her angrier, and she squeezed my arms so they felt already bruised. She pushed me back toward the pool, and I leaned forward to keep her from throwing me in again, especially this close to the stone steps where I might fall and crack my head open.

"Was it your idea?! To go swimming?" She sobbed and squinted, blinded by the sting of her tears.

"My idea was breakfast."

She let go of my arms and grabbed me by the raglan material of my red shirt, now maroon from the soak in the pool. "It wasn't enough to screw up once! You've cost me my job and my friend!"

I grabbed her wrists while she tightened her hold on my shirt, paying her back for the Kung-Fu grip she'd had on my arms a second ago. Her eyes were so full of rage I expected some vortex to break open soon, cause her hair to pull back behind her as if we were being dragged toward a hell she conjured with her mind.

"Your 'friend'!" I tried to sneer, but my lips wouldn't curl, and the uneven line of my mouth looked more like a weak Elvis impersonation.

"Yes!" She shook me and I squeezed tighter on her wrists. "He was my friend! What was he to you?!"

She let go of my shirt, wrinkled to the point of tearing, ruined and wrung dry as if put through an old-fashioned hand-cranked mangle.

"I don't know." I shook my head, looked over at his body, bloated and white, slick like a glistening perch snatched from fresh water. "I was just getting to know him."

"Trying to worm your way into the will, you mean?"

My mouth was agape, my anger rebuilding but not enough to make the first physical move, if she wanted to fight another round. She was female, and if it came down to a scuffle, it would be her word against mine about who did what first.

"You're the one worried about money while there's a body over there!" I pointed toward my uncle. "And while we're on the subject, I assume that you wormed your way into his will?"

"No." Her wrath tapered, and the tears returned, a strand of mucus from her nose somehow impossibly not hindering her beauty. "He found his way into my heart." She gave the insufficient single syllable English word the emphasis of *Corazon*, pressed her open fingers into her sternum. "Into me."

It sounded like they'd been watching some Hallmark movies as well as the old cowboy flicks, and I wanted to call bullshit. But the problem was his words were drifting to me, almost audible in the slap of the water, as if the pool was a babbling brook that kept an echo of his parting speech. "He said to tell you 'Thank you,'" I said. "And also to tell you he was sorry."

It wasn't mine to pry, to ask what he was thanking her for, or why he was sorry. And I didn't really care about the two million and change or whatever it all was.

I was thinking about the trust fund babies I'd met at school, the children of the über-rich poisoned by being born on third base and knowing in their heart of hearts they hadn't hit a triple. Money would not solve my problems, not the money of a dead man, at least, even though it spent like every other kind. Nor was the money of some wannabe-cowboy who kept my mother as a toy going to help.

I didn't know what I wanted, except out of this part of the country, this cursed desert where the white man was still an intruder and a white boy like me had neither the desire nor the will to manifest his destiny. This place sucked, and I wanted to go home. The only problems was there was no home.

"I'm sorry," Luna said, rubbing her brown dress so that the ruffled pleats created by our tussle became smooth, at least those parts of the outfit that hadn't gotten wet from our grappling.

"I'm sorry, too," I said. As I looked closer at her, I saw a blackish fleck claiming a corner of her eye, from the temple to the orbit. I apologized once more and felt it this time and meant it, contrite where before I was merely diplomatic. "Jesus, I'm sorry, Luna. I didn't mean to hit you."

I walked toward her, on the verge of tears myself now, wanting to inspect the bruise. I didn't understand how I had put it there. I'd grabbed her arms to keep her from beating my ass but… I looked down at her wrists. No marks there. Not that I didn't know my strength; I knew my strength, and I didn't think it was enough to give her the black eye.

She turned from me, glanced at my uncle's pale body, the water drying in rivulets that ran off his skin as the sun tanned him. If we didn't get him into the shade soon, it would burn him so he looked like rawhide or pemmican, unfit even for an open casket funeral, a repast only for the literal vultures instead of friends and family hungry to pick over the carcass of the estate.

Luna disappeared through the open sliding glass door. I walked over to my uncle's prone form, the husk where that fighter's soul had dwelled. I placed my hand on his chest, comforting whatever remnants of soul might remain there.

"I'm sorry, old man," I said. "You deserved better. Better than this." I looked up at the sun, which was indifferent, merciless even though it didn't have a mind with which to hate. The white-hot orb was radiant, yellow, and burning, wondering perhaps in its smoldering corona what had happened to the hearts of the virgins and the children that the devoted once offered it daily a few thousand years ago.

I squinted in its direction, knowing it was bad for my retinas to look at it without sunglasses. "Fuck you."

"Who are you talking to?" Luna had returned. Her sandals made a squishing sound as each step caused bubbles to gush from the shoes and some warm water to seep out of the leather and onto the sandstone patio.

"The sun," I said, dizzy, dehydrated, and maybe a little crazy.

"The ambulance will be here as soon as possible. They will probably have to helicopter him somewhere like UNLV for a thorough job, the kind of thing they can't do with the facilities they have around here."

"Okay."

She leaned down to me. I hovered over the body of my uncle roughly where she crouched only moments before.

Her arm strayed in my direction but missed me, as she was shaking so hard that it was difficult for her to control her motions. I moved toward her to make it easier, let her put her arm around me and leaned on her. I breathed in the acrid pungency of her armpit, the dark hair there like indigo-dyed strands of corn silk.

Sitting there was soothing, her grip on me maternal. It was nice for everything sexual finally to go still in me. I couldn't wait to be an old, impotent man with the nightmare agitation of constant horniness a thing of the past.

"The autopsy will probably show no water in the lungs."

I breathed in her smell of patchouli and honey, sighed as the scents worked on me like a bump of heroin left over in the brown paper after I had cooked the main pile up. "What does that mean?"

"It means he probably died of a heart attack, cardiac arrest, stroke maybe." She pulled back from me, but only so she could hold my head in her hand, in a two-fingered grip, light and graceful. She stared into my eyes, her own eyes wide saucers meant to not just impart, but to imprint something she knew it was important for me to hear, words that needed to remain and echo to keep me from torturing myself.

"It means it's not your fault," she said, enunciating each word slowly, as if she was teaching me English and expected me to repeat the sentence back to her. "It means he didn't drown."

She let go of my head with her hand, and I had become so accustomed, addicted to her cradling touch that my jaw responded like that of a nutcracker toy with its back lever left in the "down" position after he'd been used to shatter a walnut.

Luna laughed, maybe finding my gaping mouth, my puppy eagerness for her touch and approval to be cute. She pushed my wet hair from my eyes. "I think maybe you were right." She looked over at my uncle, and the tears flowed with the same rupturing force with which they'd first bled from her eyes. "He was just old. And he'd been after me to let him get in the water and go for a swim some for time now."

That bluish bruise on her eye was dark enough now that the tears didn't show up except as a gloss against the wound while they streamed, streaking down her cheekbone like a final coat of tempura lacquer on a religious painting.

"I think he died happy," she said, nodding in agreement with herself.

"He did," I said, stowing my final thoughts before they became words. *He died thinking of you.* Maybe saying it out loud would have flattered her, but it also might have unsettled her, and those wise words some guy said about discretion and valor applied here. She had been through enough.

My presence at this house was a headache she didn't deserve. I would get the hell out of here as soon as possible, maybe even before my suspension was up. I would remember her fondly, but only if she agreed to forget me entirely.

***

The world moved around me while I remained still. I felt like one of those scuba men figures people put in aquariums to aerate them.

Paramedics came, but it was all an unhurried formality. Some paperwork done while wearing latex gloves, a signature from Luna, natural causes the provisional ruling (barring foul play on the autopsy, I guess), and then they had gone.

The fight we'd had or whatever had gone down between us still had both me and Luna weirded out, and so after the paramedics came and went we stayed in separate parts of the house. I didn't bother to check on her, but I could hear her shifting around in the kitchen, migrating to my uncle's bedroom at some point, where I thought I faintly heard her sobbing.

Meanwhile, I stayed on a tufted satin daybed in one of the house's many rooms, looking at an open tackle box where Luna's crafts, things like glass beads and Velcro, sat cut into strips, never to be sewn into the old man's shirts. A pincushion shaped like a tomato held me rapt for a long enough time that when someone else showed up, it took me by surprise.

"Mind if I sit down?"

Cliff had a treated leather smell to him, somewhere between new car and well-worn saddle.

"Please." I scooted over and he relaxed, smoothing his twill slacks and adjusting his shirt, patterned with double exposures of palm trees from the collar to the hem.

"Well, this puts an end to our plans." He pulled out a cigar pliant as a licorice whip from being handled so much.

"You mean with the doctor?"

"Doctor?" He spoke around the cigar which caused his jaw to bulge like he had the mumps. "No, though I must tell him the news. I was talking about something else. I'd almost talked your uncle into coming with me and sitting in on a backgammon tourney in Reno." His eyes twinkled. "You know, I thought maybe after he got his super brain from Dr. Parks I could put him to work picking ponies for me or something, or at least hustle some ladies from the blue rinse brigade out of their social security checks."

My laughter startled me, relieved me a bit. It seemed to make him relax a little too. "What's blue rinse?"

The cigar in his mouth wagged. "Like Youth Dew but it doesn't smell so strong."

I didn't know what Youth Dew was, but let it drop.

He looked in the bedroom's direction, where Luna's constant footfalls suggested she was pacing hard and thinking, as she did her laps in the confines of the room where so much of my uncle's struggle occurred, where she and he had probably bonded the most.

"How's she taking it?" Cliff asked.

"I think she thinks I murdered him."

I put my head in my hands. His catcher's mitt of a left came out and pincered my neck, the opening hold in a post-fight rubdown ritual, I figured, something that took all the stress out immediately, like the Vulcan Death Grip sans the KO part. "He and I were friends for a very long time. He lived hard and was lucky to make it this far."

Cliff took his hand from my neck, worked the creases in his pants again. "Like Sinatra said, he filled his cup before his number was up. Filled his nose, too," he added, low and in a hush.

"Coke?" I said, a bit too loud.

He pressed the air with his empty and open hands palms-down, a pushup gesture meant to say, *Keep it down*. Then he spoke in the register he no doubt preferred me to be in. "He was a pioneer in that way, chased his nose up and down the Strip, when he wasn't chasing tail. His parties took as much out of him as the ring wars."

"Was he really punch drunk?" I asked, maybe tactless.

"Nah, I knew worse." Cliff looked over his shoulder, as if the missus might be there waiting to lay into him about some chore he hadn't completed. When he didn't see the battleax, he took a chance and put match to striker plate on his matchbook, held that over the end of the cigar and puffed. He spoke after getting it going. "He had a detached retina that put him out of the game. These days they can fix that stuff up. Back then, it was a career killer, and thank God it forced him to stop. A dead career's better than a dead body."

He placed his own head in his hands, just as I had a moment before, and since I lacked his touch and the wisdom to know which words to find, it meant his head would remain in-hand longer than mine had. Maybe he was thinking of guys he'd seen who'd died in their fights, or later in the dressing room, staggering out of the ring on wobbly legs and going through seizures under medically induced comas; it couldn't have been a pretty sight, whatever was flashing there now behind his forehead.

Cliff smoked, perhaps trying to work out some problem that had no resolution. Maybe whatever had Luna walking up and down had him furrowing his brow. He finally looked over at me, grateful for the reprieve from himself and the weight of his own thoughts.

"Will you come to the funeral?"

"I don't know. I have to get back to school soon."

A rare desert rain broke outside and we sat on the couch quietly listening to the whispering sounds of it coming to life, and then the sights of lightning and slanting windblown-showers bombarding the windows. It started first with a light pattering of water-drops against the glass door and windows then turned into a torrent, escalating finally into an even rarer summer squall, complete with gusts that rocked the cacti so they bowed like windsocks. The windows of the house streaked, so it looked like we were in some massive vehicle being slowly dragged through a carwash, and when it finally let up, the rain dripped for a time in sheets so slowly cascading they looked like molten liquid metal.

Cliff finally stood up and patted my shoulder one more time. I wasn't a touchy-feely person, but I somehow didn't mind it from him.

"You didn't kill him," he said. It sounded like he was saying it to reassure himself. I didn't like to think of it, but the thought came unbidden anyway that I was a suspect not just with Luna, but with him.

I should have suspected him of something in return, but I just couldn't bring myself to do that. Somebody somewhere had to not be a total piece of shit; someone had to be exactly what they presented themselves as in public. If I could just find one such soul I could hold out some hope.

"Alrighty, kid," Cliff said. "See you at the funeral. And if not there, I'll catch you in the funny papers."

"On the flip-side," I said, which was more imprecise and left the door open for the funnies or the funeral.

"I'll call the doctor," Cliff said, and disappeared from sight around the corner and into another room in the house.

"Michael, are you smoking?" It was Luna, her voice accusatory, but the edge softened by all that had happened between us, and the fear of another fight breaking out.

"It's me," Cliff said.

"Oh, Cliff, I didn't ..."

Their voices trailed off into intermingling murmurs, dulled further by the force of the storm picking back up. I stood from the settee, accidentally kicked Luna's clear plastic tackle box, grateful to be wearing tennis shoes that kept me from getting a stubbed toe.

I endured a mild head rush, thinking of Cliff's advice about when to take the eight-count when decked, and when to get up immediately. My headache tapered by the time I reached the den where the warm relics and free-floating afterglow of what had once been my uncle still lingered strongly in the room, a presence that smelled of him but also felt of him, in a less sensory but no less palpable way.

The room was windowless, the walls all wainscoting. That left the storm as something felt only in the occasional boom of thunder whose accompanying claps of lightning ended up concealed, the rain as faint as the scurrying of a dormouse making its way between walls.

Cliff entered the room, pausing on the threshold, and then crossing over in his suede Wallabee's with the same tentative step that I had taken, as if this room had gone from hangout spot to shrine and we must now show it the proper respect.

"I brought this over for him."

He held up an old black-and-white photo in a gilded oak frame, lit like a mugshot and taken from an angle that made an already-rough mug even less complimentary in its features. The man was scowling around a cigar, as if the tobacco tasted like shit but since that had been the general taste of his life he had expected little else. Both Cliff and my uncle were harder than I would ever be, but this man was harder than them, had a toughness that was part Cro-Magnon, party teddy bear. He was rotund and craggy, gave the impression that being his daughter would be constant and easy insurance against disrespect from young potential suitors outside the tenement where he lived, but that conversely trying to court her might get a kid tossed from a fire escape onto the heart of Little Italy's cobbles.

"Two Ton Tony," Cliff said, admiring the photo just as much as me. "Your uncle loved him." He nodded to himself and adjusted his clenched jaws around the cigar whose smoke he sucked. "Maybe I'll put this in the casket."

He held the photo out to me, facing the image toward me as if Two Ton might have been his patron saint. After he'd displayed it in front of me for a suitable length of time, he went back to studying the picture with his own appreciative eye. "Thank God there weren't too many guys like him left when I came along. Otherwise I'd have been out of the business."

"How do you mean?" I walked over to one of the twin chairs facing the radio beneath the lamp. I sat down in the one across from my uncle's spot, feeling it would have been sacrilege to sink into the imprint he'd left in the Gerichair.

"Tony was from a different time, a throwback even in them pier six brawl days." Cliff made his way to my uncle's seat and settled in, a right which I felt he'd earned. The framed photo rested on his camel hump of a belly, and the outcrop of fat sunk and rose in time with his breathing, or rather inhaling and exhaling of smoke from his cigar. "One time he needed thirty stitches. He told the docs to kick rocks, went back to his bar in Orange, New Jersey, and did the thread job himself." He shook his head, resisted the need to shudder from the horror of it. "No anesthesia, except for a couple shots of whiskey."

"God damn," I said.

"I remember one time he came by and saw Charlie drinking a glass of milk. Nothing out of the ordinary, but he was looking at the glass the kid was holding like it was Don Perignon." Cliff screwed his face up now, froggy, squat, and yet with a hardened charm to his mug flattened out by the look the Two Ton impression forced him to assume. "'Milk was for babies when we was coming up, and then maybe only once a week, unless it was from the tap, the tit I mean.'" He looked down at the photo, watching it as if Two Ton might come to life and wasn't only a framed and disembodied black and white bust.

"Gave Doc Parks the bad news a second ago. He'll be here soon," Cliff said. Rather than looking toward the hallway leading to the front door, he glanced toward the backdrop painting behind us, leading to the semi-secret room. The filling station was radiant with light from the sun of a permanent postwar optimism detonating over all the tract houses and Good Humor trucks. It was like an inversion of the A-bomb, a time-suspending rather than world-ending glow that, once it spread across the dome of the sky, would make everyone happy forever.

"Your mother," Luna said, only sticking her head into the room, talking to me but making eye-contact with Cliff. We still hadn't worked up the nerve to look at each other. I was afraid that her shiner would be more prominent than it looked in the soft glow of the den's lamp, though a quick glance at Cliff looking at her made me think maybe the bruise wasn't that big, and I hoped again that I hadn't put it there. I realized, as I stood, that I was asking for the benefit of two major doubts, that I hadn't killed my uncle and that I hadn't beaten up his caretaker.

I sighed en route to the kitchen, took the green phone's receiver from where it had been resting with its pigtail cord bunched and coiled on the linoleum countertop.

"Hello."

"How are things, Michael?"

I figured Luna hadn't told Debbie about my uncle.

"Things are good," I said.

There was a pause, pregnant with meaning I couldn't quite put my finger on. "And your uncle?"

"Good."

This pause was one of shock. She hadn't expected me to say that. "Well, it's a pity your uncle can't travel. He would have loved to see this piece we just saw performed here at the Théâtre des Nouveautés."

Cliff had just said that Reno would have been a stretch, so I was guessing France would not have been an easy trip to make. I figured that Doctor Parks hadn't factored jetlag or elevation or any of that stuff into his calculations to take care of my uncle's eyes and brain; he therefore might not have signed off on the trip even if my uncle had still been alive.

"It was a play about Battling Siki, a Senegalese boxer who fought for France in World War One and became world-champion. First African to do that."

"Sounds cool," I said, though I feared that, as it was the vogue for people in her set, she might come back with an African baby in tow, perhaps peeking from the berth of a white leather handbag, a bit of carryon snuck through customs at De Gaulle and brought to McCarran. Debbie could hire a nursemaid for him and park him in front of one of Big Jim's vintage slot machines when she wanted to teach him about numbers, shapes, and colors.

"Mom," I said, "I got to go." After a slight delay, I added, "Have fun in Paris."

"Say 'hi' to your uncle for me."

"Will do," I said, hanging up and thinking if things didn't go well, I might get my chance to see him again, and sooner rather than later.

***

Our time together in the den grew into something fraught and wordless, like a chess match neither party wanted to believe had reached stalemate after an investment of so much time. When Doctor Parks showed up, he wasn't sure if he was interrupting something by coming into the room where Cliff and I stared into space at nothing and didn't hear whatever was on the radio.

"Terrible," Doctor Parks said, probably just to say something. When neither of us responded, just kept sitting and staring, he finally put himself between us. He was still wearing an unseasonably warm sweater, still prickly and burred with stray pieces of unraveling fabric, only the color was pea-green today. His eyes were racoon-rimmed from sleeplessness and his skin was ruddy because the Southwestern sun didn't agree with him and he was too busy for sunscreen.

It didn't take him long to walk to the curtain, pull it aside, and disappear there. It pissed me off a little the way he just tugged that drop-cloth aside as if nothing was there, as if that tableaux didn't deserve the least bit of admiration.

We listened as Dr. Parks rummaged around, fumbled with the front of one of two slot machines, pulling his smaller contraption from the belly of the larger one. He emerged from behind the curtain, again into the den, holding in his arms the bulky device he'd used on my uncle's eyes. He cradled the thing, his hold both awkward and protective, like an AV club member who wasn't sure whether he had the authority to borrow a piece of equipment we caught him requisitioning.

I looked at the device, then at him, and said, "What made him different?"

Dr. Parks stopped his slow migration toward the door that would take him out of the den. He turned to me. "We know a couple things about that, but we'll find out more now."

Cliff looked up at the doctor. The old cut man woke from his catatonic funk, and with an unlit half-cigar waiting for flame, said, "You going to cut him up to find out more?"

The doctor held his device like it was a TV he was attempting to sneak from someone's walkup apartment via fire escape. "As per his request," Doctor Parks said, a little testily.

That stopped Cliff from saying anything else, or getting any angrier, but just barely.

Somehow the doctor's words didn't dissipate my anger. The sound of a steel guitar grew louder from the radio, or at least somehow more insistent, since no one had touched the volume knob. "What was his mind state when he gave his consent?" I asked. Cliff looked over at me, gave a slight nod.

The doctor drifted slowly back toward the center of the room, and away from the doorway where he'd been ready to leave a moment ago. He now held the device in his arms slightly higher, which, together with his changing expression, made it look like he might drop the damn thing onto my head. He literally looked down his nose at me, and maybe he had the right to, since he had seniority over me in this thing (whatever it was), as he had known my uncle longer and had involved himself here longer.

I thought of Luna again, wondered where she was. It was a psychic groping panic, like pining after a phantom limb or a quick three AM check by a geezer to make sure his dentures were still sitting in a glass of water on the nightstand. I didn't need her, and I knew she didn't like me very much, but still I needed to know that she was nearby, gaining for myself some inexplicable comfort by that fact.

The doctor brought me back to the moment, and away from the ghost of my uncle and the spirit of Luna, speaking again in that testy tone. "The only reason your uncle even had more than one 'mind state' is because of me." He tapped the rubberized box in his hands, as if he and the device were interchangeable.

"Yeah," I said, looking down, dejected and whipped for a moment, before a counterpoint occurred to me that caused me to raise my eyes to his again. He didn't like what he saw written in my face and shifted from foot to foot in his worn and scuffed loafers. "But if his mind hadn't been outpacing his body, he might not have felt the need to push himself like he did."

"Push himself?" Curiosity replaced the doctor's bile. It was scientific curiosity, but it beat the pure and defensive coldness that had reigned in his mien until a second ago.

"He needed to go swimming," I said. "He said he had his mind back, and it was time to get his body back."

"And you didn't stop him?" There was a twitch in the doctor's face, something halfway to a smile.

"If I'd tried to stop him, he'd have had his heart attack on his way to the pool instead of *in* the pool."

"So you're sure then, that he didn't drown?" The doctor tilted his head, waiting for the subtext work its way in.

I wondered how long this suspicion would follow me, and if people more powerful or dangerous than the doctor might get that idea, and want a word with me. Maybe they would want the two-million dollars and some change from me they thought I had. And I might have a hard time convincing them I didn't have it.

Shit.

Thanks, Debbie, for suggesting this little relaxing sabbatical from Redrock.

"Maybe," Cliff said, breaking his self-imposed silence, "we'll find out whether he drowned when you cut him open." The doctor could hold my lightweight gaze, but he dropped his eyes before Cliff's smoldering glare, which was so strong that it made the old-timer walleyed for a moment, the strabismus causing the eyes to swim in his skull. "Maybe you won't cut the whole body up, though."

Cliff's hands moved over his shirt. It was a gesture I already knew meant he was searching his person for the pack of matches he'd misplaced; sometimes though it meant he was seeking the cigar if it wasn't already dangling in his mouth or stashed behind his ear like a draughtman's pencil.

"Maybe you just want to slice up the brain." Cliff found his matches, hit the striker plate with a deft flourish, a flick of the wrist like a boxer chopping wood to train his hands to build snap. "Or maybe you just want the eyes."

The image of the eyes, wet and round, disgorged and gouged from the head, sliced free via scalpel and plopped in a kidney-shaped pan was too much for both me and the doctor, and maybe Cliff even though he'd been the one to put the image out there. When Doctor Parks left the room in a huff with his toy and without another word, I didn't blame him, or hate him so much.

Luna's voice echoed from the hall as she said some civil words of parting to the doc to see him out the front door and on his way back across the graveled caliche to the Volvo.

Cliff looked at me and smoked, winked.

A blue plume drifted from his thick purplish lips, seeped from his flaring nostrils. "The temporalis," Cliff said.

"What?" I squinted at him.

"The temporalis," Cliff said, and tapped the side of his head with a finger that'd strayed from the cigar he held in his hand, the digit drifting free like a gentleman's pinky when he lifted his cup of tea to sip from it. "It's the bones on the sides of your head. Your uncle's were double-thick."

"That doesn't explain it, I don't think." My voice was more petulant than I meant it to be, and I regretted my tone.

Cliff didn't take offense, though, shrugged, smoked, rocked once in the Gerichair and spoke as the chair's carriage rebounded in its return motion. "No, having a strong bone where it should be weak can make things worse." His finger that had touched the temple a moment before now brushed his chin, grazing the jawline gracefully.

"I knew a guy whose jawbone was super-thick, which meant when he got hit enough for his jaw to break, the pressure that should have escaped through a jaw crack, and *would have* on a normal man, travelled up his head looking for a place to break free." He paused, winced as he remembered what were only words to me, but was a very real image and probably even an accompanying sound to him. "That pressure found a way out through the top of his head, moved along the sutures like they were a wick, and then dynamited its way through the skull like this." His fingers formed into a claw, a fistula of nasty fused tissue imitated by his fingers dancing like a tarantula down three legs. "It was like one of those trick cigars. Just…" He struggled for words, settled for "popped," and snapped his fingers for emphasis.

I thought of a man's skull popping, as opposed to his jaw cracking, decided it was way worse. "So," I said, changing the subject, "Do you think the doctor got enough from my uncle to learn something, to help some other people?"

Cliff squinted into the smoke he'd blown in front of him, as if he could make a prediction in the air he'd puffed there. "Maybe, I hope so." He looked at me, face screwed up and sour as if he'd swallowed a pickled egg whole from some bartender's briny vitrine. "I guess we'll know if he wins the Nobel Prize, right?"

He looked off into the distance, dragged on his cigar, and when he breathed out the smoke this time it was more like a sigh of disappointment than an exhale, making my eyes water as if I was crying, shedding stinging tears hidden from him by the cloud that he'd blown.

CHAPTER EIGHT
RED BADLANDS, BAD REDLANDS

Part of the crew was waiting for me when I got back to Redrock, along with a pile of homework and a little good news to soften that blow. I got said news from Ari, a thin-featured, curly-headed Jewish kid who had the weird habit of carrying around a Ben Hogan golf club as he walked the campus cobbles. He had once almost caught Administrator Stevens on a backswing and had to serve detention for it, but it hadn't slowed down his chipping game.

"You're in Trappist Town now." He pointed the head of his wedge toward the old dormitory, the right arm on the cruciform shape of red-tiled Spanish colonial mission houses.

"Good stuff," I said.

"We moved all your stuff from your room. Kept what weed and pornos you didn't take with you, left your Gummy Bears, Walkman, and clothes untouched in the footlocker."

I nodded magnanimously. "You guys deserved some kind of renumeration."

"I figured you'd see it our way." He held his club behind his head, resting his arms on either side of the iron bar so he looked like he was standing pilloried. "Guess who your roommate is?"

He grinned until we got to the dorm, just to keep it a secret. When I opened the door to my new dorm room and saw him, I was happy enough to break into tears.

"Adam!" I dropped my bag by my bed.

"What's up?" He stood up from in front of his computer set in a freestone nook initially carved to house a little saint statue.

He came over toward me to give me a hug. I embraced him back, but carefully, the birdlike bones of his underdeveloped body feeling like they might crush if I squeezed him too hard.

"How was it at your uncle's?"

Adam stood back from me, took stock of my frame, how much weight I lost, while I marveled at the weird growth of blackish peach fuzz traversing his top lip. "He died," I said awkwardly. "My uncle, I mean."

"Did you get any pussy?" Ari asked, from behind us.

I turned around. "No, but I met a beautiful woman, and she beat me up a little."

"Did she touch your dick?"

I shrugged. "Maybe on accident while we were fighting, with her knee or something."

Adam squirmed a bit and returned to his desk; because of his hypogonadism he got uncomfortable when the subject turned to anything sexual. Unlike the gay or bi guys at school who stayed in the closet to avoid getting their asses kicked, Adam couldn't even fake his way through such a conversation. We'd all seen his hairless balls and weirdly concave chest, despite his best efforts to never shower at peak time in-dorm and to skip showers altogether during gym period.

"You guys want to toot?" Ari pulled out a glassine baggie brimming with crushed Adderall. He already had a drip leaking from his nose, and I thought I saw a bit of red waters mixed in with the translucent snot.

"You should slow down," I said, and sat on my bed. I had my books stacked high on the sienna-striped Navajo blanket. The topmost text was a glossy Social Studies book with a cover that was a patchwork collage of everything from the First Man on the Moon, to the Beatles Deplaning, and Martin Luther King Jr. pointing toward a mountaintop just over the horizon.

"I can't slow down," Ari said, sitting on my bed and taking the additional liberty of using my book to snort. "I don't have that luxury. I got to read *Catcher in the Rye* for Mr. Granski's class tomorrow."

"You should have started a couple weeks ago," Adam said, spinning in his swivel chair in front of his computer screen.

Ari shot him the stink-eye. "You should have sprouted at least a couple pubic hairs by now, but you don't see me giving you shit about that."

Adam turned back to the computer, chastised to the point of near-crying. The tears were in his eyes but he was blinking too fast to let them slip out. I shot Ari a dirty look, but his head was already down and a hundred-dollar bill was in one of his half-collapsed Michael Jackson nostrils. His Milanese Piaget watch caught fading light from the sun pouring through the room's sole gothic tracery window, the rose gold glowing like champagne foam overflowing a fluted glass.

"How much was that?" I asked.

"Free," someone said, coming in through the open door. "These diamond-mining Hymies got the De Beers concession on lock." It was Mahar, square-headed and snarling, spoiling for a fight with his sworn enemy. He wore an unseasonably heavy butter-soft Pelle-Pelle leather 8-Ball jacket, under which he could hide anything, from stuff he pilfered from a dorm room or whatever hashish he'd snuck back from Jordan.

"Mahar, what do you want?"

He stood over Ari, who was still nose-down with my social studies book. "I want Palestinian statehood, you land-grabbing kike. But I'll settle for a bump."

"Fuck you, you PLO reject." Ari took another line to the head and lifted his face toward the ceiling like a wolf baying at the moon.

"Look at that schnoz!" Mahar winked at me and Adam, neutral observers in this round of peace talks. He looked back at Ari. "Gimme a bump or I'm going to tell Stevens exactly which tile of the drop ceiling you used to hide your urine cleanser."

Ari spun the text slowly enough so that none of the remaining powder would spill off, turning the peace offering toward Mahar, who leaned and snouted it without bothering with the dollar bill.

"What I do," Ari said, "I do from the goodness of my heart, not on account of your petty attempt to blackmail me."

"Keep telling yourself that," Mahar said, lifting his head from my book and leaving its glossy surface cleaner than when I first got it shrink-wrapped from the school bookstore.

"I hide my stuff in my golf bag now."

Mahar sneered. "I've seen it. Lizard leather, pink. It's a chick's bag."

"Damn straight," Ari said. "It's got more pouches than a dude's bag, for 'unmentionables' and lipstick. More places to hide."

The sneer stayed on Mahar's face, but the intel he'd just gotten went into the mental Rolodex. "You guys be good." He shot the Churchill "V" to me and Adam and was out the door.

I stood to close the door, but Ari stopped me, letting himself out before allowing me to shut it behind him. Now it was just me and Adam.

He'd gotten control of his emotions and looked like he wouldn't cry barring any more attacks about his growth problem.

"I tried jerking off," he said.

"How'd that go?" I leaned back on my bed, stretching out at my ease and trying to forget what Ari and Mahar had been doing there a moment ago.

"Couldn't come, but it could have been the pressure."

"Pressure?" I laughed. "Were you timing yourself or leaving some posterity at the sperm bank or something?"

He tittered in a high, feminine key. "No, it was a circle jerk. Ari only had the one porno, and he wasn't sharing, so we kind of had to powwow around his screen."

"Still no internet, huh?"

Adam shook his head and his thatch of blond, broom-like hair stayed in place, a perfect bowl-cut like Moe from the Three Stooges. "Not in rooms. And I'm not whacking it in the library."

"Can't say I blame you," I said, remembering at least one case of a kid kicked out of school for doing just that. I could feel the blockage in my body and was waiting for him to go to supper or to shower, so I could crank it as I thought of the way Luna's breasts had jiggled and flailed as she tried to kick my ass, the swaybacked, serpentine wobble of her butt pillowed with soft fat as she walked away from my prone, defeated and half-drowned form.

"It's true what they say about Ari."

"What?"

Adam held up the black alpaca of his shirt with the dayglo Atari symbol in the center. "He wraps his wiener in the shirt material like it's a pocket pussy and then goes to town."

"That's got to hurt." I shook my head. The man didn't care much for lubricating his nose or his wang, apparently. And what had Adam called his dick? *His wiener*. It reminded me of the weird gulf that existed between him and me, between him and all the other teenagers at this institution. I quickly shifted the conversation away from sex, pubescence, and other things that would make him uncomfortable, to a subject that would instead put us back on common ground.

"Any news on the UFO front?"

He ceased shrinking into his shell, bloomed in his own body so that his posture was ramrod-perfect. He grinned at me with his mouth full of goofy baby teeth, and I immediately felt better, too. He gave me something like what I got from being around my younger brother, a feeling of being a useful protector for someone whose innocence, if properly defended, would also be a source of strength for me to draw on from time to time when I needed a break from my cynical self.

"I've shifted focus to mutants, nuclear-engineered mutations. I ordered a Geiger counter online. I'm going to take it on a test run over all the downwind farmsteads around here on Spring Break. Going to do lots of Arizona, maybe some New Mexico, if we have time."

"Your dad's cool with it?"

"Of course." The grin remained plastered on his face. I didn't envy Adam's war with his glands, or his body's war against him, but I was jealous of his relationship with his father, some bigwig defense contractor with Raytheon who was also an amateur stargazer. He was a good sport enough to indulge his son's conspiracy theory hobby, even if he didn't buy into it himself.

"The old man wants to snoop around Area Fifty-One." Adam kicked his desk and pushed off, spinning three-hundred and sixty degrees in his swivel chair with his feet off the ground, looking like an evil ventriloquist's dummy who'd come to life after finally escaping the onus of its operator's hand. "I told him he's wasting time. They've got greys there, and saucers, but it's needle in a haystack time. They got dummy hangars, a whole

Potemkin Village of them, for anyone lucky enough to breach the perimeter. Ninety percent of Nevada's government land."

"And the other ten percent belongs to Big Jim," I said, under my breath.

"Not just government, either," Adam said, stopping his swiveling before he got too dizzy. "Federal land, which makes it, guess what? A federal crime if you trespass."

"So if Area Fifty-One is out, what do you hope to do at these farmsteads?"

Adam's sneakered feet found purchase on the stone floor again, and he pulled himself in front of his computer screen in the cubbyhole. "Working out a theory on cattle mutilations and crop circles."

He double-clicked on some folder, said, "Come here."

"Adam, don't show me any pictures of mutilated cows, man. I'm not in the mood."

"No, these cows aren't mutilated. I think the mutilations are just the aliens' way of covering up the experiments they're doing with the government, joint exercises that are mutually beneficial for our elite and their own race."

"Sounds legit." I was beat from the extended cab ride from my uncle's house back to Redrock (charged to Debbie's credit card) and had no desire to stand up again after having just lain down in my new digs.

"Ari left his golf club," I said, trying to reach his iron where it sat beside my bed without having to sit up to grab it, and failing.

"I think some of this livestock's transgenic," Adam said, clicking through the images in the folder he'd opened. "Weird crossbreeds between Herefordshire, Black Angus, and shorthorn, from the USDA Beef Cattle Research Station."

"Transgenic?" The term was curious enough at least to bring me up onto my elbows, propping myself on the harsh blanket's itchy wool.

He saw he had my attention and turned the computer monitor my way, twisting it on its swivel. On the screen was a beefed-up cow that wasn't so much marbled with muscle as overstuffed, as if the flesh beneath its spotted coat were implants that were swelling and would soon burst.

"It's the Ah-Nuhld of the bovine world." I had a hack Schwarzenegger impression at the ready like everyone else.

Adam would have usually laughed, but he found himself too engrossed in the fate of this cow, its rapid transformation, to grant my comedy stylings the faintest giggle. "I read this book, more like a pamphlet, *The Milk we Drink*. The experts claim a lot of milk on these downwind farms has strontium-ninety in it."

"You should read less about mutant milk and more Salinger for that *Catcher in the Rye* test tomorrow."

He looked toward the door where the two visitors who'd been to our little Camp David snorting accord had been a little while before. "What about you? Do you think you can cram for the *Catcher* test between now and second period?"

"I know that book like the back of my hand," I said. I also knew it was Mr. Granski's favorite, and that when he proctored the final test on it, he even wore his Holden Caulfield hunter's cap with the earflaps down.

"Well, if you need to bone up…" Adam stood up from his desk, went to his wastebasket that had an orange and blue Knicks backboard clipped to its rubber body. He held out the trashcan to me and came to my bedside. I feared what might be there, and I gazed in reluctantly, when he got close enough and I had no choice.

"What the hell?" Pages from a book lay scattered there, some shredded, some dogeared, others flecked with blood. Just scanning the print and seeing the odd word like "phony" or "New York" let me know that it was the mangled husk of what had once been *Catcher in the Rye*.

"Ari was geeked out on Adderall last night, speed-reading, but every time he finished a page he'd either use it to stop the blood coming out of his nose or just straight up tear it out and throw it in the trashcan."

"Jesus," I said, looking at the wastebasket as Adam walked the bin back over to his corner of our room, smiling over its gross contents like he was the proud owner of a new litter of kittens. "You should probably take that out."

"I will," he said, "soon."

I lifted my books off my bed, set them down on the cold limestone floor covered with only the most threadbare throw rug, patterned with the same fractal network of red diamonds and turquoise rhombuses as the blanket covering my sleeping pad.

"So," Adam said, hesitating.

"What's up?" I folded my hands behind my head and stared up at the groin-vaulted ceiling, where some monk no doubt stared a long time ago looking toward heaven during Vespers, and where I scanned for spiders and other creepy-crawlies of the desert.

"Your uncle really died, huh?"

"Yup."

"Fucking sucks, man."

"I know," I said, and turned over, wondering if, when he took the trash out, whether I would have enough time to rub one out and wipe away the evidence with Kleenex before he returned.

"Maybe if I can figure out what the government or the aliens are putting in that milk, I can get some for myself and it can help me grow." His voice was wistful, distant, as if he was afraid that even I, his best friend, might laugh at what he had to say, what he'd probably really been thinking all along.

I didn't laugh, though.

***

No word of my uncle's funeral reached Redrock, and while I missed him and Cliff, and even Luna (but in a different way), I was also relieved to be out of the loop. I didn't understand death, except that I feared it, hated it, and didn't believe it could happen to me. Not at least until I was old, like forty or even fifty.

But word reached me of the reading of the will, that I needed to be there at the Legacy LLC firm in Reno for when it went down.

"That means you're included," Adam told me, as we packed for the trip. They had timed the reading at least so it fell during spring break, which meant I wouldn't be missing any more school. Adam's father was busy, so he elected to roll with me to Big Jim's suite at the Flaming Reno.

"I don't want to take anything from a dead man," I told Adam.

"It's not taking," he'd said, "if he's giving it to you."

A blue Lincoln Town Car with steer horns for a hood ornament picked us up at Redrock, and I explained Big Jim's MO as the chauffeur drove us wordlessly to the private airstrip. "He always said limos are for the mafia and high-school prom. He's trying to be the classiest redneck in his little jet set." I opened the sunroof en route, sat back in the blue padded leather seat, occasionally opening the wet bar compartment, which was dry but had a cut-glass decanter and some lowball glasses there for whenever some adults rode in the car.

The air-strip was a "No Tower" affair, like a lot of private airports, and the driver brought us all the way to the mouth of the hangar where the bird sat waiting, like we were some drug lords getting ready to swap prisoners. Adam looked sufficiently awed.

The driver helped us with our bags, moving with stooped deference, perhaps not sure about my relationship to Big Jim, or where his power ended and if it extended to me and my friend. I dug a twenty out of my Velcro wallet covered in zippers and the driver tapped the hard black brim of his hat in thanks before letting us get on the plane.

"This is awesome," Adam said.

"Welcome aboard," the pilot said, from the cockpit.

"Thank you." I sat on a white ribbed leather throne, with armrests made of burlwood whose lacquered swirling patterns made it look more expensive than Botticino marble. Everything that wasn't ivory-white leather or honey-brown wood had a golden edge, trim, or gilding, softened by warm lights that worked on dimmers like in the dressing room of an ageing diva who didn't want to see any of her wrinkles.

I pulled out my moleskin notebook and my pen and went over some poetry exercises Mr. Granski had given us.

"You're really getting into poetry, man." Adam leaned back in his own seat, buckling up as the plane's engines roared to life. He sounded a bit disappointed, like I would give up on UFOs. I figured I could do both, though.

"I didn't want to hurt Mr. Granski's feelings," I said, which was partly true. That dick Sergei had been sitting front and center in Granski's class, listening to the teacher praise Russian poetry hoping to get some reaction from the vulpine little Russian with grey eyes, but Sergei had just waited for him to finish his speech, and said, "Poetry…mean… nothink to me."

I'd been more attentive after that in class, just to make sure Granski didn't sink into the mire that most of these kids lived in, and which I had seen drag down several teachers, counselors, and even a Pollyannaish nurse whose brightness dimmed under the weight of countless overdoses, repeat case STDs, ignored medical advice, abused and bartered prescription meds.

"Poetry has a pattern," I said, scanning the couple poems that I'd kept writing out freehand repeatedly, filling up the margins in my book like some penitent. I counted the syllables on my hand, admired how it always came out as ten in each instance, with the same stress on each syllable. It was like math. I whispered as I spoke and rubbed the iambs between fingers as if I might break out into snapping like a Beat in a beret at any moment. "My mistress's eyes are nothing like the sun… If snow be white, why then her breasts are dun."

"That's good," Adam said. "Tell a girl her tits look like literal shit."

"Do not go gently into that good night."

"It's hard not to go gently when you're on a private plane this comfortable."

I'd been so engrossed, soaring on the words, that I hadn't noticed the plane taking off.

"You looking forward to seeing your mom?" Adam pulled a paperback Jim Marrs book from the inside of his Bugle Boy hoodie, where he'd been holding his hands like a mother marsupial keeping tabs on a newborn kanga.

"I don't have any problem with my mom," I said. "She's been at the Fifth Arrondissement and she usually comes back from there happy as hell, loaded down with art."

"That what you and Sergey were talking about?"

"Yup, the Latin Quarter and the Fifth are the same thing."

"And you believe him?" Adam flipped through his book, stopped on a severely dogeared and heavily highlighted page.

"Yeah, I mean his dad was a bigwig in the Nomenklatura. They probably did steal a lot of icons from the Russian people on their way out and sell it on the black market in Paris. Not that I think my mom would be keen to give the stolen artwork back."

"My dad went to the Sorbonne once."

"France ain't on my itinerary," I said, though I figured this aircraft could do intercontinental.

I pulled up the shade over my window, looked into the massive yawning chasm of red boulders and freestanding buttes turning orange in the fading sunlight. The jagged escarpments of the mountains looked manmade from this high up, or planned at least by some intelligence, like the ruins of massive castles rather than the result of tectonic shifts.

Adam wasted no more time. "I'm thinking the Von Däniken hypothesis is real."

"Those are pyramids," I said, "assuming the ancient aliens built them."

"You think they did?" He asked.

"No, I think ancient aliens killed Kennedy." Then, forgetting aliens for the moment, I tried combining Dylan's villanelle and Shakespeare's sonnet. "Do not go gently into my lover's hair."

"Yes, women don't appreciate it when you pee in their hair. I haven't even reached puberty and even I know that."

"You'll get there," I said.

"At least I don't have breasts." He grabbed the puffy fabric of his sweatshirt, groped himself, as if he needed to make sure the mammaries hadn't sprouted since the last time he'd checked. "Guys with Klinefelter Syndrome get breasts." He shook his head. "Ari and those guys would never let me hear the end of it."

"You'll grow," I said. "Just wait."

We both silently watched out the window as the sun washed like a wave over the valley, sweeping the red into dimmer shadow, presaging in Adam's imagination something like a giant spacecraft hovering and getting ready to land.

Lonely stands of ponderosa were the only signs of life, of green, of the presence of water. Everything else was gray stone, black volcanic tufa, and loose scree silently speaking of when oceans and magma had met here.

"You're probably right," I said, "about ancient aliens. Not just in Egypt, but here. I think they dropped a bomb here a million years ago."

He watched the same open, vast expanse of rock that looked Martian when the sun was up and gave it a bloody tinge, and turned into a lunar boneyard when the moon waxed and held sway.

"Could be," Adam said.

It grew dark enough for us to appreciate the glitter of Reno's strip when we made our approach to yet another private airstrip where Big Jim rented space. The "Biggest Little City in the World," had most of what Vegas had, in terms of hotels and casinos, but on a smaller scale, so that the skyline of glowing neon signage looked like Sin City if America had ever had a World War on its own soil and had endured air-raids that required a time of rebuilding. It was sin sedated, garishness and bright lights not totally torn down like the Tower of Babel, but chastised into something squatter and lower-profile.

"There's where we're staying."

I pointed toward the Flaming Reno, which, if you said it fast enough, let you know what chain it was a part of (the Flamingo). The yellow and orange sunburst was a rippling waterfall of light, looking like an impossibly flaming flower burning as it bloomed yet somehow never burning out.

It occurred to me then that Vegas, and to a lesser extent Reno, were Man's brightly illuminated candles lit in answer to the darkness of the desert, waiting to consume, to turn flesh to bone. No one, not even the most degenerate gambler or greediest tycoon, really thought they could beat death (maybe a crazy man, like Howard Hughes), but they knew how to keep the thoughts at bay, with discount buffets and pussy and the lights and noises of all kinds of distracting dreams.

It even worked on Adam, who sat open-mouthed with his face awash in emerald and golden light, staring down on that bright flower, which watched the approach of our airplane like a Venus flytrap waiting for some winged creature to fly too close to its hungry mouth.

CHAPTER NINE
HOW BLACK GOT GAMMON'D

The suite worked its wicked magic on Adam. Not that I was immune to what wealth could do, but I'd at least been here before twice and my mind was still on what was to come with the reading out of the will.

"Don't worry," Adam said, his voice echoing off the tiles of the jacuzzi and reaching me downstairs.

I walked up the spiral staircase to the second level, which put me at the top of the penthouse, overlooking the gold-filmed glass curtain window that faced the outdoor pool jutting into the sky like a lido deck on a cruise ship. Beyond that was the Strip.

Adam felt comfortable enough around me to wear his bathing suit, with its drawstring which he found himself forced to readjust constantly as he waded through the jacuzzi that swallowed him in its roiling blue waters. He opened his mouth, took the water that the marble Nyad resting on a blue tile pediment shot from her porcelain nipple into his mouth. He spit that out between his teeth, doggy-paddled. "We got it made," he said.

"Don't get too comfortable."

The phone rang, an old candlestick model that was an in-house direct line from the valet's stand at the porte-cochere downstairs to the rooms. I rushed past the grand piano, buttoning my blue Oxford shirt and tamping down the collar as I practiced walking in my slip-on dress shoes.

"Yo."

"The car is waiting for you downstairs, sir."

"Thank you." I hung the candlestick back on the cradle, looked at Adam where he was still swimming as happy as a fat seal in waters free of predators. "That was Jeeves. I must heed the master's call."

He'd navigated in his swim until he was beneath the white Poseidon statue whose trident pointed toward the grand piano, as if he was commanding some phantom player to tickle the ivory. "If you get enough from the will, make them an offer on this place."

He disappeared below the waterline. I took it on faith that he wouldn't drown, or that if he did, he would at least die happy. I followed the rolled steel and ribbon of glass encircling the room, leading to an elevator enclosed in a glass box in the center of the second story. I walked in the private elevator walled in mirrored vacuum plastic that made it look like living water. I pressed "G" and as it took me down, I felt like some tiny bug who'd strayed into a foamy bath and ended up trapped in a bubble and was being carried away on a draft against his will.

The way I felt might not have been too far from the way things were. I definitely didn't feel like I was moving under my power as I got off downstairs, got rotated through the revolving doors chopping like golden fan blades, pushed on the artificial gust of hot air in the lobby out into the colder street, into another Lincoln Town Car (this one black) as rapidly as a capsule package shot through a pneumatic tube.

"You in, sir?" The partition between driver and passenger sat open, but I still could barely make him out in the driver's seat, where his black leather driving gloves made a crinkling sound as he choked up on the steering wheel.

"Yes, sir."

"Beautiful day," he said, pulling out, dropping the "sir," which made me feel better.

"Yeah, it is."

I was ready to take his word for it, but looked out the window, anyway. Clouds were drifting down from the Peavine range, looking so near to us, so far from the sky and so bright white that they seemed more like smoke from cannons fired in a recent set-piece battle, or maybe belched from some skirmish reenactment happening up on the hill.

My heart did drumrolls in my chest that became a timpani-like thudding as we got closer to the law firm. I was far from equipped for this world. My hands sweated. I could hear the blood pounding in my ears. I wished I was back in the hotel with David, screwing around on the piano or in the pool or jacuzzi, scouring the wet bar to see if they'd been diligent enough to clear it out before we came, the same way they had the cars.

By the time we reached our destination I was ready to run, bolt from the car into traffic and hope that I got clocked by an oncoming Greyhound that would solve all my problems for me.

"Good luck," the driver said.

I pulled another twenty from my frayed Velcro wallet and pressed it into his hand. He winked, which made his bushy eyebrow twitch, and the faintest tug of his lip at the corner of his mouth let me know he'd have smiled more if they allowed him.

I got out of the car, walked toward something black and reflective that looked like a cross between a water fountain and an obelisk. A statue of a Basque shepherd looked out over his ghost flock, water cascading over him in waves to put our little Neptune up in the penthouse to shame.

Cliff was sitting on the edge of the fountain, wearing an old cabbie's cloth cap and bomber's jacket covered in patches and zippers. He stood up from the fountain, holding some paperwork in his hand. The cigar was in the corner of his mouth, right where it should be, smoldering like an eternal flame.

"How you doing, kid?"

"Pretty good, sir." I stuck my hand out to him. He clasped my palm in a grip that was firm but not overbearing, hinting at power, hell, probably punching power, but without the need to show it.

I nodded toward the pile of papers he had in his hands, slightly moist with backsplash from the Basque shepherd. "You got some paperwork to back up your claim?"

"This?!" He grimaced, then grinned, making the cigar dance. "Nah, I was just looking over the minutes of an old game that went down at a tourney here, seeing how black got gammon'd. Would have loved to get your uncle out here to sit in on a game with me at the Expo Center one last time."

I turned around. The Towne Car was still at the curb. I figured it would wait for me until I returned. The driver eyed me behind mirrored shades, shot a crisp salute which seemed to confirm my hunch.

I looked back at Cliff, tried to hide that I was ready to puke from nerves.

"You ready?" he asked. He stood up from the fountain, already looking for a place to grind out his stogie, so I figured he was more than ready.

"Let's go." I cracked my knuckles. He collared me in a half-headlock, half-hug and I put my hands around his waist that felt cushiony even through the heavy leather of the bomber jacket.

"Kid, you're all right." He released me to ditch his stogie in a steel pebbled sand cannister where a couple crooked cigarette butts already sat.

"Where are they?" I asked. I wasn't sure how many other people the will included, but I knew there had to be a "they."

"They're already up there." He nodded toward the doors toward which we walked, pulled by that same invisible magnet that had dragged me from Redrock to Reno and was now yanking me upstairs, into what looked like the only postmodern building in the neighborhood. It was a sculpted steel and glass cylinder about as imaginative in design as the thing where Cliff had just ditched his cigar.

He led the way, and I kept my mouth shut. Our feet went from marble to soft carpet that masked our footfalls. The heavy oak doors stood already opened on the conference room where a lawyer in charcoal grey pinstripe sat in a wingback chair. My mom and Big Jim occupied chairs that were smaller but still looked sleek and aerodynamic enough to be the leather thrones from which some captain and his lieutenant barked orders on the deck of a spaceship.

Debbie wore a red pantsuit low-cut at the neck to show off both the pearls and the silicon Jim had paid for, and the cuffs flared enough on the pants for her to look like she might be some 1970s sexy karate sidekick to the evil Texas tycoon that Big Jim presented in contrast.

If he was a villain in a movie, he would have needed a pet, but some kind of Persian cat would have been too continental. An iguana would have been more region-appropriate. His outfit was more Tom Mix than Wild Bill, a white wool cowboy suit fringed in leather, something fit more for negotiating prices on heads of cattle on the veranda than doing any branding or cow-punching out on the open range.

"Finally," Big Jim muttered, under his breath. My mom dug frantically into her purse, as if she was looking for someone's nitro pills during an emergency. She hadn't yet invented a pretext to avoid seeing me and Big Jim face off, but maybe if she kept digging she would find one in there, or waste enough time for it not to matter.

I looked from the lawyer to my stepdad to my mother. "White man say he has treaty to negotiate with my people?"

"Please, have a seat." The lawyer had spoken without betraying a hint he'd heard my words. It was clear these people were too busy and rich to pay attention to mockery in the rare instance someone aimed it their way. They wouldn't countenance even being offended by me unless I did something that would probably get the police or at least house security in here. There was a heavy carafe of water within reach on the massive Brazilian rosewood boardroom table, along with some heavy ballpoint pens, so I had a couple options.

I sat down and was grateful when Cliff took the seat next to me.

The lawyer's skin looked harder this close, more like a hide or something squamous that belonged on a reptile, but there was also a flaky, peeling quality to the flesh, as if the snakeskin was overdue to shed. He shifted in his chair, opened his single-breasted jacket and lifted one leg to cross it over the other, exposing first a bolo tie and then a goddamn sheriff's tin star pinned on his oxblood shirt, worn as naturally as someone else might sport an opal stickpin, and then a pair of high-heeled (at least for a man) cow print boots. It would have been incongruous outside the Southwest, but was probably a deliberate concession to put the new money and frontier money at ease.

"Still waiting on one more…" He said, looking at a piece of paper thin as onion skin, allowing for all the light that could breach the tower's tinted glass to break through the sheaf. It was clear the lawyer was using his paper there before him the same way my mother used her purse, to send the awkward into abeyance. Big Jim and I had anger to do that, and we were using our eyes against each other. *Fuck you*, my eyes kept saying, and his eyes would twinkle, receive the message. Then dimples deep as scars would weld themselves into his flesh of his face as the mockery of a smile spread across his lantern jaw, and he broadcasted back, *I'm fucking your mother, for now at least, and fuck you, too* and there was nothing I could do about it. Nothing legal, at least.

"There she is." The lawyer stood and extended our final guest a courtesy he hadn't bothered to give to me or Cliff, whose cigar musk had caused the lawyer (and Big Jim) to look around the room with their noses upturned, as if someone had made the mistake of stepping into a dog pile on their way up here.

"Madame."

I caught her scent before I saw her, was happy that I was sitting down since otherwise I would have been knee-knocking weak and bereft of senses. Luna was the only one tastefully dressed, wearing a cashmere knit sweater with a turtleneck that gave her swanlike throat a little extra elongation, like an Assai warrior in the early days of her ritual stretching. She wore grey tulle pants with a perfect knife-crease in each leg, golden hoop earrings and a blood-red shade on her lips whose bow was a perfect complement to the heart shape of her face. In toto she was soft, sexy, and leonine, as if she had shape-shifted from tigress and the act of sustaining human form for any length of time was taxing.

"Please sit down." The lawyer motioned toward the table, not pulling out a specific chair for Luna, which meant she had her druthers in choosing. We all watched her with gazes of undisguised and harried anticipation, like parents in a custody battle waiting for the kid to come our way.

She sat down as far away from both me and my mother as she could. She wore large oval-shaped sunglasses with tortoise shell frames that hid her eyes. Her face wore no expression, though she was straight enough in posture that I could tell she was feeling something, probably for my uncle. Probably more than the rest of us.

The lawyer wasted no more time, cleared his throat, and read from the thin sheet. "To the Bledsoe and Reeves heirs I leave my entire catalogue of fights, the right of broadcast and rebroadcast, in perpetuity, to be divided or divested as they see fit, provided whatever they decide is agreed-upon by a two-thirds majority of the named beneficiaries."

My mother emitted a small bird coo, meant, I supposed to contain her excitement at what was the first of many prizes rained on her today.

"To Luna Alvarez, I leave my house, whose deed will be transferred by the original owner who wished to remain anonymous upon purchasing said-house and wishes to remain anonymous now as the deed is transferred."

Big Jim harrumphed, stirred in his seat so that his spurs jangled. He whispered something to my mom to pacify her. I finally worked up the nerve to look over at Luna. A tear beaded and slid down a cheek that looked puffy, practically swollen, from already crying.

""To my nephew Michael, I leave all the remaining contents of the aforementioned home, except for any which Ms. Alvarez purchased during her time in my employ.'"

My mom leaned forward, staring at me down the length of the table with that crocodile smile. I looked away from her, back to Luna, whose jaw pulsed with the effort to keep from crying.

"'For Clifford Pacheco, AKA 'Cutty,' my dearest and closest companion, I leave this boxing glove.'" The print must have become smaller for the lawyer had recourse to a pair of gold-rimmed bifocals whose stems were so thin I thought he was wearing an opera lorgnette at first. "'This glove was worn by Muhammad Ali against Henry Cooper, was torn during combat and subsequently discarded by Ali's trainer An-'"

"Angelo Dundee," Cliff said, smiling more for the memories than the money.

"Please wait," the lawyer said, lowering the paper so thin it surprised me it hadn't already torn. "Until I am finished."

Cliff held up his chorizo link digits, mouthed, "Sorry" but kept it silent so that the lawyer didn't think he openly defied him.

"This glove, believed until now to be missing or lost, authenticated by Mad about Memorabilia, has a conservative estimated value on the market of one-point two million dollars."

I heard a yelp from my mother than sounded like a Pomeranian getting its foot caught in a bear-trap. Cliff looked off into the distance, still thinking about that fight.

The lawyer folded the piece of paper three times, his mouth an open aperture for some last words that needed saying.

"We'd like to contest the will." My mom sat forward in her seat, looked like she was ready to lunge across the table and maybe dance until the varnish scuffed beneath the wrath of her stilettoed heels.

"That's your right," the lawyer said. "But the testator had the requisite two witnesses, plus a third just for good measure. This third was also a licensed and practicing M.D."

"Who were the first two?" Big Jim massaged my mother's shoulder with his talon-like hand as the mascara bled from her eyes.

The lawyer looked at Luna and Cliff.

My mother stood up. "In it together, taking advantage of *my* flesh and blood!" Big Jim stood with her, held her, half in a consoling embrace and half in a clutch designed, it seemed, to keep her from lunging at the alleged coconspirators. "You!" Debbie's eyes went from wide to bulging so that fissures of blue veins danced beneath her rouged skin. She looked at Luna, who averted her eyes. "You think I don't know how you did it! What methods you…" She halted, allowing an awkward glance at Big Jim, tapering off in her speech since she might not have only been lobbing accusations at Luna.

"Let's step out for some air," Cliff said, standing and fixing his face into that grimace that always ended in a pained smile.

"Let's."

We turned, and I fought the urge to look back at Luna, just to see her once more, a glance to supplement that light flower fragrance she gave off before heading to the bank of elevators through the glass doors. But I stayed strong, didn't heed the siren call.

"Holy shit," Cliff said, shaking his head, pulling another Cubano from inside his weatherbeaten bomber. He clenched the cigar so that some wrapping flecked off, a cigarillo psoriasis, brown bits helicoptering down like one-winged moths.

"What?" I asked. The doors to the elevator opened on the lobby where the sound of Verdi leaked in on unseen speakers, some frantic catgut paean to one of the four seasons. Winter maybe. "The glove?"

"Not the glove," he said, shaking his head and walking out into the fading sunlight, the clear, crisp desert air made slightly aqueous by the splash from the fountain that sprinkled us as we walked around its rim. "Your ma." He continued shaking his head, put spark to an oversized match big as a birthday cake candle. He wagged the stick of wood until the flame became a sulfurous wisp of smoke, puffed the coal on the end of the Cuban into life just after the match-head died. "It's a pity to see her suffer like that."

"She'll live," I said.

"What about you? We must wait for your ma's case to fall flat. But after that do you need help with an appraisal of what's there? I doubt Luna wants to keep much of it, if any of it." He looked back toward the sleek black building where the rest of the adults were still working it out.

I shrugged, stuffed my hands in the pockets of my pants. "Why don't you take it?"

His jaw dropped and the cigar almost hit the pavement. "Don't be a dumbass, kid. You don't know what's in there."

He recovered his composure, lodged the cigar back where it belonged, looked around the courtyard, the mostly empty downtown where the only sounds came from birds fluttering or cooing, the hiss from steam grates, and the rustle of stray leaves from a local newspaper flying around buoyed on the breeze.

"Maybe there's the other glove from that fight in the pile," I said. "You should have the pair if there is a set."

"I don't want another glove. I want a hotdog."

He tapped me on the arm. "Let's go get a couple franks dragged through the garden, Southwest style, salsa verde y picante."

"Claro, Jefe. Andele, pues."

"Might as well live it up now that I'm a millionaire, at least in assets."

We walked toward the cart where a man in a straw boater hat and a shirt printed with Dio de la Muerte skulls worked the steam trays.

My stomach rumbled, looking forward to something greasy, not some raw, expensive, chilled seafood or an unpronounceable dish served in ludicrously meager portions brought via glass elevator to the suite by room service.

"Tardes, gente." The man wore a down-turned Zapata stache that the wind and work-sweat had cowlicked into a reverse-handlebar shape.

The surrounding street was mostly empty, the only car being a gypsy cab driving without purpose in the canyon formed by the buildings.

I looked back toward the front of the building where the law firm was, hoping to see Luna coming out through the heavy glass front door and cursing myself for being weak enough to care. She wasn't there. Neither were my mom or Big Jim. I wondered if I shouldn't be upstairs, too, if they were still up there, since maybe I needed to protect my investment. Maybe my mom's fellatio game was good enough to get the lawyer to bend the rules or "discover" some loophole in how estates got handled. I didn't know how these people operated, not exactly, but I knew the real world was a grimy place.

I turned back to Cliff, wanting to unburden myself to him, to tell him about my fear of everything, my love for Luna…

But it was too late. The cab was up onto the curb, raised on two screeching tires just as it passed the food truck toward which we'd been walking. The car was out of control, seeming to be both without purpose or even a driver, until I saw the shadow of a man's head like a berm gnome on Redrock's archery range. The car had a goal that became clearer as the driver gunning the gas got closer. The goal was us.

I didn't know I had instincts until that moment, but I rushed aside without thinking, rolling on the concrete so I scraped my elbows, bruised my hip, and heard a loud thump. My maneuver hurt so much I thought I got clipped by the old hunk of classic American steel, so hard that I hadn't even felt it when it bounced me from one side of the sidewalk to the greenstone tiles at the foot of the fountain.

But any damage I suffered I did to myself in my panicked leap.

When I regained my feet, the chauffeur from earlier was standing there, along with the guy from the hot dog stand. Birds flew up as if released for a celebration, flapping toward the eaves and gables of Reno's battlements.

Cliff lay sprawled on the ground, half on the concrete of the sidewalk and half in the gutter, blood thick as antifreeze leaking out around his limbs bent in ways that suggested someone had broken them and the laws of physics today.

I started crying like a bitch and didn't care who saw me and then felt a soft warm hand on my shoulder I knew belonged to Luna.

***

It was back to underwater time, that feeling of being the scuba man in the fish tank with everything around me moving and no ability to move myself. The presence of Luna's hand on my shoulder was light, but it felt even fainter than it should have, like a phantom limb. The unreality of it all washed over me in waves that eroded my senses one by one until everything was black and soundless. The last thing I remembered was Cliff muttering something in his Spanish that wasn't so rapid-fire anymore, as the life ebbed from him and blood spluttered from his mouth.

Luna said something back to him and he closed his eyes. The strobing blue mars lights from cop cars bounced off the reds pulsing from the EMT vans fighting to block off enough space to get the body on the gurney. The banshee wail and the honk of fire trucks finally brought me out of my stupor.

Luna had her sunglasses pushed up on her forehead, disheveling her black hair. "Are you okay?" Her hand reached for my face, wiped the cracked reddened spots on my cheeks where tears I'd forgotten I'd shed had dried.

"Where are my mom and Jim?"

She shook her head. "I don't know."

"They're at their hotel." The deep voice belonged to the driver who'd taken me here. He was shifting from foot-to-foot, looked antsy from the overtime we had forced him to put in and from being thrown into the middle of our drama.

"Do the cops want to talk?" I looked over at the barricade they'd erected, where a couple cruisers sat parked herringbones fashion and a couple plainclothes policemen sipped coffee from Styrofoam cups, lingering around the crime scene with their baggy suits and unshaven faces.

"They tried," Luna said, pulling her hand away from my face now and hugging her arms to her body, as if she was cold. "They said they'd come by the Flaming Reno in the morning."

"We should get back, sir." The driver spun his chauffeur's cap like a vinyl record, then placed it on his sweat-matted comb-over.

"Come on," Luna said. "I'll go with you."

That was enough to get me in the car, away from the crime scene and free for the moment from my curiosity.

I walked back to the Towne Car on my rubbery legs. My feet touched concrete that felt like meringue as the unreality that dwells after any violent incident was still fresh. My heart hadn't recovered its regular rhythm, and I still didn't have much of my mind back either.

The driver tried to open the rear door, but I double-timed it and beat him to it, held the door open for Luna in my first ever attempt at chivalry.

"Thank you."

I settled into the crocodile-embossed leather of the backseat, keeping the middle seat between us empty as she scooted over to the other side.

"The Flaming Reno, sir?" The driver was already back in the front seat. I realized that his question wasn't rhetorical, that I did still have a Jeeves or two at my beck and call if I wanted them, though I didn't.

"Please," I said, looking over at Luna in a half-bashful, half-proud manner, a bigwig by-proxy thanks to whatever osmosis there was between Big Jim, my mother, and me.

"Calling shots," she said.

"You're the one with the new hacienda, lady."

I was joking, or trying to keep it light, but the house weighed on her, as much as my uncle's death and Cliff's accident.

Cliff.

"Is he going to be okay?"

The car pulled out into traffic, driving away from the courthouse district to another block whose main attraction was an Ibiza-style nightclub. The hotspot pumped out Mediterranean techno and some moonflower lighting.

"Cliff's dead." She clenched her jaws to keep from betraying any more emotion, exhausted. "They're taking him to Renown Children's since it's closest."

We'd made it through the gridlock around the club where a younger corporate set was overflowing from the patio area into the street, rocking the Casbah to the sound of Euro trash *thump-thump* bass carried on a subwoofer that made our car's doors rattle.

"What did he say to you? In Spanish?"

That seemed to upset her more, but I needed to know bad enough that I didn't worry about things like mercy. I cursed myself again for my half-assed Spanish, inexcusable in this part of the country.

She laughed, her pert nose crinkling, bemusement radiating her features.

"He said he would have seen the car coming except for his dad's belt buckle."

"His dad's belt buckle?" The driver turned left, onto a shopping strip where name brand logos glowing from signs let tourists know that Reno had all the amenities of home.

"Cliff was blind in one eye. His dad used to beat him with a belt. One time the prong was poking out of the frame when his dad swung on him and…" She aimed a well-manicured pink fingernail toward her eye, let me imagine the rest.

"Ouch."

"Yeah," she said, in a voice that was deep yet feminine, slightly hoarse from screaming earlier.

"We used to talk sometimes when he was over, after your uncle had gone to bed."

I liked that she hadn't said, "After I put him to bed." She knew how to let a man have his dignity, even a nearly helpless one.

"He said during the Depression his dad would get drunk and beat him, but the worst part wasn't the beating. It was that his father would cry while he was beating him. He didn't have a job and his wife had left him." She stuttered.

My pothead brain that had mostly cleared still blanked on the words for "cry" and "rain" in Spanish, which I remembered were similar, and may have even rhymed. Euphonically they were closer to what I thought of as the act of crying than the English word. I wished I could remember them in their infinitive forms, or, since she was crying, conjugated. *Ella lluvia*, maybe? Did that mean "She cried" or "She rained"?

I wanted to console her, but I didn't know how. I looked away from her silently shedding tears, toward the driver. He was a man, so maybe he knew what to do. But they had taught him to mind his business; minding his business was very much his business, and I knew he wouldn't be any help.

The car slowed as we approached the Flaming Reno, and the rush of emotions, the adrenaline still going from the near-death by gypsy cab along with the fragrance of Luna had me going full cornball.

Lady fair, I crave a lock of your hair. I reached for her, no intention of coiling a lock of her black glorious mane, but just to touch it.

She pulled away, smiling indulgently, gathering herself up and stowing her need to sob lest I misread it as some kind of cue. She took my hand in hers, neither as a restraint against my stupid action nor as an invitation, just holding it in sympathy, the stroke of her warm brown fingers across the back of my knuckles meant to soothe me.

"I got to go," I said, as if she was asking me to stay.

She laughed. The cloud of "maybe," that threshold I could have tried a little harder to cross, had lifted. The driver sat in the front seat, the glitter of the lights fronting the casino rippling, the phosphorescence twinkling like pennies in a fountain or a sky full of stars all going supernova at once.

"I saw your school on TV, on a documentary," she said.

"Not just my school." I unbuckled my belt. "You saw my dorm. Trappist Town." I said it in Ari's voice, not letting any air into my nostrils so it sounded like I too had snorted my cartilage into collapsing.

"That's it!" She said.

"Yeah, that rich lady who founded the school liked some place she visited in Belgium, some monk's abbey, and she based part of the campus on that." I looked toward the cattle chutes out on the street, as industry people called the paths to the casinos, watched people walking on red carpeted killing floors marching to their slaughter, or at least a good fleecing if they were lucky.

"You be good," she said, touched my cheek lightly.

"You, too," I said, smiled weakly, and looked away.

She was out of the car, switching her purse strap from one arm to the other, heading toward the lead checker cab in the line at the stand.

"This is yours, sir." The driver's gloved hand came through the partition, holding a watermarked piece of paper that looked like high quality parchment printed on heavy stock.

"What's this?" I asked.

"From your lawyer."

That lawyer wasn't mine but at least he hadn't been on my mother's and Big Jim's side (or at least he didn't seem to be). I didn't correct the driver, though. It was best to make people think you had an army of lawyers, just like it was fun to pretend a moment before that I had a personal chauffeur who I could have told to take Luna and me to a fancy cliff-side bistro, but since I had business in the morning... *You know how it is, Dear.*

I studied the sheet. It was my uncle's address, where I was to peruse and then pick up the various lots of furniture, paintings, memorabilia, and curios, if my mother's and Jim's contestation got shot down, withdrawn, or the time window had closed.

I folded the paper, spoke to the driver. "What's your name, man?"

"Gordon," he said, the name spoken like a two syllable belch.

I stuffed the paper in my pocket for the moment. "Gordon, how do you feel about doing a little more driving, earning some money?"

The driver really looked at me for the first time, hawk-eyed and bushy browed, like a bird of prey sizing up the amount of effort it might take to pick off a field mouse. "I can do a little moonlighting, provided you're not asking me to be the wheelman on a jewel heist."

"Nothing like that," I said, opening my door and letting the light and sounds of the strip flood into the car's dark interior. "Just want to check on my investment."

His gloved fingers drummed the slip-covered steering wheel, did a full paradiddle. "You need me to sit tight?"

"Just for a few."

He winked one of those raptor eyes, grimaced, letting me know that he was hungry but I wouldn't be on the menu provided I fed him something that made it worth his time.

I hustled through the revolving, gold-gilded glass doors of the hotel's lobby, no longer feeling pushed along by forces I didn't see or understand. I still didn't totally understand them, but I thought I'd gotten a glimpse of them, and thought also I might counter them, push back a bit.

I walked to the elevator car in the lobby, its doors gold-plated and the rest of the car a mixture of bottlenose-blue glass chips that sparkled but contained no color, and a nacreous lacquer that made me feel like I was stepping into the locket of a rich old widow who rarely opened the face of her jewel.

My fob that overrode the elevator's normal route propelled me up into the sky, where all the glass sparkled and all the stars irradiated the night as far as the mountains hemming in the heavens on the horizon. A Bell helicopter heading toward a hospital (maybe to Children's) seemed to be at about the same level as me when the car disgorged me in the penthouse.

It was dark, and I had a bad feeling. "Adam?" Had he taken his life? I wondered. Maybe I was being paranoid, thinking death must always follow more death, or that trouble came in threes (him after my uncle and now Cliff).

I ran down the reasons he might do it even as I ran up the winding spiral staircase. The roar and whap of the helicopter grew closer, and I told myself that Adam had slit his wrists because he didn't believe me when I told him he would reach puberty and maybe surpass all of us, develop more muscle mass and thicker hair down there. Or maybe he realized that the mother ship wasn't coming, or contra Fermi's Paradox, they were coming and they would enslave us or eat us, so why not get the jump on those grey bastards? They'd been biding their time in Nevada, performing radioactive tweaks on our cattle that would have them giving nuclear milk that would curdle into something that gave us all cancer or make us mutants.

I fought off the insane thought my mother and Big Jim were in the helicopter, nosediving toward me with a chain-gun hanging from the runners, ready to Gatling me and my buddy to bloody messes just to get another heir out of the way.

I found Adam upstairs, as relaxed as I felt keyed up. I didn't want to burden him by telling him about what happened with Cliff, or that I'd suspected the worst had happened with him up here in the penthouse suite.

He sat in Jim's gold filigreed terrycloth bathrobe, monogrammed with the man's initials over the left breast pocket. He was lifting a cinnamon-covered pecan from the remains of a melting Banana Foster he'd put quite a dent in. I doubted he would finish it, since the T-Bone on the same cart looked picked clean down to the last bit of medium-rare meat, and then there were the jumbo shrimp shells swimming in horseradish cocktail sauce crowned by a celery stick stirrer.

"What's up, man?"

He looked back toward the Roman caldarium where he'd been bathing a couple hours ago. I smiled, relieved to see him alive and happy. Sure there was a lot of downside to his condition, but he could eat what he wanted, when he wanted, and didn't have to worry about gaining weight.

My stomach was aching for something, but I had too much to do. Besides that, the stupid part of my brain that wouldn't quit hoping kept telling me not to get chunky again, that Luna would appreciate a relatively flat stomach (no way I was getting washboard abs) if we got together. And that dumb part of my brain that refused to be silent grew even louder, said that it wasn't a matter of *If*. It was only *when*. And the *when* part was soon. To which I responded *Bullshit*. But the dream didn't hear me.

And since I had money, maybe I should have been willing to heed the dream's call. That was why I had marched up here with such purpose.

I walked across the marble floor, the whap of the helicopter growing fainter as my paranoia ebbed. The relief at finding Adam still alive continued to prickle my skin in much-appreciated calming nettles that reminded me of my first couple times doing heroin, where the God Morpheus massaged the limbs with one hand while sneaking a poisonous snake down my open throat with the other.

I picked up the candlestick phone from its cradle, summoned up the petulant tone I'd heard so many rich kids use with teachers and maître-ds, their money (or their parents' money) trumping age, wisdom, and dignity in this sick sky world I inhabited for the time being. I never used this tactic normally, but I had no choice now.

"Yes, sir?" a voice said on the other end.

"Debbie wants Winnie the Pooh up here in an hour with a hundred golds in the honeypot, or she says she's taking her business across the street."

"Comped and coming, sir."

I hung up.

"What's going on?" Adam had migrated from his gluttonous spread, giving up on the caramelized and glazed brown sugar leeching the very potassium out of the remaining banana that swirled in the kidney-shaped crystal dish. He'd gone back toward the caldarium, shedding his bathrobe, still wearing his swimming trunks.

"You will get a rash if you keep that thing on," I said.

"I've got baby powder," he replied, and flipped a light switch that brought the candelabra to life and started the flow of water again from the nipples of the armless Nyad. No water came out of Neptune's dick, which I thought was an oversight on someone's part.

Adam sunk back into the warm roiling waters, the geyser shooting like some artesian hot spring from the Fountain of Youth.

"You swim and you will get a cramp that soon after eating."

Adam's eyes were closed as he did the dead man's float, face up toward the frescoed ceiling. "I'm not swimming," he said. "I'm soaking."

The private elevator dinged, and the doors opened. A man in a pelisse with a golden aiguillette and an opera usher's red pillbox cap pushed a room service table toward us. They'd upholstered this one in the green baize of a gaming table rather than a white tablecloth. In the center of the deep berth wide enough to play snooker there was a ceramic Winnie the Pooh holding a honeypot brimming with ruffle-edged Bakelite chips, worth $100 each.

"Courtesy of the house, for Debbie," the man said, grinning. I picked one chip from the pot which was technically illegal, but laws were for the lower orders. And the man didn't protest when I placed it in his palm.

"A toke," I said. "From Debbie."

He grinned, nodded in supplicating gratitude to the as-yet-to-arrive hostess who staff already knew had an insatiable yen for the slots.

The rest of the chips were for the driver downstairs, whose name I couldn't quite remember in all the rush back and forth, up and down the stairs. Something like Gerald?

***

He corrected me, telling me his name was Gordon, not Gerald, after I placed the ten $100 chips in his hand. The money seemed to make him friendlier. "Your mom's got you and your friend set to go to the airport tomorrow, and if I don't take you, it's my good name, if not my Class D and E licenses."

"Shouldn't be a problem getting there and getting back. It's not that far, is it?"

Getting out of Reno around sunrise was easy. Sinners were still nursing hangovers and anyone religious was getting ready to go to their local Mormon Tabernacle or Catholic church.

"Distance isn't the problem." The chauffeur studied the address on the paper he'd given me only hours before. "It's what we're doing there." He eyed me in the rearview mirror, his fig-colored irises in shadow and nearly black under the cap's brim. Those eyes wouldn't brook much bullshit, so I didn't quite lie.

"I'm just checking up on my piece of the estate."

He eased the Lincoln onto the highway. "You got a key?"

"Yes."

That was closer to a lie, but I knew how to get through most locks with a hotel keycard, credit card, or a bobby pin. Other lock housings were easy pickings with a Peterson knife or a thin icepick. Mahar had taught me how to do it all during one tour of extra duty we'd shared at school after getting caught smoking (cigarettes) on the green space behind Trappist Town.

The car drove west, away from a rising sun the color of a blood orange. Maybe it was because it was early and the sun hadn't gained in force and heat, but it wasn't looking like itself, a near-invincible fireball. It looked frail, rather wounded and leaking its blood onto the far horizon, staining the clouds with its life-force diluted to pink as it dripped down from the shining tendrils onto the wide canvas of the bleached white sky.

The saguaros at the sides of the road were in shadow, jutting like the hands of long-buried giants finally punching their way through the hard desert rock to break free from ancient graves. The cottonwoods looked stunted, their branches wrapping around each other as if fighting for whatever meager nourishment came their way this far out in the desert. I wondered how they survived out here with so little water. They must have been like the camels of the tree kingdom.

"As long as I get you kids back on time, we're kosher." Gordon nodded to himself, gripped the wheel so that the leather-on-leather made a menacing crunching sound. I figured he could probably do a right number on my trachea, though he probably wasn't threating me, at least not consciously.

The highway started slowly filling up with big rigs, teardrop campers, and RVs. Ours was the only car that looked like a refugee from the metro area, isolated among the growing numbers of a wannabee-biker gang, weekend warriors clogging up two lanes. They rode in columns, weaving in and out of the two lanes of steady traffic, their *Easy Rider* fantasy on autopilot til they made it to the convention center or parade grounds. Once they got there, they'd compare German-made Harley's and other high-end hogs, with their leathers and black helmets that made them look more like ageing bondage enthusiasts than Hell's Angels.

I pulled my wallet out of my pocket, and Gordon's ears, trained to the sound, pricked up and his eyes fastened to the rearview again. I was looking over my cards to see which was the sturdiest and least possible to break if I tried to slide a bolt aside to get into my uncle's place. Still the hawk-eyed driver made me antsy enough to fear not toking him again, and I sanded a twenty from my dwindling stack of paper to cool him when we came to a stop.

We got off the highway, tires lurching from seamlessly asphalted hardball to caliche with a crunch to it that made it sound and feel like we'd just gotten dropped in a rover on the surface of the Red Planet. The sun, growing ever redder, didn't strain the simile budding in my mind.

The roads became a series of switchbacks that made my stomach lurch, but I didn't complain for fear that Gordon would use my bitching as an excuse to make a pit stop to get our legs back under us and grab a bite, maybe even at Sonora Bend, which I remembered as being somewhere around here.

The half-inhabited ghost town where me and my uncle had stopped for gas appeared perched on a flat limestone butte at our left, and my heart sank from my chest down to my stomach.

I missed riding in his car with him, smoking weed and watching the desert through the window, that feeling of being in a ride with the cool old man, comfortably cruising in an old American auto while the barren, dead land spread motionless around us and watched and envied the only two living creatures moving in its midst.

I'd felt wonderfully separated from the rest of humanity and linked close on some invisible line to the old man, even though I hadn't known him long. Or perhaps my mind and my heart were tricking me, because I knew that he was dead and I was due to be getting some stuff from him. People became more popular when they died, and more loved, especially when some of the still-living had been waiting for them to kick the bucket for a while.

"Any of this look familiar?" Gordon looked back at me from through the open partition between front and backseat.

"Yeah, that especially." I pointed at the lime-washed "Ghost Gulch" sign I'd first passed on my way in here with Debbie in her Land Rover.

"Good stuff." The old pro nodded in the front seat, hunched over a bit now like a Formula One racer taking a hairpin.

"That's it!" I sat up in the backseat, unbuckled my belt, held my "key" (an expired demagnetized Four Seasons card) in my closed right palm.

He slowed down as we approached the front of the hacienda. It had only been a few months since someone had been here, but those months had not been kind to the homestead. The facade looked like it could use a pressure washing, and the sand-colored mud-brick I remembered from before was leprous with black and yellow patches, standing out in pitted hexagons, like the skin of a Gila monster that'd been hiding in scrub for too long.

My uncle's car was there, draped in a khaki-colored canvas cloth sooty from neglect, sitting beneath a scalding-hot tin roof that shined. Parked in the adjacent spot was Luna's silver coup. Just like old times.

"Here." I handed the driver another twenty, said, "Sit tight."

"Everything all right?" He'd taken the bill in his right hand, which he'd ungloved after about an hour's steering. He stowed the twenty in a leather wallet more creased than a road atlas owned by a long-married couple.

"Fine," I said, and got out.

I closed my door and walked toward the front of the house. The presence of her car proved nothing. She could have left it here. She had taken a cab the other night, after she'd gotten out of the Towne Car in front of the Flaming Reno.

My shadow elongated as I walked across the driveway, stubbly with rocks and scrub that the rare wind had blown over here in the intervening time between my last visit here and this one. It felt like ages, even though it was only months ago. I was too young to have much of a gauge for what an age was anyway, and time was just something that made me taller.

I went to the front door which was open. It was a massive slab of oak fitted with some iron fixtures and a bronze knocker, so I doubted a desert wind had blown it open. I put the keycard back in my wallet and stepped inside, knew my step made an echo, even though I was still wearing my bench-made Italian shoes I'd worn to the reading of the will the previous day.

I padded softly now. All the antiques in the room sat covered either in plastic slipcovers or drop cloths like the one thrown over the old man's car out front. The only things not covered were the trophies mounted on their plaques on the wall, the stuffed heads of the big game who'd met their match in man.

The sonorant warbling of some country singer came as a soft sound barely intruding in the room, like an aural tracer left after listening to music while on strong sunshine LSD. The only problem was that I had never done acid while listening to anything but industrial or bright-eyed hippie music, like the Beach Boys or the Beatles, and this was honkytonk.

The vibrations coming from my uncle's old den weren't bad in and of themselves, but that I was even hearing them when this place should have been soundless was enough to make me feel like I'd entered a haunted version of the Grand Ole Opry.

I wanted out and knew I had to go forward.

I crossed from the darkness of the cavernous main room to the dark lamplit glow of the den where Luna sat in my uncle's Gerichair, motionless except for what it required to weep in silence. Her shoulders convulsed, and she stared down at a book she held in her hands.

She looked lost enough to not see me, or to not care even if she had noted my presence. She sat gussied up cowgirl-style, just like on movie nights and fight nights with Ole Charlie Reeves, wearing a fringed gingham skirt and gabardine shirt, both cornflower blue. Her hair was pigtailed, accenting the soft-angled curves of her face.

I didn't like to see her like this, reduced to this strange childlike state that she entered when my uncle was around, and which she had somehow reentered, if only for this moment now that he was no more. I liked her as the assertive woman slightly out of my reach and way beyond my level, pitying my attraction to her but still letting me glance, worship from a distance, and even graze her with my touch. Everyone needed a time and a place to break down, especially those who held it together so well the rest of the time, but it wasn't mine to see. I had no right to be here, despite my literal claim on some effects among which she sat.

She spoke, and her voice shook me because she'd never taken her eyes off the book, or given any sign acknowledging my entrance. "I had to come back for this." She held up the book, forlorn but possessive, as if she was showing someone a photo of her dog who'd gone astray in the neighborhood.

The title said, "Riders of the Purple Sage." The cover featured an aquatint of a suitably indigo-shaded woman on the prairie, handling big leather reins in her gauntlets that went up to her elbows. She was the centerpiece of the cover artwork so I didn't notice the man behind her at first, though as I stared at what Luna needed me to see the other cowpuncher came into relief. He wore what looked like a planter's hat, a kerchief tied around his neck, and an ear-to-ear smile.

"Riders of the Purple Sage," she said, and slowly lowered the book back into her lap, onto the wrinkles of her gingham skirt. "Zane Grey, first edition, signed."

"If he gave it to you as a gift…" I started, then trailed off. What she had shown me had nothing to do with laying claim to it. It was hers. She wanted me to bear witness to it, to its existence and my uncle's generosity in giving it to her. I regained some of my composure, still wanting nothing more than to back out of this eerie cove carved into this corner of the house, as cloister-like as the strangest candlelit nook in Redrock at midnight. "What's going on?" I asked her.

"You can have everything in here but this," she said, and lifted the book once more, holding the icon of her prairie saint in a viselike grip.

"Okay," I said, wondering why my voice had taken on the solicitous, careful tone of a hostage negotiator. "It's yours."

"Everything…" There was spite in the word, as if she was accusing me of having violated her and taken every shred of her dignity. *Everything.* I didn't like it when she said it, and I liked it even less when she said it again.

"Everything except this book, and the two million dollars in there."

She tucked the thin dusty old volume beneath her armpit, and pointed with her other hand toward that Rockwellian town, the painted portal between this cave and the hidden hole in the wall.

***

The smile on her face had nothing to do with happiness or joy. Like her uttered *Everything* a few moments before, she was reveling in something. This time I think it was my shock in discovering that I didn't know her, and that everything I'd thought I knew about her resulted from my arrogance.

I was seeing myself through her eyes as she smiled and watched me, and I looked even worse now than I did in my own eyes, which had always been bad.

When I could speak again, I did. "It's been in there the whole time?"

She ignored me, pulled the flouncy material of the canvas backdrop aside, as if she intended to tear it down as she passed through it. I stood and followed her, deaf to the sound of the rockabilly guitarist strumming on the radio, tuned in only to whatever sounds Luna made, and blind to everything but whichever motions she took.

I was careful as I passed through the watercolor Main Street to work the creases out of it like a mother fixing her son's slacks before sending him off to school.

The objects of the room sat draped in the same sheets that covered so many other things in the house. She flipped on the light switch as she entered, proving that the power still worked in the room. The juice hit the neon Sargasso cactus, which, pitched beneath its sheet and glowing green, looked like a kid reading by flashlight underneath his blanket before bedtime.

The chuckwalla carved from driftwood that had scared me when stoned scared me now that I was sober. His form lay contoured beneath the blanket over him so he looked like he was not only alive, but was hiding there and waiting to pounce on his prey.

The framed photos previously on the walls were no more, and the square shapes left there after years showed blackish imprints limned in water-damaged lines that stood out against the dusty wooden panels.

Luna walked past the slot machine, which stood there, no longer draped with a sheet and still open from where the doctor retrieved his prototype (patent perhaps pending). She ignored the old gold and silver box and pulled the Oxford cloth off of the other standup model, this one-armed bandit an exact twin to the original one.

"In there?" I guessed, propping myself against the doorframe so I didn't fall over.

"In here." She leaned down, her gingham cowgirl skirt riding high on her thighs as she crouched, exposing the tops of her knee-high red kid leather boots.

She pulled the front panel open. Inside the berth, piled like logs in a fireplace, was a stack of cash bundled in thick rubber bands. The topmost bills in the stack were hundreds, the old ones with the small faces and without holograms, with serial numbers going back probably decades. That cash had probably seen handling by keno runners, pit bosses and showgirls long-turned to dust by the Florida sun. It was literally old money, charming and with the musk of time on it like someone's stamp collection.

But it was still legal tender, which made it a lot less cute. As Luna placed a proprietary grip on it, tight as snake jaws unhinging around a field mouse, she clarified that it was hers.

Her smile, which I thought sadistic but somehow warranted, disappeared. Her eyes seemed to glow in her skull, morphing like the faceted stones on a mood ring, going from their usual brown color, blackening to onyx, flashing blue like glass marbles for a moment and then smoldering into a kind of feline jade.

"Go ahead," I said, less out of fear or the stupid, still-lingering cloud of my attraction to her, and more because I was too spiritually tired, even at this young age, to fight for money, literally or figuratively.

Her eyes stopped shifting color, or maybe I had imagined it all. Either way, the possessive rage that held her once the money was in view evaporated into something different, envy or disgust causing the corners of her nostrils to flare and the scowl on her face to deepen so I could see, for a brief flicker of a moment, what Luna would look like in fifty years.

"It must be nice," she said.

"What?" I asked. I wasn't a mind reader and didn't know what the hell she was talking about.

"To not need money, to not care. To just be blasé about the pile of cash in here."

"I'm not exactly Richie Rich."

"No, but your dad is." That scowl showed, still carved in her face; if anything it was even more deeply engraved than a moment before.

"My dad's in La Tuna."

"FCI," she said, half to herself and a half to me. "I had a boyfriend in there."

"You don't seem like the type," I said, elaborating when her eyes didn't move from mine. "I mean, to have a boyfriend in prison."

"You don't know me." She seethed as much as spoke, hissing like a guttering candle whose flame someone had sprinkled with gunpowder.

"Yeah, well, you don't know me, either. It's my stepdad you're thinking about who's paid until Kingdom Come."

"So why don't you want any of this?" She was curious, didn't quite hate me. Since I wasn't a threat to her bundle of cash, she turned from me, found an empty cardboard box on the desk where a pile of my uncle's stuff sat along with some of the good doctor's progress notes on his now-deceased patient.

"What I need I can't buy," I said.

"How romantic," she sneered, stacking the cash in the box. "I thought they sold heroin by the gram."

I blinked back tears. I almost said, *Why are you trying to hurt me?* But that would have just invited more torment from her. Had she seen me every time I'd stolen a glance at her ass? Did women somehow know, through some ether-ish frequency foreign to men, when some creep was fantasizing about them? Or maybe it was that I was a boy, and boys became men, and she had reason to hate them. Whatever it was I felt that she had punished me enough, and we were more than even.

"Fuck you," I said.

She stood with the box of money, clutched in a hold so indifferent it might as well have been a basket of dirty laundry. "I feel a little better now."

"Because I told you 'Fuck you?' It doesn't seem like a healthy thing to feel relief when someone cusses at you."

Luna walked past me and I held my breath so I wouldn't catch any of her scent, the comingling passion fruit accents of her hair and skin in my lungs. If even the faintest enchantment of her musk entered my nose, I might forget for a minute that what she was and what she smelled like were two different things.

"I'm not a healthy girl. Also, I was wondering why you were just taking all of this laying down. That you're angry makes me feel a little better. For you, I mean."

She pulled the curtain aside, tearing the watercolor town in two, rending that Main Street momentarily asunder. In the main den where my uncle's Gerichair still sat, a countryfied duet between some man and woman ragging on each other came from the radio. "You're the reason our kids are ugly, little darling," they both sang at the same time.

"I feel like I should give you something." She walked through the den and I walked out, ready to go back to the Lincoln. I wanted to get the hell away from here, back to Redrock where things were depressing, nightmarish in fact, but at least where they made some sense and the only females were my age or older matronly types. They weren't complex prickly bundles I couldn't un-riddle, like what was before me, what tortured me and what I still worshipped. Maybe I wasn't healthy, either.

"It's not my money," I said, which I thought should have settled the matter.

She shifted her weight to one leg and the strong muscles on her naturally tan thigh both corded and separated one from the other in flexing definition. Luna hefted the box, which was full enough with cash to force her to lean. "How about a blowjob?"

She had asked offhand, taxed, like she was a waitress running down the items on a menu for a picky eater who'd said "No" to all the specials.

"Fuck you," I whispered through a super-heated veil of streaming tears.

"You can't fuck me," she said. "This pussy is spoken for. And you couldn't handle it."

The tears burnt hot paths down both of my cheeks, feeling as hard as the track marks when they'd bitten deep into the tissue of my arms and were close to abscessing.

"Hey, let me show you something." She said it just as casually as she'd offered fellatio, as if she hadn't already traumatized me two or three times today and hadn't just delivered a coup de grâce. The way she talked I might have just been her girlfriend whose opinion she wanted regarding the spot where she'd moved a sofa.

I followed her, rather than going out through the front door which was closed now. Thunder clapped from the sky. The sound reverberated through the windows but the stones that made up the house stopped the force of it.

The tin Pacific Railroad sign that had been over the entryway to the kitchen, hillbilly mistletoe, now dangled from a rusty chain. It precariously swung over the door like a pendulum that would reward the careful and slice the incautious clean through to the bone.

"Watch your step," Luna said, shifting the box from one hand to another.

Greed, that universal current carrying us all, made me think of putting something in the kitchen to good use, maybe bashing her brains out with a frying pan or ramming a butcher knife through her breastplate.

I'd never been violent (unless you counted being on the receiving end of ass-whippings from bullies and my father). But I'd experienced nothing like this weird spiritual cuckolding that had me feeling like I needed to double over just to get my breath back or keep from retching up the bile of my stomach onto the slate tile. Every second that I lived without killing her seemed to siphon something from me. That she didn't fear me, or even the chance of violence coming from me, made me think if I didn't do something soon I would never have a chance for self-respect. The loathing that made me want to go back to the needle would consume me if I didn't stab her. That was the choice blooming in my brain, the knife or the needle, her death or mine.

Her boots clopped on the granite floor as she made her way over to the refrigerator, that massive black slab that looked like a cryogenic chamber, from which I half-expected her to produce my uncle's frozen and sleeping corpse, covered in blue fog and basking in gelid dormancy until the good doctor attempted to reanimate him.

Instead, she reached into the freezer where months of provisions sat still covered in permafrost. Then she moved aside a massive bag of ice and tins of concentrate orange juice and rolls of uncured bacon. She produced a small vacuum-sealed package of what looked like a baby chicken, grown enough to have evolved beyond an egg yet too stunted to cook into a proper meal.

She threw it on the wooden table and it landed with a thud. A closer look made my stomach lurch, and I flashed back on those images they sometimes slipped into the cellophane sleeves of cigarette packs to scare young girls off smoking, an eggy yellowish and translucent vein-traversed unborn baby, too young to be stillborn.

What did they call it at that stage? I'd forgotten, and knew little about feminine hygiene and sexuality, aside from what I'd picked up eavesdropping on some of my mother's recent griping with another trophy wife about menopause.

"Miscarriage," Luna said. "I didn't name it and I never told your uncle."

I sat down. I had to. "He raped you?"

"No," she said. "Not exactly."

The frost around the packaged fetus was already turning to meltwater. I backed away from it, as if even a drop of the unholy water contacting my skin might poison me. That thing had been alive, had been on its way to being human. I had no rage left for her, only fear. Even the attraction disappeared. This was too crazy, and I wanted to leave, but it paralyzed me.

"We screwed sometimes while I was sitting with him in his bedroom. He was a virile stud for an old man. Sex is hard on all men but the refractory period really kicks an old buck's ass." She giggled. "He talked a lot in his sleep after we screwed."

Luna set the cardboard box in the center of the wooden table next to the baby, took the seat opposite me, where one of my uncle's rubber sippy cups sat, skinned with an ochre film and still smelling faintly of vegetable soup even after all this time.

"He talked about boxing a lot. With the War, he didn't so much talk as scream."

"And he talked about the money?" I asked.

"He talked about the money." She folded the flaps on the box so it was closed, ready for someone to tape it shut, stow it somewhere, perhaps deposit it in a bank's safe deposit box. "The money's mine." She looked at me across the table, her game face back on, the eyes smoldering through that whole spectrum of shades once more, scrolling like fruit combinations chuntering in the face of a slot machine.

"The money's not yours. It's mine," a voice said from behind me.

The voice that had spoken wasn't earthy enough to belong to the chauffeur, Gordon. It had a Texan twang, the vowels wide as an open lasso, but leavened with something else, a sprinkle of laid-back California boy, and another flat, affectless tone that effaced most of what I'd detected. It was a tone I knew from La Tuna, from both my father speaking behind the glass and what bits of conversation I picked up from the other visitors commiserating with their jailbird family members while I talked to him.

Prison.

Only this wasn't my father.

***

The pile of chips I'd thrown to the chauffeur landed on the table with a slap, like a massive raise by a player with a royal flush. "I'm all in." The guy who'd thrown the chips gripped the big gun he needed two hands to hold properly.

It was a .357 Magnum. I didn't have to know much about guns, only movies featuring guns, to know that he could have hollowed me out at this range. Or Luna, who was maybe his intended target.

I was paralyzed and remained half-turned toward him, leaning away from Luna and the table with the box of money on it. His smile was for Luna, similar to the one she'd shown me, and while I should have been happy she was getting some of her own medicine, I wasn't sadistic enough to enjoy it. My heart hurt for her as her eyes watered.

"Don't try that crying shit."

The boyfriend was an *El rubio mejor* type, dimples on dimples smile with a dash of pomade browning his surfer blonde locks. His five o'clock shadow had the same premeditated messiness as that thatch of golden hair. It took a lot of work for him to look like he'd just rolled out of bed.

For someone like Luna I imagined he was America itself, or the promise it represented but didn't deliver, something just out of reach. His appeal was part bad boy, part Brahman snob whose disdain for her and her accent only deepened her sick attraction to him. For someone like Debbie he would resemble a model for the bodice rippers she consumed while downing box wine when the Muscadet in the cellar was no more.

Blondie would yearn to land some rich broad for more than a night, while they disdained him and used him as a boy toy, and he would take it out on any woman shortsighted enough to not see through his youth and shallowness and his own thwarted ambitions, maybe to be a rock star instead of just to play acoustic guitar at the cabana.

He didn't seem to like my scrutiny, maybe even sensed my thoughts and my reading of him. His eyes shifted to me while his gun stayed on Luna. Her hands stayed on the cardboard box. The fetal tissue was now swimming in thawed water.

"How old are you?" he asked.

"Sixteen," I said.

He sucked air, hissing through the ionized-white teeth that made up that million-dollar grin. "I don't know if I can shoot you."

That didn't quite let me off the hook and my chest was still tight when I tried to breathe. "Then again..." His blue eyes glowed until they were grey. "You might want to die after I tell you what kind of scandalous bitch you've been drooling over."

"Mark!" Luna's plea was urgent, more frightened than begging. I wanted to know what he had to tell me and I didn't want to know.

"That's it," he said, eyes and gun back on Luna again. "Use my real name so I *have* to clip this fucking rug rat."

I didn't have the balls to rush him, but a first flush of anger coursed through me. He saw it, liked it enough to lick his lips once, biting his tongue and holding it between even rows of teeth.

"You know, this bitch called me while I was in the can, said, 'I got this old man in love with me. We're going to get this geezer for everything.'"

"No, I didn't, Michael." Her voice was deadpan enough that I considered believing her. One of her pigtails had come undone and the black hair spilled from her scalp and clung to her sweat-soaked forehead in a cleaver-shaped slice of bang. "This loser was just jealous that I was doing something with my life and that I wouldn't write him or visit him enough. Someone showed him a story about me in the local paper taking care of your uncle, and he got wind of it. He-"

The guy was as lithe as he looked, switching the gun back to a one-handed hold and crossing the space between him and Luna. He delivered a backhanded row of protruding knuckles to her chinbone and cheek. The blow left a dent in her flesh that was red now and would be purple in a matter of minutes.

"*This loser* is walking with that money," he said.

"No, you're not," Luna half mumbled, mush-mouthed from the slap and sounding like she'd just gotten a dentist's shot of Novocain.

"I can stand on my head in a cell for three hours. I got the core of a fucking Himalayan yogi master. And I got a gun. But you two are going to… what? Overpower me?"

"I don't want the money," I said.

"He's got the right idea." He waved the gun, once again in a two-hand grip, in my direction, which neither I nor my pulse appreciated.

"Make your move," he said. But neither she nor I moved. He seemed assured enough of our paralysis to take stock of the room, or at least the table where the money sat in the still-closed box. He also finally noticed the thawing package where blood and water had mixed so it looked like the half-formed baby was swimming in Kool-Aid. "What the hell is that?"

I was no hero, but I was smart enough to realize that maybe the truth would either stun him or enrage him with jealousy. The words came out of my mouth even though I knew they might get me shot. "My uncle fucked her, but she miscarried. She's been keeping the baby in the freezer."

"Get out of town!" He grinned so widely that his ears twitched once, then he managed a laugh, a stuttering stoner giggle that was open and bro-like. It would have been disarming if he wasn't literally armed. He looked back at Luna. "You sick bitch!"

He crossed the table to her, coming to stand over her shoulder. He gathered the hair that had fallen from its hold in the pigtail in one hand, ran his fingers through it. Luna closed her eyes, which caused more tears to spill over the forming bruise. He pulled her hair back from her scalp in his strong hand, his knuckles still slightly skinned from where he'd hit her. She fought the shudder of disgust that morphed into a quaking shiver of the old passion.

"No way can an old limp-dicked dude do it for her." He looked at me, needing me to see this. I neither wanted to see it nor could do anything to stop it, and so dropped my eyes to the ground like the coward I was. A real man would have wanted the money and the girl. I wanted to live.

"I know Viagra works wonders, but she likes it rough and raw dog. You got to pull this little *campesina's* hair, choke her out a bit to get those endorphins rushing."

I looked up, not to watch the display for which he wanted an audience, but to get his attention. I wanted to piss him off again, hoping he would turn his anger on me and let her go.

The hand holding the gun still gripped a ponytail's worth of her perfumed black locks, the Magnum looking like a stylist's high-tech blow-dryer at work atop her hairdo. His other hand gripped her throat and she let out an ecstatic little yelp as he tightened his hold and cut off her oxygen.

"I thought you guys start fucking each other in the ass when you go to prison," I said.

Luna coughed as she tried to giggle, seeming to understand where I was going, where I needed to guide him. He loosened the hand from her throat and now that she was free she both laughed and breathed.

"The fuck do you know about prison, punk?"

"His father's in there," Luna said. That got him to tighten his hold on her throat again. With the other hand he pointed the gun at me. He was mostly muscle, marbled from calves to traps and hard enough to look like a pro fighter, a kickboxer maybe. But that was still a lot of gun for one hand, and even if he got the first shot off, he might not be capable of holding it steady for another.

But he wouldn't need two shots if his aim was true.

"You're pretty," I said. "White, blue eyes, blond hair. You fit the profile for predators. Muscles or no."

"You-"

Luna yanked her head to the side like a hunger striker resisting a force-feeding, bit the hand that had first beaten and then choked her, hard enough for the blood to ooze rather than pump from the webbing between his thumb and pointer finger where her teeth sank.

He waved his hand like it was on fire, got his paw free from her mouth for a moment, but she lunged for the flying and bleeding hand like a fighting terrier until she'd resettled her hold, this time only on a single finger rather than the whole hand. Her jaw shifted around the meat of the pointer finger she squeezed between her eyeteeth and molars. There was a crunch, like a dull knife meeting the hard crust of stale bread, followed by a howl that could have come from a coyote with its foot in the jaws of a steel trap.

Blondie hit the tile knees-first, his face up toward the ceiling as the gun skidded across the granite floor. Luna spit his finger from her mouth and it landed in the grout work between two tiles, the cracks quickly becoming a canal for the blood pumping from the sinewy root of the severed digit pointing nowhere.

"You fucking-" It was more pant than exclamation, the words of someone too faint from shock and blood loss to play tough anymore.

She stood and reached above her, to the dangling array of crockery hung on pegs. Luna selected a heavy black skillet and brought it down on his head with the force of an executioner's axe. The metal hit the occipital lobe, a "rabbit punch" as they called it in my uncle's trade. A couple blows with a gloved hand there could be lethal if applied right. Brought down with such force (and with metal rather than a padded fist) by a woman who'd been waiting quite a long while to do this had quite a different effect and the hard sutures of his skull might as well have been cardboard pieces on a jigsaw puzzle. His head cracked after the second swing of the pan. After several more I looked away.

I lost count of the blows landed, winced from the sound I yearned to block out, and when the hollow *ting!* of the skillet pounding brainpan finally stopped, I looked back over to see her breathing over the blood-soaked body. Both of her pigtails flailed undone now. As for Blondie… the skull casing had given up its contents in seeping cauliflower-textured brain that poured like pus from a wound, along with more blood to go with that which had pumped from his finger.

He was dead, not only lifeless but waxen, clammy and drawn from the rapid blood loss.

Luna looked at me, smiling and alive, her teeth covered in red gristle so thick it looked like she had chewed an entire tube of lipstick. Her cornflower blue cowgirl outfit was now dark purple from blood, the buttons on her top bursting open so that her heaving cleavage in her purple lace bra was visible, but I didn't dare more than sneak the smallest involuntary glance.

And then I backed up until I hit the far wall of the kitchen, my hands gripping the cold brushed steel of the gas range.

I was grateful to her for killing him, but terrified I would be next. I thanked God that I hadn't done something stupid like pinch her ass at any point and kept my eyes up to avoid the natural straying that would occur if I looked anywhere near her chest. Perfect gentleman, was I.

And the money?

Hers.

She dropped the pan to the floor, and it gave a loud metallic report as it spun three times, then came to rest, leaving a ring of blood in its wake as it settled and her own heaving breathing returned to something like a regular rhythm.

When I looked back up at her she had the cardboard box in her hands, opening it just wide enough to throw the thoroughly thawed-out fetus on the pile of bundled bills. The blood from her teeth had somehow become smeared across her cheeks like a poorly applied version of the painted butterflies kids sometimes get at the carnival.

"My baby," she said, as if that explained anything, and maybe it did.

I nodded, unable to speak. If I had spoken my words would have just been a litany on repeat to punctuate my terrified nodding assent. *Your baby. Your money. Your baby. Your money.* Over and over again to let her know I wasn't a threat to her, her money, or her baby.

She walked across the room, and I watched her ass one last time as it swayed like a conquering army's standard proudly planted on a hill and buckling in the wind after a long battle.

The rightful victor walked out of the house, leaving a dead man and a live boy in her wake.

I stood up, enjoying the sensation of breathing without a gun trained on me. I walked forward, through the kitchen and back into the main room. Patsy Cline was falling to pieces on the radio in my uncle's den. The buffalo and steer trophies watched me from their mounts on the walls, glass eyes haunted and snorting mouths caught in contorted rictuses of final defiance. Some taxidermist had condemned them to hold these poses for eternity, their pride a sad mockery of itself since the heads lacked bodies- hooves and horns- to back up the menacing looks that hadn't been enough to keep them from being killed and stuffed.

Through the front door I could see Luna's car going in reverse, kicking up enough dust to blind a man wearing aviator goggles. She churned up the earth, sand, and creosote with her tires, the dirt joined by whatever debris a warm foehn of a breeze pushed around as it stirred to life and began to comb the desert. The conflicting winds, manmade and natural, caused the scrub to rustle as the silver coupe disappeared on the horizon, finally switching to "drive" from "reverse" as it reached the road.

I staggered outside on wobbly legs, doing the newborn giraffe walk as I tried to process a tenth of what had just happened, and failed.

In front of me was the gypsy cab that had made half a donut in the caliche earlier when the crazy-ass boyfriend had brought the car to a halt and almost tipped it over (which, had it happened, couldn't have resulted in an injury any worse than what he got anyway). The front fender looked crumpled and dented from where it had contacted Cliff's body after jumping the curb in downtown Reno.

Poor Gordon's Continental had one spiderweb-shaped fissure in the passenger's window where the jealous boyfriend had fired a single shot. I'd mistaken the shot for a clap of thunder, but considering it came from a Magnum I could be forgiven for my error.

I had my choice now. The cab or the Continental. One car had dents in its body and was probably stolen, while the other one had a conspicuous hollow drilled into the passenger-side window. Plus, I only had my learner's permit.

Redrock wasn't too far away, and maybe there was still a working phone in the house, if I could think of someone to call.

But Mexico was also close.

I looked toward the horizon, as if the sky could tell me something, give me some sign.

But there were no omens described by the setting sun, only clouds there, forming into a mass near the vanishing point that looked like a white reef in the endless ocean my bleary eyes conjured of the desert. If I squinted a little more, I noticed the clouds looked like snowcapped mountaintops far away from the valley where my uncle's spread lay.

For the first time maybe ever in my life I had a bit of peace, and I watched the clouds pass across the canvas of the sky the way people probably did hundreds of years ago, the way now we could only watch TV or stupid videos online.

That cloud eventually formed into the shape of a prairie dog reared up on its hind legs, and I laughed as I thought about it, and I realized two things.

First, I didn't miss heroin anymore.

Second, I missed my uncle. Missed the hell out of him.

ABOUT THE AUTHOR

Joseph Hirsch is the author of several published books as well as numerous short stories, essays, and poems. He holds an M.A. in Germanistik from the University of Cincinnati.

More info can be found here
www.joeyhirsch.com

NOTE FROM THE AUTHOR

Word-of-mouth is crucial for any author to succeed. If you enjoyed *My Uncle's New Eyes*, please leave a review online—anywhere you are able. Even if it's just a sentence or two. It would make all the difference and would be very much appreciated.

Thanks!
Joey

Thank you so much for reading *My Uncle's New Eyes*.
If you enjoyed the experience, please check out our recommended
title for your next great read!

Veterans' Affairs by Joseph Hirsch

"Mr. Hirsch is a writer of uncommon talent."
– Tom Kakonis, author of the
award-winning crime novel, *Double-Down*

View other Black Rose Writing titles at
www.blackrosewriting.com/books and use promo code
PRINT to receive a **20% discount** when purchasing.